LUKE JENSEN,
BOUNTY HUNTER:
DEATH RIDES ALONE

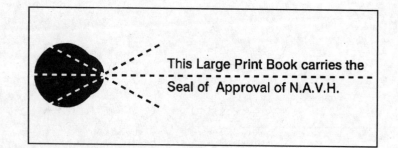

LUKE JENSEN, BOUNTY HUNTER: DEATH RIDES ALONE

WILLIAM W. JOHNSTONE
WITH J.A. JOHNSTONE

WHEELER PUBLISHING
A part of Gale, Cengage Learning

GALE
CENGAGE Learning·

Farmington Hills, Mich • San Francisco • New York • Waterville, Maine
Meriden, Conn • Mason, Ohio • Chicago

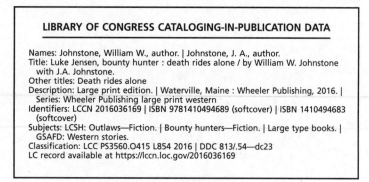

GALE
CENGAGE Learning·

LIBRARY OF CONGRESS CATALOGING-IN-PUBLICATION DATA

Names: Johnstone, William W., author. | Johnstone, J. A., author.
Title: Luke Jensen, bounty hunter : death rides alone / by William W. Johnstone with J.A. Johnstone.
Other titles: Death rides alone
Description: Large print edition. | Waterville, Maine : Wheeler Publishing, 2016. | Series: Wheeler Publishing large print western
Identifiers: LCCN 2016036169 | ISBN 9781410494689 (softcover) | ISBN 1410494683 (softcover)
Subjects: LCSH: Outlaws—Fiction. | Bounty hunters—Fiction. | Large type books. | GSAFD: Western stories.
Classification: LCC PS3560.O415 L854 2016 | DDC 813/.54—dc23
LC record available at https://lccn.loc.gov/2016036169

Published in 2016 by arrangement with Pinnacle Books, an imprint of Kensington Publishing Corp.

Printed in the United States of America
1 2 3 4 5 6 7 20 19 18 17 16

Luke Jensen, Bounty Hunter: Death Rides Alone

CHAPTER 1

Luke Jensen was in Bent Creek, Wyoming, on business. He didn't want to waste time — or bullets — killing some obnoxious young fool who didn't know any better than to prod him.

Unfortunately, it looked like he might not have a choice.

Luke stood at the bar of the Three of a Kind Saloon and toyed with a glass of exceptionally mediocre whiskey. The liquor wasn't *quite* bad enough to convince him that the proprietor had brewed it out back in a washtub and thrown a few rattlesnake heads into the mix for flavoring, but it came close.

Some decent cognac would have been more fortifying after the long ride Luke had made today, but since this was Bent Creek, Wyoming — a squalid, muddy, vermin-infested hamlet if ever there was one — and not San Francisco or Denver, Luke supposed he would just have to make do with what was available. Any port in the proverbial storm.

He threw back the rest of the rotgut in the glass, grimaced slightly, and tried to ignore the young hardcase sitting at a table behind him with some friends.

"Don't he look dangerous, dressed all in black that way?" the would-be troublemaker was saying. "And them fancy guns, well, it makes me scared just to look at 'em, boys."

The youngster's mocking tone grated on Luke's nerves. He wasn't an overly vain man, although the black hat, shirt, trousers, and boots he wore were well cared for and he had slapped some of the trail dust off of them before he walked into the saloon.

Nor were the revolvers riding in the crossdraw rig he wore as fancy as the hardcase made them out to be. They were longbarreled, .44 caliber Remingtons, nickelplated, to be sure, with ivory grips, but they weren't adorned with any elaborate engraving. To Luke they were simply the well-used tools of his trade.

None of that mattered. The kid was on the prod, and if it hadn't been Luke's clothes or guns, the harasser would have found something else to make fun of. Luke was a stranger in Bent Creek, and the young man, who probably considered himself the big he-wolf around here, had decided to goad him into a fight.

The short, fat bartender looked nervous, as if he had seen similar scenes played out in the Three of a Kind before. Most likely, he had. He picked up the bottle and gave Luke an inquiring look. Luke shook his head and said, "I believe I've had enough."

"Next one's on the house, mister," the bartender said. The words made his three chins wobble.

"Obliged, but I'll pass." The bartender clearly didn't want a shooting, so he was trying to stall for time hoping the kid would get bored and forget about starting a fight, Luke figured.

That was all well and good. The man didn't want bullets flying around his business. Luke could understand that.

But he was tired and not in the mood to be charitable. Besides, he might be able to use this to his advantage.

"I should probably be moving on . . ." Luke began. He saw hope leap to life in the bartender's eyes, the hope that Luke would leave before any gunplay broke out. "But I need to ask you one question first."

"Sure, mister. What is it?"

"I'm looking for a friend of mine who

might have come this way," Luke lied — about the *friend* part, anyway. "Medium height, brown hair, just a little on the slender side."

"That could be a lot of men. He got a name?"

"Judd Tyler."

The bartender shook his head slowly and, Luke thought, sincerely.

"Sorry, mister. Don't know the name. Anything else you can tell me about him?"

"Well, he was riding a paint pony a while back, but I don't know if he still is."

"What you should do, then," the bartender said, "is go on over to Crandall's Livery. It's the only one in town. If anybody rode in lately on a paint, Fred Crandall will know about it."

"And once again, I'm obliged to you," Luke said. The young hardcase had fallen silent, and Luke thought maybe he had lost interest.

That wasn't the case. Luke glanced in the mirror behind the bar and saw the kid watching him. The intent expression on the young man's face told him all he needed to know.

Luke caught a glimpse of his own face, too: tanned, weathered, too craggy to be called handsome, dominated by a slightly larger than normal nose with a neatly trimmed black mustache underneath it. It was a tired face, weary from the years he had lived, the miles he had traveled, and the gunpowder he had burned. To be honest, the face of a man not to trifle with.

The hardcase, though, was blinded by youth and arrogance, and as Luke turned away from the bar, the young man scraped his chair back and stood up.

"Where you goin', stranger?" he asked. A simple question, but it had an air of challenge about it.

"Over to the livery stable," Luke said, his voice deceptively mild. "As late in the day as it is, I believe I'll spend the night, so I'll need to arrange to leave my horse there."

"Well, maybe we don't want fellas like you spendin' the night in Bent Creek."

Luke smiled at the bluster and said, "Fellas like me? Just what sort of fella do you think I am?"

"The kind who thinks he's better'n everybody else. You can't fool me, mister. I was watchin' in the mirror and saw the face you made when you took your drink. You think Johnny's whiskey ain't no good."

The bartender cleared his throat and said, "I, uh, didn't notice anything like that, Tate."

"He wouldn't take a second drink, would he? Even when you told him it was on the house! Where I come from, by God, that's a damn insult."

"Where *do* you come from, Tate?" Luke asked.

The young hardcase frowned in confusion, the question clearly catching him by surprise. He said, "Why, right here in Bent Creek, of course. Born and raised on a spread a few miles outta town."

"Well, if you're actually *in* the place you come from, then you shouldn't be saying *where I come from,* because that implies it's somewhere else, other than where you are."

Tate's confusion was growing. He gave a little shake of his head and moved a step closer to Luke. Behind him at the table, his two friends had stood up as well and spread out a little. Typical tactics, Luke thought. They were ready to back Tate's play, whatever it turned out to be.

Tate scowled and said, "You're tryin' to get me all mixed up —"

"Just pointing out a slight logical flaw in your manner of speaking —"

"You high-toned son of a bitch!"

From behind the bar, fat Johnny said, "Please, Tate, if there's any more trouble in here, Marshal Donovan's liable to shut me down —"

The tense way Tate held himself told Luke that Johnny's plea wasn't going to do any good. Tate had screwed his nerves so tight inside that there was only one way to let off the pressure.

"Look, maybe I'll have that second drink after all," Luke said, turning back slightly to the bar but not taking his eyes off Tate. The move made Tate frown and keep his hand from stabbing toward his holstered gun, as it had been about to do.

Johnny had set the bottle of whiskey on the bar. Luke's left hand closed around the neck of it, and what happened next was so swift it was hard for the eye to follow. Luke twisted, whipped his arm out, and flung the half-full bottle at Tate. The bottom of it struck him in the center of the forehead with a solid thump but didn't break. The impact knocked Tate back a step. His feet tangled with a chair and he went down in an ungainly sprawl.

Even before the bottle hit Tate, Luke's hands had closed around the butts of the Remingtons and pulled the guns smoothly from their holsters. He had the revolvers leveled at Tate's friends before the two men could do more than start their draws.

"Touch those guns and I'll kill you both,

gentlemen," Luke informed them. He took a quick step forward. Tate was moving around on the floor, but his eyes weren't clear and he didn't seem to have much control over his muscles. His Colt had fallen from its holster. Luke kicked it and sent it sliding across the sawdust-littered floor.

He set himself, kicked again, and this time his boot thudded against Tate's jaw. Tate sagged back, out cold.

"Hey!" one of Tate's friends said. "You kicked him when he was down!"

"Yes, and I could have just as easily killed him. Johnny, come out from behind the bar and take their guns."

The bartender hustled to do as Luke ordered, telling the two men, "Don't hold this against me, fellas. I ain't got no choice. I mean . . . look at him. He's some kind o' gunman."

"Damn outlaw, more'n likely," one of the men said as Johnny lifted his gun from its holster.

Luke smiled and said, "I'm on the other side of the law, for the most part."

The second man's eyes widened as he said, "Hell. You're not one of them U.S. Marshals, are you?"

"Nothing that official."

"I bet he's a bounty hunter," the first man

14

said, spitting out the words bitterly. "Look at him! A born killer!"

"Yeah, Tate should've seen that," the second man said with a gloomy sigh. "We tried to tell him to leave you alone, mister. Sorry things got to this point."

"Will you quit kissin' up to him?" the first man said. "We don't have to worry about a damn bounty hunter. Ain't any reward dodgers out on us."

"What about him?" Luke asked, nodding toward the still senseless Tate.

"There ain't no charges against him. Every shootin' scrape he's been mixed up in was self-defense."

"Like this one here tonight would have been if I'd let him push me into reaching first?" Luke shook his head and went on disgustedly, "You two had better open your eyes and think about something. You keep following Tate around and giving him an audience for his little gunfights, there's a good chance you'll die right along with him one of these days. I could have killed all three of you if I'd been of a mind to."

"I reckon he could have," Johnny said. "You seen how fast he got them guns out."

"Here's something else you should remember: I'm not really that fast," Luke said. "Not compared to some I've seen."

He was talking about his brother Smoke and his other brother Matt, both of whom could have shaded Luke on the draw if it ever came down to that . . . which it wouldn't, seeing as they were all family and good friends, to boot.

"Tate, there," Luke went on, "he may be *Bent Creek fast,* but that doesn't mean he's fast enough to survive for long anywhere else."

"You're preachin' to the choir, mister," the more reasonable of the duo said. "We don't want any more trouble. Why don't we just all go on about our business and forget this ever happened?"

"That would be the smartest thing for all of you to do, including Tate." Luke lowered the Remingtons. "But if he's the sort to hold a grudge, I won't cut him any slack next time. If he's really your friend, you should make sure he understands that."

He didn't pouch the irons until he had walked to the saloon's entrance, watching the three men from the corner of his eye as he did so. Tate's two friends knelt next to him and started trying to bring him around.

Luke pushed out through the batwings and paused on the boardwalk to sigh as he looked across the street toward the livery stable. It had started raining while he was inside the Three of a Kind, so the street was even muddier than it had been when he rode into Bent Creek a while earlier. Now he was going to have to slog across there, leading the rangy gray gelding he was riding these days, and talk to the liveryman to see if he had seen Judd Tyler or the paint pony Tyler had been riding.

Luke hoped he was nearing the end of this pursuit. Tyler had a decent bounty on his head, a thousand dollars, but more than that, he was the sort of owlhoot Luke enjoyed taking out of circulation: a mad dog killer who had beaten and choked the life out of a young woman, a minister's daughter, at that. Tyler richly deserved the hangrope that was no doubt waiting for him up in Montana.

Luke led the gray toward the stable in the fading light as the rain droned around him and pelted on his hat. Bent Creek had a single hotel, so there wasn't any choice in accommodations. Luke hoped they had a bathtub. He wanted a hot soak and some dry clothes.

He wasn't so lost in his thoughts that he failed to hear the batwings slap aside suddenly behind him. He dropped the gray's reins and wheeled around in time to see the young hardcase called Tate lunge out onto

17

the boardwalk with a gun in each hand, flame spouting from their barrels as he fired.

CHAPTER 2

Could be Tate wasn't seeing straight because of the clonk on the head from the whiskey bottle, or he might have been so furious that emotion was throwing off his aim. Or maybe he just wasn't that good a shot when he wasn't facing some scared wrangler or sodbuster.

Whatever the reason, some of his bullets whined over Luke's head while others plunked into the mud in front of him.

In smooth, unhurried fashion, Luke drew his right-hand Remington, lifted it, and fired one shot.

The .44 round sizzled through the rain, punched into Tate's chest, and knocked him back against the batwings. He didn't fall through them but caught the one on his left instead, hooking his arm over it as he tried to hold himself up.

The batwing wasn't very stable, though, and neither was Tate. He swayed back and forth for a second as he struggled to raise the gun in his right hand for another shot.

Luke didn't particularly want to shoot him again because of the possibility that the bullet might go all the way through the young fool and hit somebody in the saloon, but he was about to run the risk when blood gushed from Tate's mouth and his strength finally deserted him. He pitched forward to lie facedown on the boardwalk. Both guns fell in the muddy street.

The fight wasn't over, though. One of Tate's friends, the one who hadn't wanted to be reasonable, rushed out gripping a double-barreled shotgun he had gotten from somewhere. He yelled a curse and swung the barrels toward Luke.

The Remington roared and bucked twice in Luke's fist. Both bullets drove into the shotgunner's midsection, just above his belt buckle. As he doubled over, his finger must have jerked the shotgun's triggers, because it boomed like thunder as both barrels discharged.

The weapon was pointing down now, though, and the double load of buckshot slammed into Tate's back at close range, shredding and pulverizing it. The only good thing about that grisly turn of fate was that Tate was likely dead already and didn't feel the terrible blast.

Luke stood in the warm rain, revolver leveled toward the saloon, and waited to see if the third man was going to come out. After a long moment, the batwings swung outward slowly and the man emerged from the Three of a Kind, but he immediately held his empty hands high and in plain sight.

"Don't shoot, mister!" he called to Luke. "Tate took my gun! I'm unarmed!"

"If you came to help your friends, you're too late," Luke said. His clothes were soaked now. He was wet, uncomfortable, and mad, and he felt like shooting the third man just on general principles. That would have been cold-blooded murder, though, and even bounty hunters drew the line somewhere. At least *this* bounty hunter did.

"Tate's dead, ain't he?"

"Not much doubt about that after your other friend unloaded both barrels into his back."

At that moment, the gutshot man let out a long, pain-racked groan.

"Clevenger ain't, though," the third man went on. "I just want to get the doc for him."

"Go ahead, although I doubt it'll do much good. Wounds like that are invariably fatal."

"You're sayin' he's gonna die no matter what I do?"

"The odds are overwhelmingly against him."

The third man thought about that for a couple of seconds before saying, "Well, then, the hell with it. I figure to get on my horse and head outta this town. I know when I'd be pushin' my luck to stay in a place."

"Go ahead," Luke told him. "Nobody's going to make you hang around."

The man went to one of the horses at the hitch rack in front of the saloon, jerked the animal's reins loose, and swung up into the saddle. He hauled the horse around and spurred it into a run that sent mud flying in the air from its hooves. Luke watched him disappear into the rain.

Johnny came out of the saloon, followed by a couple of the citizens of Bent Creek who had been in the saloon.

"Somebody'll fetch the undertaker for these two," the bartender said.

"One of them isn't dead yet," Luke pointed out. Clevenger was still squirming slightly and moaning, although the sounds were getting weaker.

"He will be, time the coffin's ready for him."

Luke finally holstered the Remington and nodded.

"More than likely. Do you have any law around here?"

"Town marshal," Johnny said. "Deputy rides up from the county seat once a month or so, but he was just here last week so I don't expect to see him again any time soon."

"Well, if the marshal wants to talk to me, I'll be at the livery stable or the hotel."

Johnny shook his head and said, "We all saw what happened from inside the saloon, mister. Tate and Clevenger came after you, pure and simple. I told Clevenger not to take that Greener from under the bar, but he wouldn't be stopped. You didn't have any choice but to kill 'em."

"That's the way of the world," Luke said. "Too often it doesn't give a man a choice."

He knew as soon as he stepped into the cavernous livery barn that he had found what he was looking for.

At least, there was a good chance he had, because a brown-and-white paint pony stood in one of the stalls, its serene gaze turned in his direction.

Luke had never laid eyes on Judd Tyler or on the horse Tyler had stolen to make his getaway from White Fork, Montana, after murdering poor Rachel Montgomery. This horse sure fit the description on the wanted poster currently folded up and stowed in one of Luke's saddlebags, though.

Of course, it was possible Tyler had traded horses or simply abandoned the paint and stolen another mount since fleeing from White Fork. If he had any sense at all, he wouldn't still be riding such a distinctive animal.

And there were quite a few paint horses around, Luke reminded himself. This one didn't have to be Tyler's.

The instincts he had developed from surviving for so many long years in a dangerous business told him that his quarry was nearby, though. Luke carried a number of different maps with him, and all of them agreed there wasn't a hell of a lot between here and White Fork. A few small settlements and some ranches, that was all. Tyler might not have been able to find a better horse.

It was the maps that had brought Luke to Bent Creek. He had been in another town, several days' ride south of here, when he had seen the poster on Tyler in the local badge-toter's office. Luke had studied the maps and seen that Tyler was likely to head for Bent Creek if he continued south.

Luke had ridden hard in order to get here

in time to intercept the fugitive. It had been a gamble, but he sensed it was going to pay off.

A tall, gaunt old man in overalls and a battered hat stood just inside the barn doors. His left cheek bulged out from the chaw of tobacco he had stashed there.

"Mr. Crandall?" Luke asked him.

"Yep," the man said around the chaw. He nodded toward the far side of the street, where a man carrying a black bag had just hurried up to the scene of the shooting.

Luke and the liveryman watched as the doctor dropped to one knee beside Clevenger, looked at the wounds for a moment, then stood up and shook his head at Johnny and the other bystanders. He walked off without ever opening his medical bag.

"I seen some of what happened," Crandall said. "Shot the hell outta them boys, didn't you?"

"It seemed like the thing to do at the time," Luke said.

Crandall spat a long, brown stream into the rain, then said, "Nobody's gonna miss 'em, if that's what you're worried about. Tate's been a pain in everybody's butt around here ever since he growed up and decided he was a tough *hombre*. Clevenger was mite near as bad."

25

"Tate said he grew up on a ranch near here?"

"Yeah, but his folks are dead and it's his uncle's place now, and his uncle couldn't stand him. Ran him off and told him never to set foot on the spread again. So you don't have to be afeared of anybody comin' after you to settle the score."

"I wasn't afeared," Luke said.

Crandall looked at him with narrowed eyes for a second, then said, "No, I reckon you ain't very often, are you?" Without waiting for an answer, he went on, "Lookin' for a place to put your horse up for the night?"

"That's right, and I'm in search of some information as well."

Crandall scratched his angular jaw and said, "Got some empty stalls, but I dunno about the information. Most folks figure my head's pretty empty, too."

"Oh, I doubt that very seriously," Luke said. "For example, I'll bet you can tell me all about the man who rode in on that paint pony over there."

Crandall glanced toward the paint and grunted.

"How come you want to know?"

"I think he might be a friend of mine."

Crandall spat again, said, "Man who shoots like you gen'rally don't have many friends." His bony shoulders rose and fell in a shrug. "But I just rent out stalls and take care o' horses. Fella who rode in on that paint yesterday is young, twenty-three or twenty-four, I'd say. Got brown hair. A mite on the scrawny side. Sound like your friend?"

"It very well could be. Is he still in town?"

"His horse is still there, ain't it?"

"He could have worked out a trade with you for another horse," Luke said.

"Could have, but he didn't. He seemed to set a heap of store by that animal. Said he needed to be movin' on today, but he couldn't do it. He was afraid of runnin' that paint into the ground. He was right, too. That varmint was plumb in need of a day's rest."

"Been ridden hard, had it?"

"Yep."

"Did you happen to get a name?"

Crandall waved a knobby-knuckled hand and said, "Oh, he didn't call the horse nothin', not while I was around, anyway."

"I think you know what I meant."

"A fella's got cold, hard cash, I don't need his life story or his name," Crandall said. "Anyway, he's your *friend*. Reckon you oughta know his name."

"Then maybe you can tell me where to

find him," Luke said, although he had a hunch he already knew the answer.

Crandall pointed with a thumb and said, "He's stayin' at the hotel. If he ain't there, he's likely in one of the saloons or the café. Gettin' on toward suppertime, so he might be gettin' something to eat."

Luke took a five-dollar gold piece from his pocket and tossed it to Crandall, who caught it with practiced ease.

"You'll see to my horse?"

"Sure, mister, but it ain't gonna cost this much."

"The rest of it is for your help," Luke said.

"Not sure I helped all that much. Did I tell you anything you hadn't already guessed?"

"Not really, but it was only a hunch. It's always nice to have confirmation."

Luke handed the reins to the old man, then started to turn toward the open doors.

As he did, he heard something behind him and caught a flicker of movement from the deep shadows under the hayloft. He tried to twist back in that direction as his right hand darted across his body toward the forward-facing butt of the Remington on that side.

The gun came clear of the holster, but Luke didn't have a chance to use it before something crashed against his head with enough force to make it feel like his brain had popped right out of his skull. He heard Crandall's startled shout, but that was the last thing he was aware of before he plunged into seemingly endless darkness.

CHAPTER 3

Little streaks and flashes of light popped into Luke's brain, letting him know that the darkness wasn't endless after all.

So he wasn't dead. That came as something of a surprise, but he wasn't one to be ungrateful for a stroke of luck.

"Damn it, boy, that hurts!"

Crandall's raspy old voice made the complaint. The words that answered it came from a younger man.

"Sorry, Pop. You've got to let me tie you up and gag you, though, or else I'll have to kill you."

"That's what you're gonna do to that fella? You're gonna kill him in cold blood?"

The reply didn't come right away. When it did, the younger man sounded torn.

"I don't want to," he said. "But he's got to be a bounty hunter, the way he was asking around about me. He described me to the bartender over at the saloon, and then

30

he came in here and started asking questions about my horse."

"Got paper out on you, do you? You don't hardly *look* like a desperado. You're mean as hell, though, tyin' these knots so blasted tight."

"Quit complaining, Pop —"

"I ain't your pop. And even if I was, I'd never claim a no-good whelp like you."

Crandall tried to say something else, but the words came out as a muffled jumble that told Luke he'd had something shoved in his mouth to serve as a gag.

And it was Judd Tyler who was doing the tying and gagging. It couldn't be anybody else.

While the conversation between Crandall and Tyler was going on, Luke had stayed right where he was, as silent and unmoving as he would have been if he were still out cold.

His head throbbed from being hit, but the ache was already beginning to fade slightly. He felt a little strength flowing back into his muscles. He wasn't ready to jump up and fight yet, but he was getting there.

Since Tyler was just finishing the job of securing the old liveryman, Luke figured only a few minutes had passed since the wallop that knocked him out. He didn't know how Tyler had found out that Luke was in town looking for him. He had probably overheard someone talking about what had happened in the Three of a Kind.

At the moment the how of it didn't really matter. The important thing was turning this situation around so that Tyler was his prisoner.

"I really ought to shoot this fella in the head," Tyler muttered, more to himself than to Crandall. "But that'd draw too much attention." The fugitive sighed. "I know I'm gonna regret this, but I guess I'd better tie him up, too."

That was good news to Luke's ears. He could afford to lie there and wait while he continued to recover from being knocked unconscious.

He was stretched out on his belly, with the side of his face pressed against the hard-packed dirt of the stable's aisle where he had been standing when he was struck down. It smelled faintly of all the horse manure that had been dropped here over the years.

Luke hoped once again that he would be able to get a hot bath.

Once he had captured or killed Judd Tyler, of course.

A tense moment passed. Maybe Tyler had

caught on that he was shamming and said that about tying him up just to keep Luke from trying anything. Maybe the young killer was aiming a gun at his head this very second, about to squeeze the trigger and blow his brains out.

Then Tyler grunted as he bent over, grabbed Luke's left wrist with one hand, and pulled it behind his back. He held it there while he took hold of Luke's other wrist.

That meant both of Tyler's hands were full, so he couldn't be holding a gun.

Luke exploded into action.

He bucked up from the ground and threw himself toward where his ears had told him Tyler was standing. His shoulders rammed into the man's legs at the knees. Tyler yelled in surprise and alarm as he went down.

Luke rolled over and pushed himself up. Tyler lay on his back a couple of yards away, clawing at the gun on his hip. Luke dived toward him, caught his wrist just as Tyler jerked the Colt out of its holster, and shoved the gun aside as it went off. The shot echoed from the barn's high ceiling and made the horses in the stalls move around skittishly.

Luke drove his fist into Tyler's face while hanging on to the fugitive's gun wrist with his other hand. He planned to batter Tyler into senselessness.

Tyler fought back with surprising strength. He might be slender, but evidently his muscles were tough as rawhide. He writhed partially out from under Luke and aimed a knee at his groin.

Luke wasn't able to avoid the blow entirely, although it landed higher in his abdomen and didn't do as much damage as it would have if it had found its intended target.

As it was, his grip slipped enough for Tyler to tear free. The gun in the young man's hand slashed at Luke's head in a vicious swipe.

That blow missed, too, as Luke jerked aside, but it did some damage anyway as the gun barrel crashed down on his left shoulder. Luke's entire left arm went numb, which meant he was fighting one-handed.

Tyler really turned into a wildcat then, fighting with the ferocity of sheer desperation. He punched, kicked, clawed, and even bit, clamping his teeth down on Luke's thumb when Luke tried to grab his jaw.

With a pained yell, Luke tore his hand free and hammered a punch into Tyler's midsection. His left arm was still numb and not any good to him, so he struck as hard and fast as he could with the right.

Tyler was snake-quick, though, and most of the blows glanced off.

As the two men rolled and thrashed on the floor, they wound up next to a shovel lying on the ground. Tyler grabbed it and rammed the handle into Luke's ribs.

Fresh pain shot through Luke at the impact. Tyler swung the handle at his head. After being knocked out once already, Luke knew another blow might cause permanent damage, so he ducked, hunched his shoulders, and took the blow there.

He butted his head into Tyler's face. Tyler reared back, stunned. Luke dug a knee into the wanted man's belly and grabbed him around the throat at the same time. Keeping him pinned down, Luke banged Tyler's head on the ground several times. The young man stopped fighting, although he didn't pass out. His eyes were glassy and unfocused as they stared up at Luke.

Feeling was starting to come back into Luke's left arm. He used that hand to take hold of the shovel and toss it away, out of Tyler's reach. Then he pushed himself to his feet and stood over the young man. Both of Luke's holsters were empty, as was the sheath where his knife rode.

A pitchfork leaned nearby against the gate of one of the stalls, though, so Luke reached over and took hold of it. He held the fork's sharp tines poised over Tyler's chest and said, "Stop fighting, or I'll remind myself that the bounty on your head is payable dead or alive."

Tyler was still mostly out of it, but he was able to lift a hand and gasp, "No . . . no more! Don't kill me!"

Luke stepped back but kept the pitchfork ready. He glanced around, saw that Tyler's Colt had wound up several yards away during the fight. The fugitive was unarmed, unless he had a hideout gun somewhere on him.

A man appeared in the stable's open doors. For the second time today, Luke had a shotgun pointed at him, but this Greener was in the hands of a bulky, middle-aged man with a star pinned to his vest under the open rain slicker he wore.

"What the hell!" the lawman said. "Throw that pitchfork down, mister, or I'll blast you."

"Take it easy, Marshal," Luke said. He tossed the pitchfork aside. "I'm not the man you want." He nodded toward Tyler. "This one is. He's a killer, wanted up in Montana."

"How in blazes do I know that?" the marshal asked as he came farther into the barn. His face was broad and florid, with the bulbous nose of a drinker. He went on, "I come in here and find ol' Fred tied up and one stranger about to skewer another stranger with a pitchfork. Maybe I oughta just shoot the both of you."

"That might simplify your life, but it would be the wrong thing to do. If you'll allow me to reach into my saddlebags, I can show you the wanted poster on this man. Not only that, if you'll remove Mr. Crandall's gag, I'm sure he'll be glad to tell you that we were the ones who were attacked."

"We'll just see about both of those things. You stand right there where you are."

The marshal moved over to the stool where Crandall was perched with his hands tied behind his back and a dirty rag stuffed into his mouth. The lawman pulled the gag out, and Crandall started spitting. He kept that up for several seconds, then glared toward Tyler.

"That fella is tellin' you the truth, Marshal," he said. "The varmint on the ground is the one what caused the trouble. He must'a snuck in the back while me and that *hombre* in black were talkin', then he jumped out and walloped him on the head with a shovel."

The marshal frowned and didn't look

convinced. He said, "I need some names here."

"My name is Luke Jensen," Luke introduced himself. He pointed at the fugitive. "That's Judd Tyler. He's wanted in White Fork, Montana, for murdering a young woman."

Tyler had gotten enough of his senses back to respond to that charge. He pushed himself up on an elbow and said, "That's a damned lie!"

"Like I said, Marshal, I can prove it if you'll let me show you that wanted poster."

The lawman continued to frown for a moment, like maybe thinking didn't come that easy for him, but then he jerked his head in a nod and told Luke, "Go ahead and get it. But try anything funny and I'll blow your head off."

Luke's gray hadn't spooked during the ruckus. It had stood stolidly during the shoot-out in the street a short time earlier, too. Luke liked that about the horse.

He unfastened one of the saddlebags, reached inside, and brought out a folded sheet of paper. He unfolded it and held it out to the marshal.

Lowering the shotgun, the lawman stepped forward and took the wanted poster from Luke. He studied it for a long moment, moving his lips a little as he read. Then he looked down at Judd Tyler.

"You'll see that the horse in that stall over there matches the description on the poster," Luke said, pointing at the paint, "and Mr. Crandall can confirm that Tyler is the one who rode it into town yesterday."

"He sure as blazes did," the old liveryman said. "Now, is somebody gonna get these dadblasted ropes off 'a me? It's mighty uncomfortable, bein' tied up like this."

The marshal grunted, handed the reward dodger back to Luke, and said, "All right, Jensen, why don't you give Fred a hand? I'll keep an eye on Tyler."

"Make it a close eye," Luke said. "He's tricky."

"Huh. Bein' tricky when there's a shotgun pointed at you don't get you anything except a load of buckshot."

Luke went behind Crandall and quickly untied the ropes around the old man's wrists. As Crandall was flexing his newly freed arms and muttering, Luke asked, "Did you see what he did with my guns and knife?"

"Dropped 'em over yonder in that feed bin."

Luke retrieved the weapons. He felt better when he was armed again. He kept his right-hand Remington out. He found his hat, which had been knocked off when Tyler clouted him with the shovel, and clapped it back on his head, wincing a little at the pressure on the goose egg that had risen where he was hit.

"I assume you can lock up Tyler in your jail, Marshal?"

"Yeah, I guess that'd be all right. Name's Donovan, by the way. Chet Donovan."

"I noticed telegraph wires leading into town. I hope you won't mind sending a message to White Fork, Marshal, to let the authorities know that Tyler is in custody here. And that I'm the one who captured him, of course."

"Of course," Donovan said. "Wouldn't want to forget that, would we . . . bounty hunter?"

"Perhaps it's not an honorable profession in the minds of many . . . but it *is* an honest one."

"Whatever you say." Donovan jerked the shotgun's twin barrels at Tyler and went on, "Get up, mister."

Tyler climbed to his feet. He seemed a little shaky from the pounding he had taken, but his voice was firm and clear as he looked at Luke and said, "I meant it when I said that was a damned lie, you know."

"You mean about you being wanted in Montana?"

"I mean about killing Rachel Montgomery. I never did it, Jensen. I didn't kill her."

Marshal Donovan made a disgusted noise in his throat and said, "Every killer claims the same thing, I reckon. Get movin'. You're goin' behind bars where you belong."

CHAPTER 4

Luke left the gray at the livery stable with Fred Crandall's promise to take good care of the animal, then accompanied Marshal Donovan and Judd Tyler to Bent Creek's jail.

A squat, stone building housed both the marshal's office and a small cell block. Donovan prodded the prisoner into one of the cells and slammed the barred door after him.

"There," the lawman said with some satisfaction. "He ain't goin' anywhere, the dirty killer."

Tyler let out a weary sigh and said, "I didn't —"

Donovan held up a hand to stop him.

"You might as well not waste your breath, kid. I can read. I saw what that wanted poster says."

"Just because it's printed on a wanted poster doesn't mean it's true."

"I never saw one yet that wasn't."

Luke could have pointed out that the marshal was wrong. Not every man whose name and description turned up on a wanted poster was really an outlaw. His own brother Smoke had had paper out on him at one time, but it had been issued by a crooked sheriff who wanted Smoke dead.

Just in general, though, Donovan was right. Luke had no doubt of Judd Tyler's guilt.

"Marshal, I'm wet, I'm covered with mud and who knows what else, and I'd like nothing more right now than to wash up and get into some clean clothes," he said. "I'll leave Tyler in your care, and I'm obliged to you for your help."

"He ain't goin' anywhere," Donovan said again. "Nobody's ever busted outta this jail. Of course, I ain't had too many murderers locked up in it."

Tyler looked like he wanted to say something, but then he just shook his head and went over to the bunk bolted to the wall to sit down with a sigh.

Luke and Donovan went out into the marshal's office. Luke said, "You'll take care of sending that wire for me? I'm sure the law in White Fork will want to hear the news that Tyler's in custody from the proper

43

authorities here."

"Sure, but I got to warn you, there ain't no direct line from here to there. I'll have to wire Cheyenne, and they'll route it around some way to get the message to Montana. I wouldn't expect to hear back before tomorrow mornin' at the earliest."

"Tomorrow will be fine," Luke said.

"You understand, too, I ain't takin' responsibility for this prisoner. I don't think there's a chance in hell of him gettin' out, but if something happens and he does, don't come cryin' to me about your blood money."

"A lawman's natural animosity toward bounty hunters was bound to crop up eventually, I suppose. Don't worry, Marshal. I appreciate your help and the use of your jail, but we'll consider Tyler my prisoner, not yours."

Donovan nodded curtly and said, "That's the way it'll be, then."

Luke left the jail, but before he did, he glanced into the cell block one more time. Tyler was still sitting on the bunk, shoulders slumped, head drooped forward, the very picture of despair. There wasn't an ounce of defiance in him, Luke thought . . . which made Tyler a little different from most of the outlaws he dealt with.

He hoped that Tyler wouldn't take it into his head to hang himself in the cell or find some other permanent way out of the fate that awaited him. That could complicate matters.

But when you came right down to it, the wanted poster *did* say *Dead or Alive*.

The Hotel Beale was kind of a fancy name for a one-story, false-fronted building of raw lumber that had turned gray from the weather, Luke thought. The fella who owned it had probably named the place for himself, a hunch that was confirmed when the slick-haired gent behind the desk in the lobby introduced himself as Jefferson Beale and added, "The proprietor of this fine establishment, sir."

"Well, I'm sorry to come into your fine hotel in such a disreputable state, Mr. Beale," Luke said as he replaced the quill pen in its holder after signing the registration book. "Would it be too much to hope that you have a place where a man can take a hot bath?"

"Indeed we do," Beale replied with a note of pride in his voice. He handed Luke a key from the board hanging on the wall behind the desk and went on, "You'll be in Room Six, that's right down this hallway to the left here, and if you go all the way to the other end of the hall, you'll find a washroom with a tub. I'll tell the boy who works for me to start heating some water. He can gather up your, ah, soiled clothing as well and take it to be cleaned."

"I'll be very obliged to you for that, Mr. Beale. Do you have a dining room as well?"

Beale shook his head and said, "No, but the Keystone Café is only two doors away and serves quite respectable food, as long as you're not expecting the same quality of fare you'd find in, say, San Francisco."

Beale seemed to think that his hotel *did* compare to the hostelries you'd find in San Francisco, which Luke thought was a far cry from the truth, but he didn't see any point in saying that to the man. He just nodded, said, "Thank you," and headed down the hall to his room with his saddlebags slung over his shoulder, key in one hand, Winchester in the other.

The room was furnished simply with a four-poster bed, a chair, a wardrobe, and a couple of throw rugs on the floor. It was clean, though, and the bed looked relatively comfortable.

Luke stowed his gear in the room, propping the rifle in a corner and hanging his gunbelt with its attached holsters and the sheath for the knife over the back of the room's single chair. He brushed his hat as clean as he could and hung it on a bedpost.

Then, carrying one of the Remingtons in his right hand, he walked down the hall to the washroom, which was a shed-like affair with a galvanized metal tub sitting in the middle of it. A freckled, red-haired boy about twelve years old was pouring water from a bucket into the tub.

"Howdy, mister," he said. "The water's just startin' to get warmed up good. I'll be back with more. You probably don't want to get in there yet." His eyes widened as his gaze landed on the gun in Luke's hand. "You're the fella who shot Tate Winslow and Dan Clevenger a while ago!"

"That's right," Luke said.

The boy's young face creased in a scowl. He said, "They had it comin'. Tate kicked my dog once, really hard. And Freckles hadn't done nothin', didn't even get in Tate's way. He just felt like doin' it, the sorry varmint."

"What happened to the dog?"

"He's all right. I was afraid for a while he was gonna die, but he got better. Still walks with a limp, though."

"I'm glad to hear that he made it. What's your name, son?"

"Hardy, sir. Hardy McCoy."

"Well, Hardy, if I had known that Tate was the sort who'd kick a boy's dog for no reason, I might not have cut him as much slack as I did."

"I'm just glad he's dead. He killed five men, and not a one of 'em deserved it."

"It sounds as if the world is better off without him," Luke agreed solemnly.

"I'll fetch some more hot water."

Steam was curling from the surface of the water by the time Luke stepped into the tub and lowered himself all the way. He felt better almost instantly as the heat loosened some of the kinks in his muscles.

He had pulled a three-legged stool over next to the tub and placed his Remington on it. Old habits died hard, and Luke intended to die the same way when his time finally came.

Hardy brought in a couple of thick white towels and hung them on hooks on the other side of the tub. He said, "I'll take those muddy duds of yours down to the Chinaman."

"Will the laundry be open this late?"

"Oh, sure. Heathen Chinee don't keep regular hours like normal folks. They work all the time."

"Industriousness is to be admired," Luke said.

"Huh? Oh. Yeah, I guess so."

Luke chuckled as Hardy gathered up the dirty clothes and went out.

He wished he had thought to bring a cigar and some matches with him. There was nothing like a good smoke while soaking in a hot tub. He supposed he could send the boy to his room to fetch a cheroot when Hardy got back, but that seemed like too much trouble. Luke closed his eyes and just enjoyed the lassitude that crept over him instead.

Several minutes later he heard a floorboard creak. Since Hardy was back, Luke supposed he could go ahead and ask him to get a cigar.

"Hardy, if you wouldn't mind —"

The unmistakable sound of a gun being cocked made Luke's eyes snap open. His hand moved instinctively toward the gun on the stool, but a harsh voice ordered, "Don't do it, you son of a bitch, or you'll just die that much quicker!"

Luke's hand froze before it could close around the Remington's ivory grips.

Gloom had settled over the room. Lamps in wall sconces burned in the hallway, but not in here. The glow from the open doorway silhouetted the man who stood there but kept Luke from being able to make out any details about him.

There was enough light to strike reflections from the barrel of the gun in the man's fist, though. The weapon thrust forward, unmistakable in its menace.

"I did five years in the Texas pen because of you, Smith," the man went on. "Five years of hell! All because of some stolen cows and a damn bounty hunter."

"You're the one who decided to steal those cows," Luke said. He had absolutely no memory of what the man was talking about, but he had brought in a few rustlers from time to time, so he was sure the man was right and Luke had turned him over to the law.

"I hear you're usin' a different name now," the gunman went on. "That don't matter. As soon as you walked into the Three of a Kind, I knew it was you, Smith."

"It's true I once called myself Luke Smith. And it's true I'm a bounty hunter. But if there's no paper out on you now, friend, you don't have anything to fear from me. You've come to Wyoming, made yourself a new start in life —"

"Shut up! I'm not afraid of you. Every miserable day I spent in that hellhole, I swore to myself that I'd even the score with you if I ever got the chance." The gun in the man's hand shook a little from the depth of his rage. "Well, now's my chance, and I'm gonna enjoy watchin' you die —"

"Hey, mister, what're you —"

That was Hardy's voice from down the hall. The boy was back from the laundry and probably coming to see if Luke needed anything else. He couldn't have expected to see a man with a gun standing in the doorway of the washroom.

The gunman's head jerked toward the boy, and the barrel of his revolver shifted in that direction as well. That instinctive reaction was his undoing.

Luke's hand moved like lightning, snatching up the Remington. The would-be killer snarled a curse and tried to bring his gun back into line, but it was too late.

Flame spurted from the Remington's long barrel as the roar of the shot filled the room. The bullet drove the man backward. He hit the wall on the opposite side of the hall, bounced off, and finally pulled the trigger of his gun, but the slug smacked into the floorboards at his feet. He crumpled into a heap.

Luke was already on his feet by the time the man hit the floor. Water sluiced from his body as he stepped out of the tub. He kept the gun trained on the man who had wanted to kill him, but the *hombre* didn't move and it appeared he never would again.

"Holy cow!" Hardy yelled from the hall. "Are you all right in there, Mr. Jensen?"

"I'm fine, Hardy," Luke said as puddles began to form around his feet. "Run fetch the marshal, will you? And he'll probably want to bring the undertaker with him, too."

Hardy poked his head around the corner of the doorway to stare at the sight of Luke standing there holding the Remington. He said, "I reckon you're done with your bath, huh?"

"The water was starting to cool off anyway," Luke said with a shrug.

CHAPTER 5

"Let's see," Marshal Chet Donovan said. "You ain't been in Bent Creek two full hours yet, and this is the third fella who's tried to ventilate you and wound up dead his own self instead. I reckon this must be a pretty common thing for you, Jensen."

"More so than I'd like," Luke said. "It's a hazard of the job, I suppose. When you put men in prison for a living, some of them are going to get out eventually and carry a grudge."

"Huh. Imagine that. You wouldn't have to worry about problems like that if you just killed 'em all and brung in their bodies. That's what most bounty hunters do, ain't it?"

"I can only speak for myself, Marshal," Luke said. "I don't kill a man unless he forces me to it . . . or unless he becomes really annoying."

He was joshing about that last part, but

Donovan looked like he believed him and Luke didn't bother correcting the mistaken impression.

Luke had dried off and dressed in his spare underwear, shirt, and trousers while he was waiting in the hotel's washroom for the marshal to arrive. He had the Remington tucked into his waistband now, since his gun rig was still back in his room.

Jefferson Beale stood to one side, all but wringing his hands as he looked upset that such a thing could have happened in his establishment.

"I don't know how this is possible," he said. "I didn't see this man come in, and I was at the desk the entire time."

"You have a rear door, don't you?" Luke asked.

"Well, yes. I suppose that's the explanation. This man saw you in the saloon, recognized you, followed you over here, and sneaked in the back to see if he could find you. It was your bad luck that he did . . . and his bad luck that he probably considered you defenseless since you were in the bathtub. In the poor light he might not have noticed that you were armed."

"I'll take every bit of luck on my side I can get," Luke said.

"You ain't plannin' on killin' anybody else

while you're here, are you?" Marshal Donovan said.

"I didn't *plan* on killing any of those three," Luke told him.

Donovan nodded toward the dead man who was still lying on the floor. He had sent Hardy to fetch the undertaker, but the boy hadn't returned yet.

"What's this one's name?"

Luke opened his mouth, then frowned before saying anything. When he spoke, he had to restrain the impulse to chuckle.

"You know, I have no earthly idea. He said I was responsible for him spending five years in a Texas prison for rustling, but he never mentioned his name or how long ago that was."

"And you've put so many *hombres* behind bars you don't remember most of 'em."

"Sad but true," Luke admitted.

With a clatter of rapid footsteps, Hardy came down the hall from the lobby, trailed by a short, plump man in a sober black suit. The boy's companion bore a certain resemblance to the bartender in the Three of a Kind, and Luke wondered if they were related. Brothers, maybe.

"I told Herbert to take my wagon around back," the newcomer said as he looked down at the corpse. "That'll be closer and handier, and I didn't figure you'd want us carting him out through the lobby anyway, Jefferson. That would look a mite bad."

"I appreciate that," Beale said. "Anyone in the hotel business knows you're going to have guests die from time to time, but that's no reason to call attention to it."

"This fella wasn't a guest," Donovan said. "Just another would-be killer who ran up against somebody better with a gun." He looked at Luke. "You want me to go through my stack of wanted posters and see if he's got any bounty on his head?"

"That would be very kind of you, Marshal."

Donovan sighed and said, "Man oughta collect what he's owed . . . even if he earned it with a bullet."

Full night had fallen by the time Luke was fully dressed and ready to go out again. The rain had tapered off to an intermittent mist that created a soft halo around the lighted windows of the businesses that were still open.

Luke was glad to see that the Keystone Café was one of them. He stepped through the café's door into warmth and the appealing smells of stew, coffee, fresh-baked bread, and . . . was it pie? Yes, he decided, some sort of fruit pie.

The place wasn't busy on a damp night like this. A couple of men sat at the counter, but all the tables with their blue-checked tablecloths were empty.

An attractive woman with dark brown hair stood behind the counter talking to one of the customers as she topped off his coffee cup from a tin pot. She looked at Luke and smiled.

"Come on in," she told him. "Still enough stew in the pot for a few more servings."

"Judging by the aroma, that's good news," Luke said as he took off his hat.

"Judging from your use of the word 'aroma,' you're not from Bent Creek."

"Hey, Mary, you shouldn't oughta say things like that," the customer objected. "We can talk good."

"Of course you can, Bert," the woman said. "I was just being polite to the stranger, you know."

"Oh. That's all right, then."

While Bert turned his attention back to the piece of pie on a saucer in front of him, Mary looked at Luke, smiled, and mouthed *Not really.*

He managed not to laugh as he slid onto one of the stools in front of the counter and placed his hat on the empty one beside him.

"What can I get for you, Mister . . . ?"

"Jensen," he said. "Luke Jensen. A bowl of that stew would be fine, along with a cup of coffee and . . . is that fresh-baked bread I smell?"

"It certainly is."

"A nice, large hunk of bread, then, and we'll follow it all with a slice of peach pie like our friend Bert is enjoying."

"I'm afraid they're actually canned peaches, not fresh," Mary said.

"But she fixes 'em up mighty nice," Bert added.

"I never doubted it for a moment," Luke said.

She told him, "I'll be right back."

The other customer, a dour-faced, older man sitting farther along the counter, waited until Mary had gone through a door into the kitchen before he looked at Luke and said, "You're the bounty hunter, ain't you?"

"I am," Luke said.

"The one who killed Tate Winslow." The words didn't come out as a question.

"That's right," Luke said. The old-timer didn't look like the sort to start trouble, but you never knew.

"That's one killin' that was long overdue, if you ask me."

"That seems to be the consensus."

Bert said, "You do talk a little funny, Mr. Jensen. Like a schoolteacher. You ever teach school, sort of on the side, I mean, to go with your bounty huntin'?"

Luke had to laugh this time as he shook his head.

"No, Bert, I've never been a schoolteacher. I was well acquainted with one once, though. A beautiful young woman named Lettie. That was long ago and far away, though, before the war. Practically a different lifetime. Since then, I've ridden a lot of lonely trails. It didn't take me long to discover that a solitary man's best friend is often a book. I make sure to carry several with me all the time."

"Oh. Reckon that makes sense. I like to read, too. I send off to New York for them yellow-backed novels from Beadle and Adams. Got one right here." Bert reached to his hip pocket and pulled out a small book bound in yellow paper. "It's about a gunfighter named Smoke Jen— Hey, you and him got the same last name! How about that?"

"Yes," Luke said, still smiling. "How about that?"

Mary's arrival from the kitchen with a bowl of stew and a saucer with a large piece of bread on it saved Luke from offering any explanations . . . not that he was likely to. He didn't go around telling folks that he was Smoke Jensen's brother. For many years, he had kept his relation to the Jensen family to himself, for reasons he'd considered good at the time.

That had changed, but he still wasn't very forthcoming by nature.

He also didn't say anything about how those lurid, fanciful novels were sometimes a minor thorn in Smoke's side, bearing as they did little resemblance to anything remotely truthful about his life and career.

"Mr. Beale at the hotel recommended your café, and I'm glad he did," Luke said after he had sampled the thick, savory beef stew. "This is excellent."

Mary smiled and said, "Well, Jefferson Beale took a trip to San Francisco once, and it almost ruined him. He thinks everywhere should be like that, even Bent Creek. But he's a good man, despite those lofty ambitions. He usually manages not to be *too* pretentious."

The old-timer finished his coffee and left. Bert polished off the last of his pie, put a silver dollar on the counter, and said, "I'm obliged to you, as always, Mary. Good night."

"Good night, Bert," she told him.

The little bell over the door jingled as he went out. Luke said, "I appear to be your last customer of the day."

"You don't have to hurry. Just take your time, Mr. Jensen." She took a cup down from one of the shelves behind the counter and poured coffee in it. "In fact, I'll join you, if you don't mind."

"By all means. It's your café."

"I like having a few quiet moments at the end of the day like this." She took a sip of the coffee. "Especially with pleasant company."

She was a very attractive woman. Luke couldn't help but notice that. Old enough that there were a few lines on her face, a few strands of gray in the glossy brown hair, to give her character. Warm brown eyes with the gleam of intelligence. A womanly body under the gray dress and white apron she wore. No wedding ring, but Luke couldn't imagine a woman such as this never marrying, which made him think she was probably a widow. Taken all together, it was enough to make a man contemplate the different ways he might enjoy her company.

Before Luke could venture very far down that intriguing mental path, however, the bell over the door jingled again.

"Drat," Mary said under her breath. "I knew I should have gone ahead and locked up when I had the chance." Then she put another of those bright smiles on her face and went on, "Good evening, Marshal."

"Evenin', Mary," Chet Donovan said as he clumped into the room on muddy boots.

"Can I get you something? Coffee? Maybe a piece of pie?"

"Wish I could, but I'm really lookin' for your customer there."

"Me?" Luke said, raising an eyebrow.

"Yeah, I got an answer from up in Montana a lot quicker than I thought I would. Those wires must'a really been singin' tonight. Anyway, I heard from the sheriff in White Fork. Fella by the name of Axtell."

"Did he authorize the payment of the bounty for Tyler?"

"Nope," Donovan said.

"What?" Luke frowned. "Does he doubt that we have the right man? Did you describe the prisoner to him in your wire?"

"Of course I did. Told him I was sure the fella we've got locked up is Judd Tyler, and that the prisoner didn't even bother denyin' it. Evidently that don't matter."

"Why not?"

"Because Axtell claims there's a special condition on that bounty. It's payable only when Tyler is delivered personally to him in White Fork, and not before." The marshal grunted, and after a second Luke realized the sound was a laugh. "Looks like you're gonna have to be takin' a trip up north, Jensen, if you want to collect your blood money."

CHAPTER 6

This was an unexpected annoyance. Due to the fact that men on the run from the law often ran far and fast, Luke seldom delivered a prisoner to the jurisdiction in which the reward had been posted. Usually it was enough just to lock a captured fugitive in the nearest jail — or deliver his corpse to the handiest undertaker — and have the local authorities contact the law where the fugitive was wanted.

That was what he had done here, and in the normal course of affairs, the sheriff in White Fork would have contacted the bank here in Bent Creek and authorized payment of the bounty.

Clearly, that wasn't going to happen.

"Did the telegram say why that's a condition of the reward?" Luke asked.

Donovan shook his head and said, "Nope. Just that that's the way it is." The marshal rubbed his chin. "It's hard to tell much from words printed on a telegraph blank, but I got the feelin' Sheriff Axtell's anxious to see Tyler locked up in his jail. The boy killed a young woman, right?"

"The daughter of one of the local ministers."

"That's a mighty raw thing to do," Donovan said. "Fella like that sure deserves to hang. Bent Creek's a peaceful town, but if word gets around about what Tyler's done, folks are liable to start askin' themselves why we don't just go ahead and string him up here, since he's got it comin'."

"I'm not going to lose my prisoner to a lynch mob," Luke snapped.

"Damn right you're not. I never had a prisoner yet taken out and escorted to a necktie party, and we ain't startin' with Tyler. But I'd just as soon not tempt fate. I want you to get him out of there bright and early in the morning. You can be on the trail north at first light."

Mary had listened quietly to the conversation between Luke and Marshal Donovan, but now she said, "Isn't that rushing things, Marshal?"

"Maybe. But I don't want any trouble in my town, so the easiest way to prevent it is to send it packin'."

"That's a shame," Mary said as she looked

at Luke.

He read quite a bit in her warm gaze, so his voice held genuine regret as he agreed, "It certainly is."

"I reckon you'd best spend the night on the cot in my office," Donovan went on. "That way you can keep an eye on Tyler, just in case anybody gets any ideas."

"I assumed that you —"

Donovan held up a hand to stop Luke.

"I told you, you could lock him up in my jail but I ain't takin' any responsibility for him. He's Montana's murderer, not mine. I plan to go home and get a good night's sleep, and when I get to the office in the mornin', I'd just as soon find that the two of you are gone."

Luke could see that like the bulldog he resembled, Donovan wasn't going to let go of something once he had his jaws set in it. With a sigh, Luke said, "All right, Marshal. I'll head over to the jail just as soon as I finish this excellent meal."

"Mary *does* dish up some good grub," Donovan said. "I reckon I can watch the prisoner for a little while so you can eat. Just don't linger too long."

Donovan left the café. Luke shook his head gloomily and told Mary, "And here I was, looking forward to sharing some more stimulating conversation with you."

"So was I," she said with a sigh of her own. "You don't know how much I was looking forward to it, Mr. Jensen."

The rain had stopped completely by the time Luke walked up the street to the marshal's office a short time later. He had said a bittersweet good-bye to Mary, who told him her last name was Baxter and confirmed that she was, indeed, a widow, her husband having passed on five years earlier.

"You have to promise me, Mr. Jensen, that if you ever ride through Bent Creek again, you'll stop and have another meal with me," she had said to him before he left the café.

"You have my solemn word on that, Mrs. Baxter," he had told her. "But you may not be here by then. Surely some man will have come along by then who's smart enough to marry a woman like you."

"Some may want to," she had said with a faint smile, "but none of the eligible bachelors around here interest me in the least, and I'm not going to marry just any saddle tramp who comes drifting through."

"That's their loss," Luke had said, lifting his coffee cup to her and then drinking the last of the strong, black brew.

He wasn't the sort of man who wallowed in regrets, but he was sorry to leave the Keystone Café.

He forgot about that when he heard an ugly murmur of voices up ahead and looked toward the marshal's office. He walked faster as he spotted a group of men gathered in front of the stone building. That was hardly ever a good thing.

The office door was closed. One man stepped up, hammered a fist on it, and called, "You might as well open up, Chet. We heard you've got a woman-killer in there, and we intend to see that justice is done!"

No response came from inside. Luke hoped that Marshal Donovan was still in there and hadn't slipped out the back. His instincts told him the lawman wouldn't abandon a prisoner to a mob, even a prisoner that he didn't particularly want, but Luke didn't know the man well enough to be certain.

The man who had knocked on the door pounded on it again, and the other men began to shout for Donovan to open up. They were so caught up in what they were doing that they didn't notice Luke approaching them from behind.

Enough light spilled through the windows

of the marshal's office for him to see that several members of the mob were armed with rifles and shotguns. He didn't spot any handguns, but some of the men might be wearing them under their coats. There were ten men in the group, which meant the odds against him would be pretty high if it came down to a fight to protect Judd Tyler.

Just thinking about that put a bitter, sour taste on his tongue. Luke didn't want to risk his life on behalf of such a vile human being . . . but he might not have any choice.

He had his right hand on the butt of one of the Remingtons when someone inside the office jerked the door open. Chet Donovan's bulky figure appeared in the doorway, the twin barrels of his Greener jutting out in front of him. The townsmen flinched back from the shotgun, as anybody in his right mind would do when threatened by a weapon like that.

"You men back off!" Donovan ordered. "Have you all gone loco? How long have I been the marshal here in Bent Creek? Well, how long?"

"Nigh on to seven years, Chet," one of the men answered in a surly voice.

"That's right, and in those seven years, have you ever known me to allow a lynchin'?"

"You never had a varmint like that fella Tyler in your jail before!" another man said. "The talk's all over town about him. He killed a girl up in Montana!"

"A preacher's daughter!" a third man added.

Donovan said, "That's what he's accused of, and that's what he'll answer for . . . up in Montana where he done the crime! He hasn't done anything in Bent Creek but stable his horse and sleep in the hotel."

"They're liable to let him go up there."

"What in the hell makes you think that?" Donovan asked with a frown.

"It's a long way to . . . whatever the name is of the place he ran away from."

"White Fork," Donovan said. "So?"

"You send him back up there, he's liable to get away before they can hang him."

"You mean put him on trial, don't you?"

The man Donovan was talking to waved a hand in dismissal and said, "Put him on trial, hang him, what's the difference? It all ends up the same way, with a killer dancin' at the end of a rope where he belongs!"

"First you say they're gonna let him go, then you say they're gonna hang him. Make up your damn mind." Donovan scowled at the men in front of him. "I'll tell you what's really goin' on here. You fellas are bored!

You don't want those folks up in White Fork to have all the fun of stringin' up a killer. You don't care if Tyler's guilty or innocent, you just want to see him hang!"

A stunned hush fell over the crowd at that bitter accusation. After a moment, one of the men said, "Hell, Chet, if that was true, it'd make us terrible people."

"Damn right it would. And I know better, because I've knowed most of you for the whole seven years I've been here. You're not terrible. You just let yourselves get stirred up. And now you're gonna settle down, go home, and forget about all this."

A broad-shouldered man with a surly expression on his rugged face said, "Any man who'd kill a defenseless girl deserves to die!"

"You'll get no argument from me about that, Hobson, but it ain't up to us to see it done. Now, are you gonna back off, or are we gonna have trouble here that we'll all wind up regrettin'?"

Luke sensed that the issue hung in the balance. These men were starting to see the error of their ways, but with the stubbornness of typical Westerners they didn't want to admit that they'd been wrong.

Maybe he could tip the scales, he decided. He stepped into the edge of the light that came from the open doorway and raised his voice to say, "Besides, gentlemen, the marshal and I have you in a crossfire, if it comes to that. Between his shotgun and my Remingtons, things can get very ugly, very fast."

"It's that bounty hunter!" a man said.

The burly man called Hobson turned and sneered at Luke.

"What's the matter, bounty hunter?" he asked. "Afraid if we take care of Tyler, you won't get your reward?"

"That's not even a consideration right now," Luke said, mostly honestly. "Lynching is murder! If you string up Tyler, whether he deserves it or not, you'll be killers. Only it won't be just an accusation. It'll be a fact."

"I'm done with this," one of the men suddenly muttered. "I'm going home."

"Me too," another one said, and as Luke had seen many times before, once the mob mentality began to crack, it fell apart in a hurry. One after another, the men strode off in different directions into the night, until only Hobson and a couple of others were left.

"You fellas might as well go on home, too," Donovan told them. "You can see for yourselves that there ain't gonna be any lynchin' tonight."

"Never thought I'd see you sidin' with a damn bounty hunter, Donovan," Hobson blustered. "Or protectin' a killer, either."

"I'm protectin' the law, that's all." Donovan glared at Luke. "And I don't much like what I'm doin' right now, either. I just got crowded into it."

"Well, it's a sad day for Bent Creek, that's what it is."

"Go back to your blacksmith shop," Donovan snapped. "And I'll try to forget about you runnin' your mouth that way."

The three men finally turned away from the open door of the marshal's office. Donovan lowered the shotgun a little. Luke hadn't had to draw either of his guns. He stepped aside to let Hobson and the other two pass.

Hobson, who was evidently the town blacksmith, stopped and glared at Luke.

"I don't like killers," he said, "and I don't have a damn bit of use for bounty hunters, either. I'd have more respect for a buzzard feedin' on the carcass of a dead dog!"

"Then I suppose it's a good thing I don't give a damn about whether you respect me," Luke said.

He knew even as the words came out of his mouth that he shouldn't have said them.

He was perfectly capable of ignoring arrogant loudmouths like Hobson and carrying on with his business.

But it had been a long day, he'd been shot at and hit in the head, he'd had to kill three men, he was facing a long ride up into Montana Territory before he could claim the reward he had coming, and he'd had to say good night much too prematurely to a sweet, nice-looking widow woman. He was in a piss-poor mood, no doubt about it.

So, truly, deep down, he didn't mind all that much when Hobson's face flushed with rage and the big blacksmith shouted a curse and charged him, mallet-like fists swinging wildly.

CHAPTER 7

Marshal Donovan yelled, "Hobson! Damn it!" but the man ignored him and continued his bull-like charge.

Luke stepped nimbly aside, avoiding one of Hobson's punches and blocking another with his left forearm. That left his right fist free to snap forward in a sharp jab that landed squarely on Hobson's nose.

Luke felt a satisfying crunch as the blow flattened Hobson's nose and caused blood to spurt over his knuckles. Hobson's head jerked back, but his momentum carried him forward. Luke twisted out of the way, thrust out his leg, and tripped the blacksmith. Hobson went down face-first in the mud.

"If you have any sense, mister, you'll just stay there," Luke told him.

He didn't actually expect Hobson to follow that advice, however, and not surprisingly, his hunch was right.

Hobson got his hands underneath him

and pushed himself up. He shook his head as he got to his feet, slinging mud and blood off his face. His heavy breathing rasped and whistled through his broken nose.

Hobson staggered forward in lumbering fashion, pawed mud from his eyes, and swung his head from side to side as he searched for Luke.

"Isn't one of your duties as marshal to break up fights?" Luke asked Donovan.

"Maybe, but right now I'm concentratin' on guardin' that prisoner in there, the way you wanted me to," the lawman said with an ugly smirk on his face.

"In other words, if Hobson gives me a thrashing, there's nothing you can do about it."

Donovan shrugged beefy shoulders and said, "I already told him to go home, didn't I? Not my fault if he don't listen to reason. And since I don't have a deputy . . ."

Luke let out a disgusted snort. Donovan was enjoying this too much.

But there was nothing Luke could do about it now. He had goaded Hobson into a fight, and he was going to have to see it through.

At least Donovan apparently wanted it to be a fair fight. He told the other remaining members of the mob, "You boys just stay outta this. It's between Hobson and Jensen."

The men nodded and backed off. Neither of them looked like he had the least bit of desire to get in the middle of this fracas.

Hobson's furious but befuddled gaze finally fell on Luke again. He clenched his fists and started toward the bounty hunter. His muddy face twisted in a snarl as he launched a roundhouse punch with his right hand.

Luke started to duck under the sweeping blow, only to realize too late that Hobson was trickier than he looked. The blacksmith's left came up and crashed against Luke's jaw. The punch drove him off his feet.

He landed on his back in the muddy street. His head was spinning from the impact of Hobson's fist, but Luke's senses settled down in time for him to see the big man rushing at him, evidently intending to stomp him into the muck. Luke got his hands up and grabbed the work boot coming toward his face. He twisted and heaved, and Hobson splashed into the mud again with a startled yell.

Luke wasn't going to let it go now. He was good and mad for a lot of reasons, and he let his anger boil up.

He rolled over and dived at Hobson, landing on top of him. Mud covered both men, making them resemble hogs in a wallow. Luke hooked a left into Hobson's midsection, then battered his face with a series of rights.

Hobson reached up in desperation, caught hold of the front of Luke's shirt, and heaved him to the side.

Luke rolled over a couple of times and came to a stop on his belly. Hobson scrambled after him and practically crawled up Luke's back. He looped his forearm around Luke's neck and jammed it up under the bounty hunter's chin. Luke's head began to pound almost immediately as Hobson cut off his air.

Knowing that he would pass out in a couple of minutes if Hobson continued choking him like that, Luke drove an elbow back into the blacksmith's belly, once and then again. It was like hitting a slab of beef. Hobson didn't even seem to notice.

Losing consciousness was the least of his worries, Luke realized. If Hobson kept up that pressure on his throat for very long, it could be fatal. Luke grasped and tore at the man's arm, but it didn't budge.

Why the hell wasn't Donovan breaking it up? Hadn't the battle gone on long enough?

Luke didn't know the answers to those

questions, but he figured that his life was in his own hands, as usual. He struggled to draw his knees up underneath him, then pushed with them and his hands. The ground was too muddy for him to find good purchase at first, but then he braced himself and was able to lift his weight and Hobson's as well.

It was a feat of herculean strength and took every bit of power Luke could muster, but he got to his feet. With Hobson still choking him, Luke began pushing both of them backward, driving his boot heels into the mud. He couldn't afford to slip now. If he went down again, it would be the end.

He hoped he was oriented correctly and remembered where things were that he had noticed earlier. If he had figured wrong, it might mean his doom.

Hobson tried to stiffen his legs, but he couldn't channel all his strength into choking Luke and still prevent being pushed backward. The back of his legs suddenly hit the end of the water trough Luke had been aiming for, and when Luke surged against him, Hobson couldn't maintain his balance.

Both men toppled into the water.

The sudden dunking was finally enough to loosen the blacksmith's grip. Luke tore free, twisted around, and clamped his right hand around Hobson's neck as the man came up gasping for air. Luke forced him back down, and now it was Luke's turn for his arm to be like a bar of iron as he held the blacksmith's upper body submerged in the dirty water.

Hobson began to thrash wildly, but Luke didn't let go. His chest heaved as he continued gasping for the life-giving air that he now denied to Hobson. Fury filled him. He had come close to death many times, but it still always made him mad.

Two pairs of hands grabbed him, locking on to his arms and hauling back with grunts of effort. The men dragged him off of Hobson, who came up out of the water sputtering and gasping.

Luke was angry enough he probably could have fought his way loose from the men holding him and gone after Hobson again, but the more rational part of his brain had started to reassert itself.

"That's enough, damn it!" Marshal Donovan bellowed. "You almost killed him, Jensen!"

Luke turned a baleful glare toward the lawman and rasped through his aching throat, "You didn't stop him when he was about to strangle me."

"You're a bounty hunter passin' through

town. He's our blacksmith, for God's sake! Our friend and neighbor! We need him around."

The dip in the water trough seemed to have taken all the fight out of Hobson. He had managed to climb out of the trough but had slipped down and now sat beside it, hanging on to it to keep himself upright.

The two men who had hold of Luke let go of his arms and stepped back as Donovan motioned to them with the Greener's twin barrels.

"You still want Tyler and me out of here at first light, Marshal?" Luke asked.

"You damn well bet I do," Donovan said.

"That's fine . . . because Bent Creek is the sorriest settlement I've seen in a long time, and I'll be glad to put it behind me!"

For the second time today, Luke was filthy. He was sure the clothes Hardy had taken to be cleaned earlier weren't ready yet, so he supposed he would just have to remain uncomfortable in the wet, muddy garb he had on.

"There's a canvas tarp in the back," Donovan said as they entered the marshal's office. "I'll get it and put it on the cot. It might be a little musty, but I don't want you gettin' mud all over everything."

81

"I suppose I should be grateful you're not making me sleep on the floor."

"Don't think I didn't consider it," the marshal said.

He returned the shotgun to a rack on the wall, then fetched the tarp from a small storage area behind the office and tossed it on the cot that sat on one side of the room.

"You're on your own now, Jensen."

"From what I can see, I have been ever since I rode into Bent Creek," Luke said.

"Well, nobody invited you here, did they?"

Without waiting for an answer, Donovan left the office, closing the door behind him.

Luke barred the door. He had put his hat back on after the fight; now he took it off and shook his head in disgust as he looked at the mud daubed on it. He didn't know when he'd get a chance to clean up.

He went to the door of the cell block and looked through the small, barred window. A lantern with its wick turned low sat on a stool in the aisle between the cells. Its dim glow revealed Judd Tyler stretched out on the bunk in his cell, face turned to the wall.

If all Luke had been able to see was a bundle of blankets, he would have been suspicious, despite Marshal Donovan's claim that no one could escape from this jail.

Tyler's head was visible, though, above the blankets, and as Luke watched, the prisoner shifted a little in his sleep, snorted, and then settled down again in deep, rhythmic breathing.

Whatever Tyler had done, it wasn't keeping him from getting a good night's sleep, Luke thought. But that wasn't unusual in hardened criminals, who seemed to feel little or no guilt over their violent behavior.

Luke turned away from the cell block and grimaced at the sticky feel of his clothes.

Help came from an unexpected source. A light tapping sounded at the door. Luke frowned, went to the wall rack, and took down the scattergun Donovan had put up there a few minutes earlier.

Lynch mobs usually didn't knock so softly, but Luke didn't want to take a chance. Some of the men from earlier might have returned to try a trickier approach.

The door was thick enough that Luke wasn't worried about anybody shooting through it. He stood there with the shotgun in his hands and called, "Who is it?"

"Mary Baxter."

The soft reply made Luke's eyebrows arch in surprise. The café owner's voice was about the last one he had expected to hear again tonight.

"Mrs. Baxter, what in the world are you doing here?"

"I brought you some clean clothes. They're some of my husband's things. They might be a little small for you, but at least they're clean and dry."

"You're alone?" Luke asked.

"Of course. Who else would be with me at this time of night?"

Luke leaned the shotgun against the wall, then lifted the bar across the door. He picked up the Greener again and held it in his right hand while he used his left to twist the key in the lock.

"It's open," he said.

Mary Baxter came into the office carrying a bundle wrapped in canvas. She had taken off the apron and replaced it with a light jacket.

"How did you know I needed clean clothes?" Luke asked her as he put the shotgun back in the rack.

"I heard the commotion as I was locking up the café and saw you rolling around in the street with Clete Hobson. Honestly, at first I didn't know whether to laugh or be horrified. Then I realized it was a serious fight. I thought he was going to hurt you."

Luke put his left hand to his throat and

said, "It wasn't for lack of trying that he didn't."

"Anyway, I saw how you'd gotten mud all over and I knew you were going to be spending the night here in the marshal's office, so I thought you might be more comfortable in clean clothes. I went home and got these."

She set the bundle on the desk.

"I suppose I should be going now . . ."

"Why don't you wait around for a few minutes while I get cleaned up?" Luke suggested. "There might be some coffee left in the pot over there on the stove."

Mary smiled and said, "I'm not sure I want to drink any coffee that's sitting in a pot in a lawman's office."

"I can tell you from experience that's probably a wise way to feel," Luke told her. He picked up the bundle of clothes. "I think I saw a little washbasin in the back. Just let me lock and bar the door . . ."

"I can do that."

"You're a woman of many talents, Mrs. Baxter."

"You don't know how many, Mr. Jensen."

"I wouldn't mind learning. Perhaps we could start by calling each other Mary and Luke?"

"I think that would be a very good start," Mary said. "But only a beginning . . ."

CHAPTER 8

Mary brought breakfast from the café for both of them, early the next morning. Luke hated to impose on her, but he asked her if she could bring something for Judd Tyler, too.

Even cold-blooded killers had to eat . . . until they kept their date with the hangman.

"I'll bring a couple of extra biscuits for him," she said, "but he can drink whatever sludge is left in Marshal Donovan's coffeepot."

"You won't get any argument from me on that score," Luke said with a smile.

The sun wasn't up yet when Mary came back with a tray containing plates of ham, fried eggs, and biscuits, along with a fresh pot of coffee. She and Luke sat down at the marshal's desk to enjoy the breakfast.

Luke washed down some of the food with a sip of coffee, sighed in satisfaction, and said, "After last night and this meal, I truly do feel like a new man."

"I'm glad I could . . . reinvigorate you," she said.

"Oh, you did that just fine, sure enough," Luke said. "I'll never forget you, Mary."

"But those memories won't be enough to make you hurry back here to Bent Creek, will they?" she asked with a faint wistful tone in her voice.

Luke shrugged and said, "My work takes me a lot of different places. I don't usually know where I'll wind up next, let alone six months or a year from now."

"Well," she said, a little cooler now, "you know where to find me."

Luke thought it best to concentrate on his food for a few moments after that exchange.

When they had finished eating, Mary said, "I need to get back over to the café. I usually have it open for business before now."

Luke put his empty plate and coffee cup back on the tray.

"I can't thank you enough for everything."

"You don't have to," she told him. She came up on her toes and kissed him as he bent his head toward hers. "Good-bye, Luke Jensen."

"Good-bye," he said, feeling more solemn than he usually did when he said so long to a woman.

She paused at the doorway and looked back at him.

"On my way to the café, I'll stop at the hotel and find out if Hardy can bring your clothes over here. You can just leave my husband's things here in the office and I'll get them later."

"I'm obliged to you for that, too."

"Good-bye, Luke," she said again as she went out. Luke just nodded. There wasn't anything left to say between them, at least not now. Maybe someday.

Although he doubted if he would ever be that lucky.

Off and on during the night, he had heard snores coming from the cell block, so he knew Tyler was still in there. Mary had left the extra biscuits on a napkin. Luke picked them up and went to the cell block door, unlocking it with a key from the ring that hung on a nail on the wall behind the marshal's desk.

"Rise and shine, Tyler," he called to the prisoner as he swung the door open.

He was ready for trouble, even though the likelihood of it was very small. A man in his line of work didn't live very long by being careless.

In this case the caution wasn't necessary. Tyler was still stretched out on the bunk.

He pushed the scratchy wool blanket aside, rolled over, stretched, and groaned as he sat up. His mouth opened wide in a yawn.

"I never did get a good night's sleep on a jail cell bunk," he said.

"And why does it not surprise me that you have experience spending the night in a jail cell?" Luke asked, although the question was strictly rhetorical.

"I've had a few scrapes with the law. I won't deny that."

"You mean like murdering a young woman?"

Tyler came sharply to his feet, crossed the cell, and gripped the bars as he glared at Luke in the dim light.

"I told you, I didn't kill Rachel. I never killed anybody, and for sure not a preacher's daughter!"

"You just admitted to being an outlaw."

Tyler leaned forward as his hands tightened on the bars. He said, "I've rustled some cows in my time, sure, and I even held up a few stagecoaches. I'm not proud of those things, but I won't deny that I did them. But murder . . ." He shook his head. "I'm not a killer, Jensen, but right now I don't give a damn if you believe me or not."

Luke held out the biscuits and said, "Here. Have something to eat and cool off."

For a second, Tyler looked mad enough to turn down the biscuits out of sheer spite. But then hunger won out and he relented. He snatched them from Luke's hand.

Luke had kept his other hand on a gun butt while giving Tyler the skimpy breakfast. If the prisoner had tried anything, he would have gotten a .44 round to go with his meal.

Tyler retreated to the bunk to gnaw sullenly on the biscuits. After a moment, he asked, "Do I get any coffee?"

"If you can call it that," Luke replied. "I'll bring it to you."

As he started to turn away from the cell, Tyler said, "Hey, wait a minute. Have you gotten a reply back from the telegram to White Fork?"

With everything that had been going on the night before, obviously no one had said anything to the prisoner about the wire from Sheriff Axtell in Montana.

"Actually, I have," Luke said.

"Gonna get your blood money?"

Luke made a disgusted sound and said, "Everybody keeps asking me about that. It's a perfectly legal reward for the apprehension of a criminal. The tradition dates back centuries to England —"

"Yeah, well, I don't give a damn about what they do in England."

"In that case . . . no. Sheriff Axtell in White Fork didn't authorize payment of the reward."

That seemed to surprise Tyler. He frowned, swallowed the last bite of biscuit, and said, "Why not?"

"It seems there's a provision stating that you have to be turned over to him personally before the reward will be paid."

Tyler's eyes got wide. Even in the bad light, Luke could tell that the young man's face had turned pale. Tyler said, "No. Hell, no!"

"What do you mean? You had to be aware that if you were captured, you'd be taken back to White Fork for trial. I admit, I'm a bit annoyed by this development. I expected that the sheriff up there would send some deputies to collect you, or come himself. But I suppose I can deliver you if that's what I have to do."

Tyler leaned back against the wall and started to laugh, although there was no humor in the sound. In fact, it was downright bleak. Luke put up with it for a moment, then said, "What's so blasted funny?"

"You, Jensen," Tyler said. "You're a damned fool. You really think you're gonna ride up there and get that reward?"

"That's exactly what I think."

"Well, you're wrong. You'll never make it to White Fork alive, and neither will I! Axtell and that gang of murderers he calls his deputies will see to that!"

Before Luke could ask what Tyler meant by that brazen claim, someone knocked on the office door. He had locked it after Mary left, and since Donovan surely had his own key, that meant the visitor was someone else.

Luke turned and walked out of the cell block, but it was hard to put Tyler's stricken expression out of his mind. The prisoner really had looked terrified for a moment.

Drawing one of the Remingtons, which he had carefully cleaned and oiled during the night, Luke asked through the door, "Who's there?"

"It's me, Mr. Jensen," a young voice answered. "Hardy McCoy. I got your clean clothes."

Luke glanced at the heap of muddy clothing he had discarded after the battle with Hobson. They were piled in the corner, and there was no time to get them cleaned at the local laundry. He would have to stuff them in his saddlebag and take them with him when he left with Tyler. Maybe when they came to a stream, he could stop long enough to rinse the dried mud out of them.

Keeping the revolver in his hand, Luke unlocked the door and opened it. Hardy stared at the gun as he came in carrying a paper-wrapped bundle with twine tied around it.

"You figurin' on shootin' somebody else, Mr. Jensen?" the redheaded boy asked.

"Not unless I have to."

"Well, I sure won't give you no cause to ventilate me."

Luke chuckled and said, "I didn't expect that you would, Hardy. You're up awfully early."

"Naw, Mr. Beale gen'rally has me up and workin' at some chore before the sun rises. I'm an orphan, you know, and he gives me a place to sleep, so I got to work for my room and board."

"A boy like you, who's accustomed to hard work, will go far in this world," Luke told him.

"I hope so. I wouldn't mind seein' Laramie or Cheyenne one of these days."

Luke laughed again, holstered the Remington, and took the bundle of clothes from Hardy. He gave the boy a silver dollar and said, "My saddlebags and rifle should still be in the room I was supposed to use last night. Can you get them and bring them over here?"

"Sure thing, Mr. Jensen!"

Hardy hurried out. Luke took advantage of the momentary privacy to get out of the borrowed duds and pull on his own clothes. He had put his hat near the stove overnight, so the mud was dry on it. He was able to knock most of it off by swatting the hat against his leg.

Once that was done, he took a tin cup off a small shelf and poured what was left in the coffeepot into it. The brew looked pretty thick and unappetizing and didn't smell much better, but Tyler could drink it or do without.

Luke took the coffee into the cell block. Tyler had come back to the cell's door and gripped the bars again.

"Listen, you can't take me back to White Fork," he said. "Take me anywhere else and let 'em put me on trial there, but don't go to White Fork."

"Because we'll be killed on the way." Luke held out the cup.

Tyler reached through the bars, took it, and gulped down some of the cold coffee. He didn't seem to care what it tasted like; he just wanted its bracing effect.

"You don't know the whole story, Jensen. I told you I didn't kill Rachel Montgomery, but I didn't tell you who *did*."

Luke was a little intrigued by that, despite all the desperate lies he had heard over the years from criminals he had captured. Judd Tyler was probably lying, too, but he was putting on a good act. He looked and sounded like he was genuinely innocent and feared for his life.

"We have a long ride in front of us, Tyler. You'll have time to tell me plenty of stories. More than I really care to listen to, I imagine."

Tyler's face twisted in a grimace as he said, "You're gonna get us both killed, that's what you're gonna do."

Before either of them could say anything else, the door of the marshal's office opened. Luke turned in that direction and saw Chet Donovan coming in. The lawman stopped just inside the door and scowled.

"I thought I told you to be outta here with that prisoner by now, Jensen."

"We were just getting ready to leave, Marshal," Luke said. "How does it look out on the street? Any sign of lynch mobs?"

Donovan let out a contemptuous snort and said, "At this hour of the mornin'? Some folks are still asleep, and the ones who are awake ain't in any mood to start trouble."

"Did you have a chance to look through

your collection of wanted posters last night before the trouble started?"

"For that fella you shot in the hotel, you mean?" Donovan shook his head. "I looked, but I sure didn't find any paper on him. Reckon you won't get to collect on that corpse." He jerked a thumb over his shoulder. "I stopped by the stable and told Fred Crandall to saddle your horses, if you hadn't already been there and picked 'em up. So they'll be ready to ride by the time you get over there."

"I'm obliged to you for that, I suppose."

"I don't want your thanks, I just want you gone." Donovan came on into the cell block, drew his revolver, and unlocked the cell. "Get outta there, Tyler. You're not gonna be stinkin' up my jail anymore, you killer."

Tyler gave Luke a desperate glance and said, "Jensen . . . ?"

Luke pulled out one of the Remingtons and said in a hard, flat voice, "Let's go."

CHAPTER 9

As Donovan had promised, Crandall had Luke's gray and Tyler's paint saddled and ready when the two of them, accompanied by the marshal, arrived at the livery stable.

"Hear tell you had some more trouble last night," the old-timer said to Luke.

"Some."

"There's been more excitement in Bent Creek since you rode in than we usually have in a month of Sundays."

Donovan said, "A hell of a lot more excitement than we need, if you ask me."

"Now, Chet, you got to admit, things around here can get to be a mite borin'," Crandall said.

Donovan *harummphed.*

"That's just the way I like 'em," he said.

Hardy McCoy appeared in the stable's open double doors, weighed down by Luke's saddlebags and rifle. As he came in, the boy said, "I spotted you fellas comin' over here,

Mr. Jensen. Here are the things you sent me to fetch."

"Thanks, Hardy," Luke said. He'd kept his gun out while they were walking to the stable, but now he pouched the iron and took the saddlebags and Winchester from Hardy. "You're an observant, enterprising lad. I appreciate all your help while I've been here."

Hardy looked up at him and asked, "You wouldn't need a partner in your bounty huntin', would you?"

"You already have a job at the hotel."

"Yeah, but I think it'd be fine sport to hunt down desperadoes like you do."

"It can be," Luke said, "but it's a bit too dangerous for a boy. You'd best grow up some more first."

Donovan said, "Don't listen to him, Hardy. Bounty huntin's no life for anybody. It's just one step above bein' an outlaw yourself."

Luke wasn't going to waste time arguing with the marshal, who clearly didn't like him and never would. Instead he slid the Winchester into its sheath, slung the saddlebags over the gray's back and fastened them in place, and then said to Tyler, "Mount up."

"I sure wish you wouldn't do this, Jensen,"

99

the young man said. "Take me anywhere else you want and turn me over to the law there. I won't give you a bit of trouble, I swear. But if you head for White Fork, you're damning us both."

"I said mount up." Luke's tone left no room for argument.

Tyler sighed, put his foot in the stirrup, and swung up into the saddle on the paint's back.

Luke took a pair of handcuffs from one of his saddlebags and said, "Put your arms behind your back."

"You're gonna cuff me like that?"

"I am."

"How am I supposed to ride?"

"I'll be leading your horse," Luke said. "You won't have to do anything except enjoy the ride."

Tyler sighed and said, "It's gonna get mighty uncomfortable, riding like that."

"Maybe, but you'll be alive. That's more than Rachel Montgomery can say."

Tyler scowled but didn't say anything else. He had that air of despair about him again as he put his hands behind his back as Luke ordered. Luke snapped the cuffs around his wrists.

He mounted up and took the reins of

Tyler's horse as Crandall handed them up to him.

"I'd tell you to be careful . . ." Donovan said as his beefy shoulders rose and fell. "Except I don't really give a damn."

"You're a fine example of a peace officer, Marshal," Luke said. The sarcasm practically dripping from the words made the marshal's face redden. "Exactly the sort that Bent Creek deserves, I'd say."

Before Donovan could respond, Luke heeled the gray into motion and rode out of the stable, leading the paint behind him.

Hardy McCoy stepped into the doorway, waved, and called, "So long, Mr. Jensen!"

Luke turned in the saddle enough to lift a hand in farewell, then glanced at the café as he rode past it. The windows were brightly lit, the curtains were pushed back, and he could look inside and see Mary behind the counter, pouring coffee, serving food, and talking with the customers who were already there.

For a second he wondered what it would be like to pull his horse to a stop, step down from the saddle, go inside, into that light and warmth, and just forget about everything else. The lure of that thought was strong . . .

But he was smart enough to know that it

wasn't going to happen, and even if it did, things probably wouldn't work out the way he hoped they would. He was too old, too hardened by life to change.

Anyway, justice was a powerful lure as well, and Judd Tyler deserved to swing for what he'd done.

Luke kept moving, riding out of Bent Creek as the eastern skies turned red and gold with the approach of dawn.

Tyler didn't say anything as they traveled north with the sun rising on their right. Luke glanced back at the prisoner from time to time and saw that Tyler was riding with his head drooped forward. The brim of the young man's hat shielded his face.

Luke didn't think Tyler was actually sleeping. After a while, his curiosity got the better of him, so he let the gray drop back a little until he and Tyler were riding almost side by side.

"You were so eager to convince me of your innocence," Luke said. "What happened to that, Tyler?"

"Figured I'd be wasting my time," Tyler replied without looking over at Luke. "Your mind's made up. Anyway, the only thing you're really interested in is that reward money."

"That's not strictly true. Naturally, I'd like to be paid for my efforts in apprehending you, but I want to see justice done as well."

"Neither one of those things is going to happen if you take me to White Fork." For the first time in a while, Tyler's head lifted and he looked at Luke. "But if there's any chance that money might make a difference . . . I told you I rustled cattle and held up some stagecoaches. I've still got most of the loot from those jobs. I cached it somewhere nobody'll ever find it. Let me go and I'll tell you where to find it. It adds up to more than the bounty on my head."

Luke laughed.

"Of course it does," he said. "And if I take your word for it and let you go, when I get to the place where the money's supposed to be, I'll find an empty hole in the ground . . . if that much." He shook his head. "I wasn't born yesterday, Tyler. Don't insult me by taking me for a fool."

A look of anger flashed across Tyler's face. He said, "I can't take you to where the money is hidden, or I would. But it's too close to White Fork. There's too much of a chance we'd be spotted. Axtell and his deputies will already be setting out to ambush us."

"That's the second time you've made it

sound like Sheriff Axtell and his men are outlaws."

Tyler snorted in contempt.

"They might as well be. They're not honest lawmen, that's for damn sure. Gus Axtell may wear a sheriff's badge, but everybody around White Fork knows that he really works for Manfred Douglas."

Luke shook his head and said, "I don't know who that is."

"Douglas is the big he-wolf in those parts. Owns the Circle M ranch, the biggest, richest spread in that part of the territory. He owns at least half of White Fork, too. Nobody dares cross him."

"Except you," Luke guessed.

Tyler shrugged and said, "I rustled more Circle M stock than from any of the other ranches around there, I reckon, but that's because Douglas's herd is way bigger than anybody else's. Besides, I figured he'd miss it less. I didn't really want to hurt any of those little greasy sack outfits."

"Charitable of you," Luke said.

Tyler glared at him and said, "Just because I drove off some cows that didn't belong to me doesn't make me a terrible *hombre*."

"Just a dishonest one."

"Well, I never claimed different, did I?"

"Go on with your story," Luke told him.

"This Manfred Douglas has Sheriff Axtell in his pocket, you said."

"He damn sure does. And Axtell keeps the peace, I reckon you've got to give him credit for that. But that's because everybody's afraid of him and his gunslingin' deputies. Enough people have disappeared after giving Douglas trouble that folks figured out mighty quick it wasn't smart to cross Douglas, Axtell, or any of those gunslicks wearing a badge."

"From the sound of it, you think Douglas is going to order Axtell to kill you before you can stand trial . . . and me, to boot, since I'll be with you."

"That's exactly what's gonna happen. In fact, as soon as Axtell got that telegram from the marshal in Bent Creek, I'd bet my hat he rode out to Douglas's ranch as fast as he could to give him the news. Douglas has probably issued the order already."

"The order to bushwhack us?"

"Yep. There are still some honest people in White Fork, even though they don't cotton to the idea of standing up to Douglas. But if the truth comes out about what really happened to Rachel Montgomery, that might stick in their craw bad enough that they'd stop letting Douglas and Axtell run roughshod over them."

Luke frowned in thought for a moment and then said, "You're about to tell me that Manfred Douglas killed the Montgomery girl, aren't you?"

"No. Not the old man. His son Spence." Tyler grimaced. "The sorriest son of a bitch who ever drew breath."

They had been riding along at an easy pace as they talked. Bent Creek was several miles behind them now. Luke saw a line of cottonwoods and other trees up ahead and knew they probably marked the course of a stream.

He said, "We'll stop up there, let the horses get a drink, and rest for a few minutes. And I need to wash out those clothes that got covered with mud last night, too. While we're there you can tell me the rest of the story."

"You mean you're actually starting to believe me, Jensen?"

"I wouldn't go that far," Luke said. "But I'll admit, you have me a little intrigued. I wouldn't mind hearing more."

"It's a pretty ugly story."

"Most of the ones that involve people dying are," Luke said.

CHAPTER 10

"It's a funny thing," Tyler said as he sat with his back leaned against a cottonwood trunk. "I don't recall seeing an actual creek anywhere around Bent Creek."

"You're right about that," Luke said. He was hunkered next to the stream, which was five feet wide and a foot deep. If this creek had a name, he had no idea what it was.

As he continued washing the mud from his spare shirt, he went on, "But that's not unusual. I recall visiting a settlement down in Texas called Shady Hill. The country there was flat as a table, and there wasn't a tree in sight to provide shade."

"Chasing after some *bandido,* were you?"

"That's right. A man named Enrique . . . something or other. Don't recall the last name."

"Do you remember what happened to him?"

"They hanged him in Del Rio."

Tyler clucked his tongue and said, "Bad luck for Enrique. He was probably guilty, though."

"Of half a dozen brutal murders. Beyond the shadow of a doubt."

"See, that's the difference between him and me," Tyler said. "I'm innocent. Of murder, anyway."

"You were telling me about that," Luke said as he straightened from kneeling on the creek bank and hung the wet shirt on a tree branch next to the trousers he had already washed. "About Spence Douglas."

"Yeah." Tyler sighed. "I don't suppose you'd take these handcuffs off?"

Luke shook his head and said, "I don't suppose."

"Well, I guess I'll just have to put up with 'em, then, although it's a mite hard for me to talk without using my hands. I'm the naturally expressive sort, I reckon."

"Just get on with it," Luke said. A few yards away, the two horses continued cropping peacefully at the grass growing along the creek bank.

"Spence and I grew up together, in a way," Tyler began. "We're about the same age. He's less than a year younger than me, I think. We both went to the little schoolhouse there in White Fork, for a while, anyway. So

108

we knew each other, but we were never really friends. You see, even though the Circle M wasn't as big and successful back in those days, it was still a nice operation, so Spence was the son of a respected rancher. And me? I was just the saloonkeeper's boy."

"Wait a minute," Luke said. "You just referred to Manfred Douglas as a respected rancher. I thought most of the folks around there either feared or hated him . . . or both."

"Things were a little different then," Tyler said with a shrug. "But I'm gettin' to that."

"Go ahead."

"Spence was a hellion, right from the start, before he was even out of knee pants. He was always getting into fights and stealing. If he saw something he wanted, it didn't matter to him that it might belong to somebody else."

"Sort of like a man who rustles cattle and holds up stagecoaches," Luke pointed out.

Tyler made a face and said, "Yeah, yeah, I'm a fine one to be talking, I know. But I was never as downright *mean* about it as Spence always was. Anyway, every time Spence got into some sort of trouble, his pa came into town to straighten it out, usually with half a dozen men from his ranch crew with him. They were a pretty salty bunch. People got used to overlooking all of Spence's little scrapes because they didn't want to make trouble for themselves. And Manfred Douglas got used to people doing whatever he wanted."

"Power corrupts," Luke muttered. "And absolute power corrupts absolutely."

"Yeah. Over time, Douglas started figuring his word was law. From there, it was a pretty short step to making sure his own personal pick wound up as sheriff. Gus Axtell used to work for him, before he pinned on a star."

"I assume we'll be getting to the part about the young lady soon?"

"Rachel," Tyler said, and there was a little catch in his voice as he spoke the name. "Prettiest, sweetest girl you ever saw. A couple of years younger than Spence and me. Her pa answered the call and came to preach in White Fork when she was about twelve. I reckon I fell in love with her the first time I laid eyes on her."

Tyler jerked a little, shook his head, and looked like he couldn't believe he had just said that. He went on quickly, "Listen, Jensen, don't get the idea that I've been pinin' away for her all these years. I had a crush on her, sure, but I got over it. A girl like her, a preacher's daughter, never would have thought of a boy raised in a saloon as anything but a friend, if that much. I knew that and didn't waste my time chasing after her." He paused. "She *was* a pretty good friend, though, to just about everybody who knew her, including me. The only one she couldn't stand —"

"Was Spence Douglas," Luke finished for him, confident that the guess was correct.

"You're damn right. Spence rubbed Rachel the wrong way. She hated his arrogance and meanness, but there was nothing he could do about that. It was just part of him. An ugly part."

"But that didn't make Spence want her any less, did it?"

Tyler frowned at him and asked, "How'd you know that?"

"It seems rather obvious. I've read the Bard, and this story has definite overtones of Shakespearean tragedy."

"I wouldn't know about that," Tyler said, "but yeah, Spence wanted her, sure enough. And she didn't want to have anything to do with him. Then Manfred decided it was time to send Spence back east to school. He wanted his son to be a college man. I don't think Spence wanted to go, but he couldn't stand up to Manfred any more than the other folks around there. He went."

"It seems to me that Miss Montgomery should have married someone else while Spence was back east," Luke said. "That would have solved her problem. I'm surprised it didn't occur to you to suggest that."

"I told you, she and I were just friends," Tyler snapped. "By that time, my pa had lost his saloon in a poker game and crawled into the bottom of a bottle, and I was doin' whatever I had to, to take care of myself, whether it was legal or not. Even if I'd thought Rachel would give me the time of day, I didn't have a damn thing to offer her. I thought too much of her to ever do anything like that. And even though she had plenty of suitors, she didn't like any of them enough to get hitched up with them."

"So she was still single when Spence Douglas came back from college, and he immediately started pursuing her again."

"Say, you *are* good at figuring these things out, Jensen. Spence wasn't gone all that long. He got in some sort of trouble at that college and got booted out, which didn't surprise anybody. This was one time his pa couldn't do anything about it, either. So when Spence got back, he went after Rachel again, but she didn't like him any better than she did the first time around. And

Spence . . . well, he just couldn't stand that."

Luke had been prepared to scoff at whatever wild yarn Judd Tyler tried to spin to justify his crimes, but instead he found himself genuinely interested in the young man's story. He wasn't sure he was prepared to *believe* it just yet, but so far the tale had the ring of truth about it.

Certainly, during his years on the frontier Luke had run across numerous cattle barons like Manfred Douglas, ruthless and full of themselves, willing to use any means necessary to destroy anyone who dared to oppose them. Usually Luke tried to steer well clear of that sort, but he knew his brother Smoke had clashed violently with them many, many times.

"What happened?" Luke heard himself asking when Tyler paused again.

"Spence tried to court Rachel. He put the word out to all the other young fellas in the area that they'd better stay away from her if they knew what was good for them. Some of the ones who didn't take that advice wound up getting the stuffing beat out of them by Sheriff Axtell's deputies. Rachel heard about that and it made her plenty mad. When Spence showed up at her pa's house to call on her, she told him he was wasting his time and he might as well go away. He stomped around and told her she'd change her tune soon enough."

"I didn't even know the young woman, and I could have told Spence a heavy-handed approach like that wasn't going to work," Luke said.

"It sure didn't. But that didn't stop him from being more determined than ever."

Luke frowned and rubbed his chin.

"How do you know what Miss Montgomery told young Douglas? You weren't there, were you?"

Tyler looked a little uncomfortable — and not from the handcuffs — as he said, "Rachel told me about it. Like I said before, the two of us were friends."

"The minister's daughter and the young rustler and bandit?" Luke arched a skeptical eyebrow.

"Rachel didn't care about any of that! She knew me from back when we were all kids and always tried to tell me that I had a good heart, I'd just made some bad decisions. She said it was never too late to turn back to the straight and narrow."

"An admirable sentiment, but I've known men who couldn't find the straight and narrow if they searched for it for the next hundred years."

"Yeah, and Spence Douglas is one of

'em," Tyler agreed. "Anyway, the next big thing that happened was the church social. Rachel's pa isn't one of those preachers who's against dancing, so they had some fiddle players there and there was plenty of do-si-doin' going on. Spence showed up with a few of the Circle M crew, and he was dressed to beat the band, wearing one of those fancy shirts he likes. This one was decorated with silver conchos and fringe. Looked downright silly to me. He was bound and determined to dance with Rachel, too. He wouldn't take no for an answer, and she wound up slapping his face in front of everybody to make him back off."

"Was his father there at the social?" Luke asked.

"No, Manfred doesn't go in for things like that. Probably would have made things worse if he had been . . . although the way it turned out, I don't guess it could have been any worse." Tyler took a deep breath and went on, "Spence flew off the handle. No telling what he might've done if his pa's men hadn't been there. They dragged him out, but not before he did a bunch of yelling and cussing, right there in the church.

"That sort of put a damper on the evening. Folks tried to carry on, but their hearts weren't in it anymore. The social broke up after a while and everybody went home. Rachel stayed behind to clean up, though, and I . . . well, I stayed to help her."

Tyler had said twice that there was nothing romantic between him and Rachel Montgomery, but even if the rest of his story was true, Luke wasn't sure he believed that part of it. It seemed to him, judging by Tyler's voice and the look in his eyes when he talked about Rachel, that he'd been in love with her, even if nothing had ever come of it. Even if he never would admit it to himself.

But after listening to him, Luke was finding it more and more difficult to accept the idea that Tyler would have harmed the young woman.

"When we were finished, I would have walked her home," Tyler went on, his tone becoming bleak now. "I told her I wanted to. But she said there wasn't any need for that, since her pa's house was close by, just a couple of hundred yards away on the other side of some trees. Anyway, nobody would ever bother her. Everybody in town loved her." Grim lines appeared on Tyler's face as he continued, "So I let her talk me out of it. If I'd insisted . . . Ah, hell! If I'd done a lot of things different in life, everything would change, wouldn't it?"

"A dilemma that nags at the mind of almost everyone, I expect," Luke said. "Not very many people are able to live without regrets."

"I damn sure can't, and what happened that night . . . that's the worst of 'em." Tyler took another deep breath, as if he were having to force himself to go on. "Rachel went one way and I went the other, but I hadn't gone very far when I heard a horse moving around in that grove of trees between the church and the parsonage. I told myself it wasn't anything to worry about and went on, but it nagged at me enough that I stopped again, and that's when I heard Rachel cry out.

"Well, I was on foot, but I ran as hard as I could to get back there. I didn't see her on the road, but I remembered that horse I'd heard and went into the trees to look for her. About that time I heard hoofbeats again. Somebody was riding off in a hurry. And then I . . . I practically tripped over Rachel's body. I dropped to my knees beside her. She wasn't moving or making any sounds, so I got a match out and lit it, and I saw that somebody had choked her . . . choked her to death."

Tyler was choked as well, so wrought up with emotion that he could barely get the words out. If this was all some elaborate lie, Luke thought, just an act that Tyler was putting on, he was doing a fine job of it. Every word had the deep ring of truth to it.

"I reckon I knew in my heart she was dead, but I felt like I ought to try to get help anyway," Tyler continued. "I got up, and then I heard horses again, more than one this time, so I went toward them and realized too late it was some of those Circle M boys. I thought they must have come back to look for Spence. They spotted me, and one of them yelled, 'It's that bastard Tyler! He killed the preacher's girl!' "

"Wait a minute," Luke said. "How did they know —" He stopped as realization soaked in on his brain. "Oh."

"Yeah," Tyler said. "The only way they could have known that Rachel was dead was if Spence told them . . . and he wouldn't have known if he wasn't the one who killed her."

"That's entirely logical," Luke said, "but it's not exactly proof, not without some testimony to back it up. And from everything you've said, it's not very likely any of Douglas's men would be willing to testify against his son."

"George Armstrong Custer will climb up out of his grave and go back to fighting the

Indians before that happens."

"What did they do when they saw you?"

Tyler said, "They hauled out their guns and started blasting away at me. Things couldn't have worked out any better for 'em. All they had to do was kill me and claim they'd found me with Rachel's body. Nobody in White Fork would ever doubt that I killed her. I'm just a no-account, the son of a drunk, and a pretty shady character, to boot. And quite a few folks saw me stay behind at the church to help Rachel clean up. They knew the two of us were there alone. It'd be a pretty simple story: I made advances to her, she ran off into the woods to get away from me, I caught up with her and killed her." Tyler shrugged. "They'd bury me in a plain pine box, and that'd be the end of it."

"But you got away."

"I ran like the very devil himself was right on my heels. Those bullets were flyin' all around me, but somehow they all missed. I made it to one of the hitch racks in town and grabbed the first horse I saw." Tyler nodded toward the paint, still cropping at the grass. "That was the only stroke of good luck I had that night. That pony's damn fast, faster than any of the mounts those fellas who came after me were riding. I got away."

"And made it as far as Bent Creek."

Tyler sighed and said, "Yeah."

"It didn't take long for Sheriff Axtell to get those reward dodgers spread all over this part of the country."

"Of course it didn't. I know Spence. As soon as he realized what he'd done, he went crying to his pa for help. And old Manfred, he told Spence not to worry about it, that he'd take care of everything. He put a bounty on my head and Axtell spread the word, and they figured either some bounty hunter would kill me and shut my mouth for good . . ."

He gave Luke a long look.

"Or else I'd be caught, in which case they set up the bounty so whoever grabbed me would have to take me back to White Fork to get paid. That'd be you, Jensen."

"But you figure I'm not taking you back to stand trial," Luke said.

"Hell, no! They can't afford to let me get up in front of a judge and tell everybody what really happened."

Luke tugged at his earlobe as his forehead creased again in thought. He said, "You didn't *see* Spence Douglas kill the girl. Even if you had, Spence could just insist that you're lying to save your own skin, and everyone would believe him. It's a classic case of your word against his . . . and I don't believe you're going to come out ahead in that contest, Tyler."

"You're right. But you see, Jensen . . . I have *proof* that Spence killed Rachel, and that's why they have to kill me — and you, too, in case I told you about it — before we ever get to White Fork."

"What sort of proof?"

Tyler shook his head in slow determination.

"I'm keeping that to myself. No offense, Jensen, but I don't know that I can trust you a hundred percent. You've listened to my story, and I'm obliged to you for that, but you might turn around and try to strike some sort of deal with Manfred Douglas."

"Would that work?"

"No, he'd just kill you anyway, or have you killed, once he was sure I was dead and Spence's neck was safe from a hangrope."

"Then I'd be a fool to try that, wouldn't I?"

"I already told you you're a fool to even start for White Fork."

Luke walked over to the horses to tighten the cinches on their saddles, which he had loosened earlier. They had stayed here beside the creek longer than he'd intended while he listened to Tyler's story, but that had given the horses plenty of time to rest and his clothes had dried some, too.

While he was doing that, he thought about everything he had heard, and when he turned back to Tyler, an idea had formed in his mind.

"I'll make a deal with *you,* Tyler," he said. "You mentioned a cache of loot from your rustling and holdups."

"Yeah. I don't know how much it is, exactly. Close to two grand, I'd say. And it's all yours if you'll let me go."

"That's not going to happen. But here's my proposition: I'll take you to White Fork, get you there safely, and make sure that you receive a fair trial. If I do that, you'll pay me that money you have hidden."

Tyler stared at him, then said, "Have you not been listening to a thing I said? Manfred won't ever let the case go to trial. He'll have Axtell ambush us before we even get close to White Fork!"

"Axtell may try," Luke said, "but I'm confident I can get you there. I've delivered prisoners in dangerous situations before."

"You don't know what you're biting off here," Tyler said with a shake of his head. "Why would you do such a thing?"

"Because I'm curious. I want to find out what actually happened to Rachel Montgomery, and a trial seems like the best way to get to the truth."

"You want to do it . . . for her sake?"

"You could put it like that," Luke said.

Tyler stared at him for a long moment before saying, "I still think you're loco . . . but you've got a deal, Jensen. If we make it to White Fork and I get to stand up and tell the truth in a court of law, that cache of loot is yours. And if that happens, you'll have earned it, by God!"

CHAPTER 11

The terrain between Bent Creek, Wyoming, and White Fork, Montana, was pretty varied, including ranges of hills and small mountains, broad, semi-arid basins, badlands cut by rocky ridges, and stretches of a more hospitable nature with enough graze to support cattle. It wasn't really difficult for traveling, but Luke wasn't able to set a very fast pace, either.

It had taken Tyler ten days to cover the distance between the two settlements, but he'd been pushing the paint pony as hard as he dared. Luke didn't see any reason to do that, so he figured they would take a couple of weeks to reach their destination.

They made camp the first night on the shoulder of a ridge, under an outcropping of rock that shielded them from the wind and also would make it more difficult for anyone to spot the small campfire Luke built.

"You're a careful man," Tyler commented as he sat on a rock with his hands still cuffed behind his back and watched Luke fry the bacon Mary brought with the dry clothes.

"I've had to be, in order to survive. You've been on the dodge enough you ought to understand that."

Tyler sighed and said, "Yeah, I do. I've spent some cold, lonely nights listening to the owl hoot and hoping a posse didn't catch up to me."

"You seem like a reasonably intelligent young man. You could have done something besides becoming an outlaw."

"What? Clerk in a store? Eat a bellyful of dust following cows around?" Tyler shook his head. "I'm not gonna live like that. And I'm sure as hell not gonna push a mop and work as a swamper in a saloon. That's about the only other thing I'm qualified to do."

"If you say so," Luke said. "You've made your own bed."

"Damn right I have." After a while, Tyler added, "Don't think I'm satisfied with the way things have turned out, though. I'm not. I just don't see what I can do about 'em now."

"As long as you have that murder charge hanging over your head, you can't change anything else. But once you've faced up to it . . . if you're cleared . . . you can do whatever you want to, Tyler."

The young man shook his head and said, "Nobody around White Fork's ever gonna give me a fair chance, even if I'm able to prove that I didn't kill Rachel."

"Then go somewhere else and make a fresh start." Luke waved a hand to indicate their surroundings. "My God, you've got the whole frontier to pick from! Why do you think people started coming out here in the first place? They wanted new lives, new opportunities."

"Is that why you came west, Jensen? To start a new life as a bounty hunter?"

"There were things in my situation that would have made it difficult for me to stay where I was."

"Well, I didn't want to leave White Fork." Tyler sighed. "But now I reckon I've got no reason to stay, do I?"

Luke understood then. Tyler hadn't set off in search of a new beginning because he wanted to stay close to Rachel Montgomery. Even if he had convinced himself he could never have a life with her, at least he could see her and talk to her now and then, like on the night of the social.

"First things first," Luke said. "Let's just get you there and see to it that the truth

126

comes out at the trial."

Tyler merely shook his head, clearly thinking it was foolish to believe that would ever happen.

The night passed peacefully, and they started on the trail again early the next morning.

"You've ridden this country since I have," Luke said. Tyler was beside him, rather than trailing behind. "Are there any actual settlements between here and White Fork?"

"A few wide places in the trail, that's all. Can't hardly call them settlements. Just trading posts with maybe a saloon attached, or a blacksmith shop, and a few cabins. I didn't spend much time in any of them, just bought some supplies and moved on."

"You didn't rob the stores? That seems more like your usual approach."

Tyler glared and said, "I told you, I did whatever was necessary for me to survive, but I never stole when I had money and could avoid it. I never wanted to bring trouble to honest, hardworking people."

"And I suppose you didn't want to draw a lot of attention to yourself, either, being a man on the run and all."

"Well, yeah, that's true, too."

"We'll need to stop and pick up some supplies along the way. I'm glad to know I shouldn't have to defend you from any more lynch mobs."

"No . . . only from Axtell and those other cold-blooded killers working for Manfred Douglas."

"We haven't seen any sign of these dangerous phantoms so far."

"Hasn't been enough time for them to get down here in these parts yet. But they're coming this way, and we're headed right toward them. You just wait, Jensen. Problem is, by the time you see them . . . it's probably gonna be too late for us to save ourselves."

Over the next couple of days, Tyler kept up a litany of complaints, most of them centered around the pair of handcuffs he wore. Luke had to take the cuffs off every now and then so that Tyler could attend to his personal needs, but when he did that he made Tyler get down on his knees first and then lean forward so he couldn't move fast. Then and only then would Luke unlock the cuffs, key in one hand and a Remington ready in the other.

Luke listened to Tyler's grousing as they rode along until he was ready to gag the young fugitive as well as cuff him. He threatened to do just that. The threat shut

Tyler up for a while, but gradually he began to complain again.

"I'm not saying you have to take them off entirely," Tyler said as they rode toward one of the pine-dotted ridges that crossed their trail. "Just let me wear 'em with my hands in front of me. That way, my arms won't be pulled back behind me unnatural-like, and I can at least hold on to the saddle horn when I need to. It's sure tiring, riding this way."

"With your hands in front of you, you can grab a gun or swing a punch," Luke said. "With your hands behind your back, all you can do is annoy me with your constant bellyaching."

"And here I thought you believed me when I told you what really happened back in White Fork. I'm mighty disappointed in you, Jensen."

"I'll try to live with that disappointment," Luke told him. "As for that yarn you spun . . ." They hadn't really discussed Tyler's story since that first day on the trail. "I found it . . . believable. That doesn't mean I think you were telling the truth, but at least it wasn't a blatant pack of lies."

"None of it was a lie. I wouldn't dishonor Rachel's memory by lying about her."

"We'll see," Luke said.

They reached the ridge, climbed to the

top, and Luke reined in as he saw that the far slope was too steep for them to descend right here. They would have to ride along the narrow top until they found easier terrain. It was a matter of whether they should turn right or left, and since the drop-off was almost sheer in both directions as far as he could see, the choice was a toss-up.

Luke decided to head right. He moved his horse in that direction, then tugged on the reins of Tyler's paint and guided the pony around him, putting Tyler between him and the drop-off.

"What's that for?" Tyler asked.

"Just in case you get any ideas about crowding me and my horse off that cliff," Luke explained.

Tyler craned his neck to look down the steep slope and said, "Hell, I wouldn't do that, Jensen. The fall might kill your horse, and I told you . . . I'm no killer."

Luke grunted, but he couldn't stop a faint smile from tugging at his lips. He tightened his grip on the reins and nudged the gray into motion. He led the paint behind him and to the left.

"This is pretty damn nerve-rackin'," Tyler said after a while. "I don't care for riding this close to the edge."

"You'll be fine," Luke told him. "Just

don't try anything funny and you won't be in any danger."

"This pony can be a little skittish at times."

Luke sighed and said, "Fine." He veered the gray slightly to the right and tugged on the paint's reins. They were closer to the other slope now, but although it was steep, it was nothing like the one on the far side of the ridge.

Tyler started singing some ballad about a lonesome cowboy and the *señorita* he had left behind on the border. Luke hipped around in the saddle to frown at him.

"Are you trying to signal somebody?"

Tyler stopped singing and asked, "Why do you say that?"

"I figured such caterwauling had to have a purpose."

"Caterwauling, is it? I've been told I have a fine singing voice."

"I've attended the opera in both San Francisco and Denver," Luke said. "That's fine singing. I've even heard Lily Langtry perform. So I know something about the subject."

"Well, I'm stuck travelin' with a sour-faced ol' bounty hunter. Got to do something to pass the time."

"Yes, but you sound like you're passing a

stone. Figure out something else to distract yourself."

"Fine, fine," Tyler grumbled.

Luke turned around to face forward again, and as he did, he realized that he had drifted pretty close to the slope while he was talking to Tyler. Suddenly he sensed as much as heard sudden movement behind him. As he twisted in the saddle, he saw Tyler gouging his heels into the paint's flanks to send the startled pony leaping forward and to the right. Tyler yelled at the top of his lungs to spook his mount even more.

The gray outweighed the paint, but the smaller horse was moving faster as it rammed into Luke's mount. The collision staggered the gray, and as close to the edge as it was, it began to lose its balance. The horse let out a shrill whinny as it reared up and started to fall. Luke hauled back on the reins and tried to bring the gray under control, but it was too late.

He cursed as he kicked his feet free of the stirrups and threw himself to the left, out of the saddle. He had lost his grip on the paint's reins, but he couldn't worry about that now. If the gray fell on him and rolled over him, it would break bones and crush organs and doom him to a painful death.

Luke leaped clear as the horse began to

slide down the slope. He landed hard and awkwardly, stunning him for a moment. As he lifted his head he spotted Tyler riding hell bent for leather along the ridge, risking a possibly fatal fall himself because his hands were still cuffed behind his back and he couldn't control the animal. He had to trust to the paint's nimble hooves to keep them upright.

Luke scrambled to his feet and yanked out one of the Remingtons. He lifted the revolver and sighted over its long barrel at the fleeing Tyler as he pulled back the hammer. His finger was about to tighten on the trigger when he let out another curse and lowered the gun.

Tyler was already out of good range, he told himself as he jammed the Remington back in its holster. His lack of a shot had nothing to do with him not wanting to put a bullet in the young man's back.

He turned instead to see what had happened to the gray. The horse was about twenty feet down the slope, struggling to stand up. Luke hurried down, grabbed the reins, and helped as much as he could. Within moments, the gray had its legs underneath it again.

Quickly, Luke checked the horse for injuries. He fully expected that the gray had broken at least one leg in the fall.

Miraculously, though, the animal's bones seemed to be intact. Luke led the gray up the slope, watching how it moved. The steps were a little tentative at first but didn't appear to be pained. The horse shook its head, blew out its breath, and looked aggravated, but as far as Luke could tell it was all right, which made him heave a sigh of relief.

He looked along the ridge, but Tyler was no longer in sight. Luke could still hear the faint rataplan of hoofbeats, though, so he knew which direction the fugitive had gone.

Occasionally in the past, a prisoner had gotten away from him. That always angered Luke. He had gone after those outlaws and captured them again, every time.

It looked like he was going to have to do the same thing with Judd Tyler.

"Hate to ask it of you after you took that tumble, big fella," he said to the gray as he swung up into the saddle, "but I hope you've still got a run in you. We've got us a tricky little son of a bitch to catch!"

CHAPTER 12

Luke rode for about another quarter of a mile before he came to a place where the slope on the far side of the ridge was gentle enough to descend. He knew Tyler must have gone this way, and the few hoofprints his keen eyes were able to spot confirmed that. He turned the gray and started down after the fugitive.

They hadn't gone very far when the trees thinned out enough for Luke to be able to see out into the basin at the bottom of the slope. He spotted the rapidly moving shape of Tyler mounted on the paint.

Tyler was headed north, the direction he didn't want to go, but Luke could see some badlands in the distance and he figured Tyler thought he could lose any pursuit in there and cut either east or west, depending on the terrain.

Of course, at this point Tyler didn't know what had happened back there on the ridge.

As far as he knew, the gray had broken a leg . . . or Luke had broken his neck. Tyler couldn't be sure anybody was even after him.

But he rode like the wind in case somebody was.

Luke thought about pulling his Winchester from its sheath and trying a long shot but discarded the idea. Tyler was almost a mile away. If Luke had had one of those Sharps Big Fifties like the buffalo hunters used, he might have given it a try, especially since he had the advantage in height.

It would take a miracle to hit Tyler with a Winchester from this distance, though, and he figured he had already used up his share of those today when the gray turned out to be uninjured.

Luke heeled the horse into motion again. Tyler was getting farther away with each passing second . . .

The basin was several miles wide. Tyler was halfway across it by the time Luke reached the bottom of the ridge. He urged the gray into a run, knowing that the odds of him being able to catch Tyler before the fugitive reached the badlands were small. He was going to give it a try anyway, if he could manage it without riding the gray into the ground.

Luke knew he couldn't afford to do that, either. Out here, a man afoot was often as good as dead.

The gray responded gallantly, stretching out its long legs as it flashed across the ground. Luke leaned forward in the saddle and tried to keep his eyes on Tyler. The basin wasn't absolutely flat; it rose and fell in places, and from time to time Tyler would ride into a depression and drop out of Luke's sight, only to pop back up again a moment or two later.

Tyler was running the paint at a full-out gallop and probably had been ever since he'd reached the bottom of the ridge. It was true that the pony had been able to rest for a day in the stable at Bent Creek, but before that had been more than a week of hard riding. Luke could only hope that his gray had more reserves of strength right now than Tyler's paint could muster.

That seemed to be the case, as the gap between them began to shrink. Not by much, at first, but as the chase went on, Luke could tell the paint was faltering more and more. He closed in, but only a few hundred yards were left before Tyler reached the badlands. If he made it to that area of twisting, brush-choked gullies, spiny ridges, and towering spires of rock, there would be a lot of places for the fugitive to hide.

Luke knew he was close enough now that he could have tried a rifle shot, but he didn't want to kill Tyler. Sure, if he delivered Tyler's corpse to Sheriff Axtell in White Fork, there was a chance Axtell would pay the bounty and that would be that.

But there was also a chance Axtell would try to kill him, figuring that Tyler might have told him the story about Spence Douglas being the person who had actually murdered Rachel Montgomery.

That all depended on whether or not Tyler had told him the truth, Luke realized. If Tyler really *had* killed the girl, then Luke was in no danger. He could kill Tyler, take his body to White Fork, collect the reward, and move on.

But if Tyler was right . . . if Spence really was the killer . . . Axtell wouldn't want to risk that story getting out, and the only way to insure that would be to get rid of Luke, too.

There was simply no way to be sure.

So again, it all came down to Luke's nagging desire to discover the truth. The best way to do that was to bring Tyler in alive . . . and then see what happened.

Tyler had almost reached the edge of the badlands when the paint stumbled. If his hands had been free, he might have been able to tighten up on the reins and help the pony regain its balance.

With the cuffs on his wrists and his hands behind his back, however, all he could do was the same thing Luke had done a short time earlier. He jerked his feet out of the stirrups and leaned to the side, rolling out of the saddle as the paint went down.

Even from a distance, Luke could see how hard Tyler slammed into the ground when he landed. The young man's momentum made him roll over several times before he came to a stop on his belly. Luke hoped that Tyler hadn't broken his damned fool neck with this attempted getaway stunt.

The gray thundered up to the fallen man. Several yards away, the paint had already stood up. Luke bit back a curse as he saw the way the animal was favoring one leg. If that leg was broken, then Tyler deserved a swift kick in the rear for dooming such a gallant little horse.

Tyler still hadn't moved. Luke swung down and let the gray's reins dangle. The gray wouldn't go anywhere. Luke drew his right-hand Remington as he strode over to Tyler.

"Get up, you young idiot!" he said.

Tyler didn't respond. Luke studied him closely. The fugitive's head seemed to be at a normal angle on his shoulders, so he hadn't broken his neck. His back rose and fell, so he was still breathing. More than likely, the hard landing when he toppled off the horse had stunned him.

Luke hooked a boot toe under Tyler's right shoulder and rolled him onto his back. That position put more pressure on Tyler's arms and shoulder sockets, and the pain roused him. He let out a groan as his eyes blinked rapidly and then stayed open.

"What the hell were you trying to do?" Luke asked.

Tyler groaned again, then said, "And you call *me* an idiot. I was trying to get away."

"With your hands cuffed behind your back?"

"I figured . . . I could worry about that later. Get me up, Jensen. It hurts like hell . . . laying here like this."

With a disgusted look on his face, Luke holstered the revolver and went around behind Tyler.

"Don't you try to kick me or anything else," he warned. "If you give me any more trouble, I'm going to wallop you with a gun butt, tie you facedown over your saddle, and

140

take you back to White Fork that way."

"My horse . . . is he . . . ?"

"I don't know. He could have a broken leg. I hope you're satisfied with yourself."

Luke got hold of Tyler under the arms and lifted him, then set him on his feet. Tyler swayed and might have fallen if Luke hadn't grasped an arm to steady him. He picked up Tyler's hat and slapped it roughly on the prisoner's head.

"Anything broken or ruptured?" he asked.

"I . . . I don't think so. I just kind of got the wind knocked out of me."

"Then just stand there and don't move while I check on your horse."

Luke went over to the pony, talking quietly and reassuringly as he approached. The paint was a little wall-eyed, but he didn't try to shy away as Luke snagged the reins. He checked the right foreleg, which was the one the pony was favoring, running his hands over the leg with an expert's touch.

"Is he all right?" Tyler asked, sounding genuinely worried. "Is it broken?"

"I don't *think* so," Luke said. "He's liable to be pretty lame for a few days, though."

"Thank God."

"And no thanks to *you*," Luke snapped. "You're the one who risked all of our lives by trying to get away."

Anger flashed in Tyler's eyes. He said, "Well, what would you have done, Jensen? My life's hanging by a thread! My only real chance was to get as far away from White Fork as I could, and now you're dead set on taking me back there!"

"I told you that I'd get you there safely and see to it that you get a fair trial."

"Oh, sure, I'm supposed to take the word of a bounty hunter that he'll do his best for me! Men like you don't give a damn about anything except money! You don't care about the truth."

"It just so happens that I do," Luke said.

"Yeah? Then why wouldn't you ever say that you believed me when I told you what happened?"

"*That's* why you damned near killed both of us and our horses? Because your feelings were hurt when I didn't tell you I believed you?"

Tyler glared at him and said, "Have you ever been accused of something you didn't do, Jensen?"

"As a matter of fact, I have. More than once."

"And you knew everybody would just figure you were lying about it, because of who you are?"

"You're the one who keeps calling me a

bounty hunter, like it's some sort of obscenity," Luke pointed out. "If you're asking do I know what it's like to have people look down their noses at me, then the answer is yes. Hell, yes."

That brutal honesty seemed to embarrass Tyler a little. He frowned and looked down at the ground.

"I didn't mean for anybody to get hurt," he muttered. "I was just scared and wanted to get away."

"As far away from White Fork as possible, right?"

"Yeah."

"Do you actually believe that would have done you any good?" Luke asked. "Think about it for a minute. Axtell has already got wanted posters out across Montana and Wyoming, and probably in Idaho, too, for all I know. Maybe over in Dakota Territory as well. And those posters will spread out until they can be found from the Rio Grande to the Milk River. No matter where you went, Tyler, you'd still be a fugitive."

"A lot of outlaws lie low and never get caught. Hell, I might have even made it to Mexico."

Luke shook his head and said, "That might stop the law, but it wouldn't mean anything to a man like Manfred Douglas. If he's afraid that you can put his son's neck in a noose, he's not going to stop at anything to prevent that. The regular bounty won't be enough. He'll hire men to find you. Trackers. Killers. And then one of these days, no matter where you go, somebody will walk up behind you and put a bullet in your back. Or you'll step out into a street and a rifle shot from a hundred yards away will blow your brains out. *That's* the kind of life you have to look forward to if you try to run and hide."

"What do you think I ought to do, then?" Tyler asked in a challenging tone.

"Go back and fight. Make sure all the honest people in White Fork know what really happened. You *did* say there are still some honest people there, didn't you?"

"Yeah," Tyler said, frowning. "Judge Keller's a good man. He's his own man, too. Douglas never bought and paid for him, although I reckon he tried, and he knows he can't afford to have the judge killed. Judge Keller's one of the founders of White Fork. Been in that part of the country longer than almost anybody else. Folks wouldn't stand for it if anything happened to him."

"There you go," Luke said. "Present your case to Judge Keller, and let the hand play out. That's your only chance to have a real life again."

"To do that, I have to make it to White Fork alive."

"Leave that to me," Luke said. "And if you try anything else . . . maybe I'll just shoot you in both legs. You can still testify in court, whether you can walk or not."

CHAPTER 13

The basin was almost bare of vegetation. Clumps of hardy grass were the only things that grew here. Luke didn't want to venture into the badlands while Tyler's horse was lame, so even though it galled him to be going backward instead of forward, they turned around and started across the basin toward the ridge.

Luke made Tyler walk, saying, "You're the one who lamed that pony. The unfortunate beast shouldn't have to carry your weight until his leg is better."

"You mean we're just gonna make camp and *stay* here?"

"That's right. For a day or two, anyway."

Tyler shook his head and said, "We'll be sitting ducks for Axtell and his deputies."

"Let me worry about that."

"You'd damned well *better* worry. Your skin is on the line, too, you know. Now that I've told you the truth, you're a danger to

Spence Douglas just like I am."

Luke was walking, too, since the gray also needed a chance to rest. He held the reins of both horses. Like most Westerners, he didn't care for walking instead of riding, but sometimes there was no other choice.

"See, you've got me roped in on your problems so I don't have any choice but to keep you safe," he told Tyler. "The truth has to come out, one way or the other."

"Unless both of us are dead. Then it'll be buried right along with us."

"Maybe you should tell me what that proof is you have of Spence's guilt."

"Not hardly. That's my ace in the hole. As long as I've got it, I have something to bargain with if I have to."

"Do Spence and his father *know* you have it?"

Tyler frowned.

"Well . . . I'm not sure. They might. On the other hand, they might not."

"Talking to you is rather infuriating."

"Well, then, let's trudge along in silence, why don't we?" Tyler suggested.

Luke was fine with that.

It took almost an hour for them to walk back across the basin with Luke leading the two horses. When they reached the base of the ridge, Luke found a clearing in some brush and trees and picketed the animals there. He unsaddled them while Tyler sat on a slab of rock that had tumbled down the ridge at some point in the distant past.

"If you took these handcuffs off of me, you could put me to work," the young man said.

Luke gave him a disbelieving look.

"You tried to escape not much more than an hour ago, came damn close to killing me and my horse in the process, and you're already pestering me again to get out of those cuffs?"

"I'm just sayin', you're having to do all the chores. You take care of the horses, you do all the cooking and anything else that comes up. Doesn't seem fair."

"If I started worrying about whether or not life is fair, I wouldn't have time for anything else," Luke said. "Just sit there and pipe down."

"You're the boss."

Luke gave each of the horses a good rubdown, then poured water from one of the canteens into his hat and let them drink. He needed to find a spring or a creek, he thought. He and Tyler had enough water for the time being, but they would have to replenish their supply before too much longer.

He built a small fire, put coffee on to boil, and broke out a small pot and a bag of beans. Since they were going to be here for a while, there would be time to soak and cook the beans instead of having to get by on bacon and biscuits and canned peaches and tomatoes. He might even rig some snares, he thought, and see if he could catch a rabbit or a prairie chicken. Some fresh meat would be nice.

"Might as well sit back and enjoy it," Luke told Tyler. "We've got all the comforts of home."

Later that afternoon, after they'd eaten their midday meal, Luke fetched his rope from his saddle, looped it around Tyler's torso, and then tied it securely around the trunk of a small pine tree.

"Why in blazes are you doing that?" Tyler asked as he glared at Luke.

"Because I aim to do a little scouting, and I don't want you to wander off, or even to be *tempted* to wander off."

"Where would I go, out here in the middle of nowhere, with my hands cuffed behind my back?"

"That question didn't seem to bother you earlier, when you nearly killed me and my horse."

149

"You keep bringing that up. You're both all right."

"No thanks to you," Luke said. He picked up his Winchester. "Just sit there and keep your mouth shut. If anyone's prowling around who might wish you harm, you'd be a fool to start yelling and attract their attention." He smiled. "And let's face it, Tyler . . . right now, it's very likely I'm the only one out here who actually *does* have your best interests at heart."

"Yeah, yeah, I suppose so. Maybe I'll take a nap."

"That's a good idea."

Luke left the camp on foot and headed along the base of the ridge, exploring through the brush and the small, scrubby pines. He thought he might find a spring, and sure enough he did, half a mile from the campsite. The water bubbled out of a cleft in some rocks and formed a small pool at their base.

It would have been nice if the spring was closer. Of course, he could move the camp over here, he thought, but he didn't really want to do that. The cover wasn't as good. The brush and the trees were thick enough around the spot where he'd left Tyler that they wouldn't be spotted easily.

Luke had brought a couple of the mostly

empty canteens with him. He filled them and slung them back over his shoulder by their straps. He could bring the others later and fill them, then top them off again whenever he and Tyler were ready to move on.

Or rather, when the horses were ready to move on, he thought. Tyler would never be ready. Even after everything he had told the young man about the miserable life of a fugitive, Luke figured that Tyler still didn't want to go back to White Fork.

While he was looking for a spring and then filling the canteens, he had remained alert, listening for the sound of horses or anything else that might represent a possible threat. Other than a few birds flitting around and some small animals rustling in the brush, he hadn't heard anything. He and Tyler might as well be the only human beings for a hundred miles or more, Luke thought, and that was just the way he wanted it for now.

He heard snoring as he approached the camp, and when he stepped into the clearing he saw that Tyler had made good on that comment about taking a nap. The young man had his back against the tree trunk, his head down with his hat brim shading his face, and his legs stretched out in front of him, crossed casually at the ankles. As always, there was no sign of a guilty conscience plaguing Judd Tyler's slumber.

Luke checked the horses, found that they were grazing peacefully, and set the canteens aside. He reached into one of his saddlebags and pulled a small, leather-bound volume of poetry and short stories by Edgar Allan Poe. Settling down in a comfortable spot on the ground, he took advantage of the relative peace and quiet and began to read.

The rest of that day and the next two were more of the same. Luke read and slept while Tyler alternated between sleeping and complaining.

"Damn it, can't we at least play cards or something?" Tyler asked on the second afternoon. "Anything to pass the time."

"That would require turning you loose, and I'm not going to do that," Luke said as he rested his back against a tree trunk. He had finished the slim volume of Poe and was rereading one of his favorites, the *Meditations* of Marcus Aurelius.

"Well, then . . . how about reading whatever that book is out loud?"

Luke raised an eyebrow and said, "I'm not sure you'd enjoy it very much."

"It's some kind of story, isn't it?"

"Not exactly. It's a volume of philosophy

written by Marcus Aurelius."

Tyler shook his head and said, "Don't reckon I've heard of him."

"He was one of the emperors of Rome during the second century."

"Long time ago, huh?"

"Seventeen hundred years or so."

"They fought a lot of wars back then, right? With swords and spears and stuff?"

"And stuff," Luke said dryly.

"I saw a picture in a book once of a thing called a chariot. Kind of like a buckboard, only those old fellas stood up on it and used it for fighting. Looked like it might be fun to race around in one of those things. Any chariots in that book you're reading?"

Luke tried not to sigh in exasperation. He said, "No, this is a collection of Marcus's thoughts about stoic philosophy."

"Don't know what that is," Tyler said with a shake of his head. "I don't recall ever hearing anything about it, so why don't you explain it to me?"

"It's about how everything in the universe is connected, and how the trials and tribulations of this earth are temporary. Marcus says that we ought to do the best we can with the things that we can control, and let everything else take its natural course without worrying too much about it."

"Sounds kind of like preachers I've heard. They always like to talk about how everything's gonna work out all right in the end if you just believe hard enough. You say this fella was a king instead of a sky pilot?"

"Emperor," Luke said. "Of the Roman Empire."

"Well, if it's all right with you and Marcus, I'm gonna keep on worrying. When you've got a bunch of polecats who want you dead, you'd be a damn fool not to."

Luke didn't say anything, but he thought that while Marcus Aurelius had had to deal with all sorts of trouble during his reign, he'd never been saddled with anybody like Judd Tyler.

The next morning after breakfast, Luke led both horses around and studied their gaits, then decided it would be all right to move on as long as he didn't set too fast a pace and they stopped frequently to let the mounts rest.

"I'm going to refill these canteens, and then we'll get started again," he told Tyler.

"I'll be glad to get moving," the prisoner said. "I don't like just sittin' around doing nothing."

"At least you were able to catch up on your sleep," Luke told him.

"Well, yeah, there's that."

Luke picked up his Winchester, slung the two canteens over his shoulder, and started walking toward the spring.

He still didn't hear anything out of the ordinary, although when he looked across the basin he thought he saw a tendril of gray smoke climbing into the morning sky from the hills on the other side of the badlands. Somebody probably had a camp over there, but that didn't mean it was anybody who was looking for him and Tyler.

Of course, it didn't mean they *weren't* searching for the two of them, either.

Luke filled the canteens. As he walked back toward the camp, he heard something that made him pause and frown. It took him a moment to realize that Tyler was singing again, the same sad ballad of lost love that countless cowboys had crooned to sleeping herds as they rode nighthawk.

Luke shook his head and started on, then stopped again. This time his muscles tensed and his hands tightened on the Winchester. A few days earlier, when Tyler had started singing Luke had asked him if he was trying to signal somebody.

Was it possible that Tyler remembered that conversation and was trying to signal him now? The only kind of signal Tyler would be sending was a warning.

Luke didn't have to think about it for more than a second.

He levered a round into the Winchester's chamber, then turned and began climbing the slope, catfooting through the brush and making as little sound as possible. He worked his way around until he was above the camp and then eased down toward it.

The singing stopped abruptly. Luke heard the ugly sound of something, either a fist or a gun, striking flesh.

"I've had enough of that," a harsh voice said. "You can't carry a tune worth a damn, boy."

"But I told you," Tyler said, "Luke's used to me singing. That's how I pass the time, since I can't do much of anything else while I'm handcuffed and roped to a tree. If he doesn't hear me singing, he's liable to figure something's wrong."

Another man said, "Yeah, Dave, we don't want Jensen to figure out we're waitin' for him. I've heard that he's a pretty tough *hombre*."

"He's a damn bounty hunter," the man called Dave muttered. "I'm not afraid of him."

"Bein' careful doesn't mean you're afraid."

"All right, blast it." Luke heard the famil-

iar sound of a gun's hammer being ratch-
eted back. "Go ahead and sing, Tyler. But if
you try anything tricky, the first bullet's
goin' right through that brain of yours!"

CHAPTER 14

With all the stealth he could muster, Luke moved closer to the camp. He was careful where he put his feet with every step. After the canteens bumped together once with a faint thud, he took them off and silently set them aside. The men down below didn't seem to have noticed the sound.

The Winchester was ready to fire, so he didn't have to make any racket by working its lever.

All he needed were some targets.

So far he had heard the voices of two men, but that didn't mean they were the only ones down there with Tyler. Luke had no way of knowing how many foes he was going to face until he reached a spot where he could see, hopefully without being seen.

Other thoughts were racing through his brain. Dave had called Tyler by name. The other man had mentioned Luke's last name. That meant they weren't just drifting owlhoots bent on robbery and murder, which had been Luke's first thought.

No, they were here after Tyler, and they had known that Luke would be with him.

The only explanation that made any sense was that either Sheriff Gus Axtell or Manfred Douglas — or both — had sent the men to dispose of Luke and Tyler before they reached White Fork.

Just like Tyler had been saying was going to happen all along.

They must have really fogged it down here in a hurry, or else they had been somewhere in the stretch between Bent Creek and White Fork, along the Wyoming-Montana border. Axtell might have gotten word to them some way, possibly by fast rider.

Or maybe they had been somewhere east or west of here, in a settlement with a telegraph office, and Axtell had contacted them that way and ordered them to intercept Luke and Tyler.

Those possibilities wheeled through Luke's mind, but at the same time he knew the answer didn't actually matter. What was important was that at least two ruthless killers were only a few yards away, waiting for him to show up so they could fill him full of lead.

Tyler had started singing again when Dave

ordered him to, but now he made a croaking sound and stopped.

"Blast it, singing is thirsty work," he said. "There are two of you fellas. One of you can keep an eye on me while the other fetches that canteen over there."

A grim smile tugged at the corners of Luke's mouth. That was pretty slick work on Tyler's part, letting him know how many gunmen there were. Luke was sure now that Tyler had lied to the men and broken into song so that Luke would hear it and figure out something was wrong.

"You can have a drink once we're finished with Jensen," Dave said. "Go ahead and sing. I reckon I can stand that godawful warblin' a little while longer."

"Luke should be back soon," Tyler said, then launched into a different tune. This one was about a girl some cowboy had left behind, too, but it was a lot bawdier than the first one. Tyler's voice rose even louder.

With that racket to cover up any little sounds he might make, Luke eased aside some brush and peered through the narrow gap he had created.

Tyler was still tied to the tree, right where Luke had left him. Standing beside the prisoner and holding the muzzle of a Colt mere inches from Tyler's head was a tall, gaunt, gray-faced man wearing a black vest and a high-crowned black hat.

On the other side of the camp, near the horses, was a shorter, stockier man with a shock of fair hair under his thumbed-back Stetson. His face had a brutal stamp to it, but overall he didn't look as threatening as the tall gunslinger.

Both men wore badges pinned to their shirts.

That sight made Luke grimace. Even though he had known that Sheriff Axtell's deputies were nothing more than hired killers, at least according to Tyler, those badges were going to make things more difficult for Luke. From where he was, he probably could have drilled the man holding the Colt to Tyler's head, then swung the Winchester and downed the other one before the shorter man could draw his gun.

He couldn't shoot them both down in cold blood if there was even the tiniest fraction of a chance that they were honest lawmen, though.

Tyler's voice was starting to quaver. The bawdy song trailed off. He said, "Honest, fellas, I can't keep singing like this."

"You'll sing until Jensen shows up," Gray Face said.

"What are you gonna do when he does?"

The other man laughed and said, "What do you think, Tyler? The sheriff's orders were pretty clear. You and Jensen both got to die."

Well, that ended any speculation, Luke thought as he knelt in the brush. These men were killers, and so was their boss. He could forget all about those badges . . . unless he wanted to use them as targets.

"You don't have to kill him," Tyler said quickly. "There's no need for that. He doesn't know anything."

"You expect us to believe you didn't shoot your mouth off to him about what you think happened to the preacher's girl?" Gray Face asked.

Tyler's features hardened in anger. He glared up at the man and said, "You mean what I *know* happened. And no, I didn't say anything to Luke. So if you just go ahead and kill me, then light a shuck out of here, you can forget about him."

Tyler was either stalling for time or genuinely trying to save Luke's life, he thought. Maybe some of both. But either way, the killers weren't having any of it.

"The hell with this," Gray Face said. "Larrabee, you get over there in those trees. I'm gonna go ahead and put a bullet in Tyler's head. If Jensen's not already on the way back here, the shot ought to be enough to bring him in a hurry. After I kill Tyler, I'll fade back into the brush on this side of the camp, and we'll have Jensen in a crossfire."

"Sounds good to me, Dave," Larrabee agreed with a savage grin. He turned to head for the trees.

At that moment, Luke stood up and brought the Winchester to his shoulder in a smooth motion. He knew he didn't have any margin for error. Gray Face — he was so sinister-looking Luke couldn't really think of him by such a commonplace name as Dave — had his gun pointed at Tyler's head, and it wouldn't take much pressure on the trigger to make it go off.

Luke had to keep the man from ever pulling that trigger.

The Winchester cracked. The bullet took the gunman in the side of the neck and bored on through to explode out on the other side. The way the man dropped like a puppet with its strings cut told Luke his shot had smashed Gray Face's spine, just as he had hoped it would. The gun fell unfired from the man's suddenly limp hand.

Before Gray Face even hit the ground, Luke turned toward the other would-be killer. He worked the rifle's lever with blinding speed. Larrabee tried to twist back toward him and clawed at the gun on his hip, but Luke was too fast. The Winchester blasted again. This time the slug smashed into its target's chest.

The impact knocked Larrabee back a step, but he didn't go down. As his eyes widened in shock, instinct kept him fumbling for his gun. He grasped the butt and pulled the weapon from the holster.

As the barrel started to come up, Luke fired again. This time the bullet struck Larrabee in the center of the forehead and pitched him back off his feet. Luke knew he would never get up.

As Luke stepped out of the brush, he trained the Winchester on Gray Face. He was almost positive the man was out of the fight, but almost wasn't quite good enough. Almost could get a fella killed.

"Son of a *bitch*!" Tyler said as he looked up at Luke. "That was some shooting. I was starting to think you weren't gonna get here in time to keep those varmints from killing me."

"There were only two of them?" Luke asked.

"Yeah, as far as I know. I only saw two, and they didn't say anything about anybody else being with them."

Luke stopped beside Gray Face and

looked down at him. The crooked deputy was still alive, staring up with a horrified expression on his face.

"I . . . I can't feel anything!" he gasped.

"That's because I blew your spinal cord in two," Luke told him. "You're pretty much a dead man. You'll suffocate in a little while because your muscles can't make you breathe anymore."

"You . . . you can't leave me like this! You got to . . . end it. Put me out of my misery." The man groaned. "You'd do it for a dog, or a horse."

"I'm very fond of dogs and horses," Luke said. "I don't really give a damn about hired killers."

"Please, mister . . . if you want me to beg . . ."

Tyler said, "Go ahead and shoot him. His name's Dave Simms. He's one of Axtell's deputies, and there's no telling how many men he's killed because Axtell or Manfred Douglas ordered him to. He's lower than a snake's belly."

"If that's true, maybe it would be better if I let him die slowly and painfully —"

"No!" Simms interrupted. "You can't . . . It ain't human . . ."

Luke lowered the rifle and drew one of his Remingtons instead. As he pointed it at

Simms, he said, "Spence Douglas killed Rachel Montgomery, didn't he?"

"I . . . I don't know. Not for sure. I wasn't there that night. None of us who work for Axtell were. It was . . . it was Circle M riders who found Tyler . . . close to her body."

"But I'm sure you've all talked about it. Spence was waiting in the woods for Miss Montgomery to walk by. He lured her in there somehow and then the two of them argued, probably because she told him she didn't intend to have anything to do with him. Then, like any spoiled brat who's been told he can't have what he wants, Spence threw a tantrum. He took hold of her by the neck and squeezed until she was dead."

Sitting against the tree, Tyler closed his eyes and shuddered at the harshness of Luke's words.

"I don't know, mister . . . Truly, I don't. But I'll say anything you want . . . if you'll just end this . . ."

Luke sighed and said, "Even if you knew the truth and admitted it, I suppose it would be hearsay evidence and not admissible in court. I wouldn't have minded having the confirmation, though, just for my own peace of mind."

He lined up the Remington, pulled back the hammer, and squeezed the trigger.

Tyler's eyes were still closed, but he jumped at the roar of the gun.

"Is it over?" he asked as the shot's echoes faded away.

"It's over. Like he said, I would have done as much for a dumb animal."

Tyler opened his eyes and seemed to be careful not to look at the bloody corpse a few feet away.

"You can't *not* believe me now," he said. "You've seen it with your eyes, heard it with your own ears. Axtell sent these two to kill us, and Axtell works for Manfred Douglas. Everything I told you is true."

"Looks like it," Luke said as he reloaded the chamber in the Remington. When he was finished, he slid the gun back into leather.

"Then you're gonna let me go now. You know I'm not a killer."

"You still have to answer to that murder charge, whether you're guilty or not. We've talked about this, Tyler. That's the only way to get the truth out into the open and clear your name."

"What if I don't care about the truth anymore? What if I just want to get out of here while my hide's still in one piece? That offer still stands, Jensen. Turn me loose and I'll tell you where to find that loot I hid."

"You're going to tell me that anyway, once I've made sure you've gotten a fair trial. *That* was our deal."

"You are the damn stubbornest —" Tyler stopped and sighed. "All right. But if we're still heading for White Fork, we'd better get started. If there are any more of Axtell's men in these parts, they might have heard those gunshots."

"You're right about that," Luke said. "I'll get the horses saddled." He started to turn away, then paused and looked back at Tyler. "It sounded like you were actually trying to save my life a few minutes ago, when you were talking to these two."

"Yeah, I guess I've kind of gotten used to you, Jensen." Tyler hesitated, then asked, "Does that make a difference?"

Luke shook his head and said, "Nope."

CHAPTER 15

Luke found the horses the two crooked deputies had ridden. The animals were tied in the trees, out of sight. He led them back to camp, figuring that he and Tyler could ride them for a while and let the gray and the paint continue to take it easy.

The extra supplies and canteens of water the men had been carrying would come in handy, too, and Luke also took the guns and ammunition that had belonged to the dead men.

He planned to leave the bodies right where they had fallen. The wolves and the buzzards could have them.

Luke boosted Tyler into the saddle of one of the extra horses and swung up on the other one. He led the gray and the paint as they started across the basin toward the badlands.

"Did those two happen to mention how they found us so quickly?" he asked.

"They bragged on it some, in fact," Tyler said. "Axtell sent deputies out all over Montana and Wyoming to look for me, as soon as I got away from White Fork. Those two had ridden down to Casper, southeast of here, where there's a telegraph office. Since they were the closest, Axtell told them I'd been captured in Bent Creek and was being taken back to Montana, so they hurried to catch up to us."

"Which they probably wouldn't have been able to do if you hadn't pulled that fool stunt and lamed your horse, delaying us by a couple of days."

"Well, I couldn't have very well predicted any of that, now could I?" Tyler asked in a testy voice. "Anyway, if it hadn't been Simms and Larrabee, it would have been somebody else, soon enough. I'm sure by now Axtell has gotten in touch with all his men, and they'll be closing in on us from all directions. He's bound to have sent men south from White Fork, too."

"So no matter what we do, we're riding into a trap."

Tyler blew out an exasperated breath and said, "Good Lord, Jensen. Ain't that exactly what I've been telling you, right from the first?"

"Traps can be sprung, if the quarry is wily

enough." Luke paused. "That was pretty smart, warning me the way you did and letting me know how many of them there were."

"Well, I was hoping you'd hear me singing and catch on to what I was trying to tell you. I knew it was a long shot, but I figured it was the only one I had." Tyler shrugged. "If it hadn't worked, I was gonna wind up dead anyway, so it didn't hurt anything to try, did it?"

They rode on and reached the badlands a short time later. The rugged terrain made for slow going. Luke didn't try to get in a hurry. Even with a couple of extra mounts, he didn't want anything to happen to any of the horses. It would be easy for an animal to stumble and hurt itself on such rough ground.

They spent most of the day carefully working their way through the badlands. Late in the afternoon they emerged into the eastern edge of the low hills that gradually rose to the west into the Bighorn Mountains. The route they were following ran more toward due north. Luke knew they would reach the Powder River soon, and he figured they would follow it all the way into Montana Territory.

He started looking for a good place to

spend the night but hadn't found anything suitable by the time shadows started to creep over the landscape. Luke was about to decide they would have to camp out in the open and do without a fire, when he spotted a gleam of light up ahead in the gathering gloom.

"Do you see that?" he asked Tyler.

The young man squinted and said after a moment, "Yeah. Doesn't really look like a campfire, does it? It's too steady for that."

"That's because it's the glow of lamplight through a window," Luke said. "We're looking at either a homestead or one of those trading posts you mentioned."

"Come to think of it, that might be old man Pettifer's place on the Powder River. I've heard of it, but I didn't stop there on my trip south."

"Malachi Pettifer?" Luke asked. "He's still alive?"

"Oh, yeah. Still alive and still catering to a certain sort of trade, if you know what I mean."

"I get your drift," Luke said. "You're talking about outlaws. Pettifer had a reputation as a man who'd sell supplies and provide sanctuary to anybody and then forget they'd been there if the law came looking for them. That was over in Kansas a few years ago, though."

"Reckon things might've gotten too hot for him there and he moved north and west," Tyler said. "All I know is what I was told, which was that a fella on the dodge could stop there if he needed to."

"But you didn't stop."

Tyler shrugged and said, "I didn't need to. I still had enough supplies. And I figured it was best to keep moving as much as I could."

"Well, we're going to need to keep moving, too. If we ride in there and you're handcuffed, anyone who's there will figure out pretty quick that I'm a bounty hunter. That's liable to not sit very well with Pettifer's customers."

"You could turn me loose. You could pretend that you're on the dodge, too. Hell, it'd give us a chance to sleep in a real bed for a night and maybe pick up some extra supplies."

"We're not running low on anything now," Luke pointed out. "And you haven't given me a lot of reason to believe that you're trustworthy."

"That was before this morning. You saved my life, Luke. Simms and Larrabee would have killed me."

"They would have killed me, too. I was

acting in my own best interests."

"Yeah, but I know now that you believe me about Spence and Rachel," Tyler said. "And *you've* convinced *me* that the only way I'm ever gonna have any sort of life again is to get up in Judge Keller's courtroom and prove that I'm innocent. I can't do that on my own. I need your help, Luke. If I double-crossed you, it'd be the same as cutting my own throat."

What Tyler said made sense, Luke supposed, but he still wasn't ready to trust the young man. Not only that, but Pettifer's trading post was a haven for outlaws. Some people who weren't lawbreakers probably stopped there, too, but there was a good chance most of the old man's customers were on the dodge.

Which meant that if Luke walked in there, there was also a good chance he might run into somebody with a grudge against him, the way he had back in Bent Creek when that *hombre* had tried to kill him in his bath.

"Forget it," he said. "We're going around the place."

"But . . ." Tyler let his voice trail off and then sighed. "You're not gonna change your mind, are you?"

"Not without a good reason," Luke said.

Unfortunately, a short time later he got

that good reason.

The gait of the horse he was riding suddenly changed. The horse lurched, took another few steps, and then stopped. Luke frowned and muttered a curse.

Tyler's horse had stopped, too.

"What's wrong?" the young man asked.

"I don't know." Luke dismounted. He could tell there was something wrong with the horse's left front leg. He picked up the hoof to look at it in the rapidly fading light.

All it took was a glance to see that the iron shoe on that hoof had come loose and was barely hanging on.

Tyler had leaned over in his saddle to take a look, as well. He whistled and said, "That's gonna need some work before that horse can go much farther."

"Yes, I know," Luke said, not bothering to keep a tone of disgust out of his voice. "I shouldn't be surprised that a no-account gunman wouldn't take good care of his mount."

"That horse belonged to either Simms or Larrabee. Skunks like that, if they can't eat it, take it to bed, or shoot it, they just don't give a damn about it." Tyler paused, then went on, "You know, a while back a fella told me that Pettifer's got a forge at his place. He doesn't do any blacksmith work

175

himself, but he's got all the tools there for somebody else to do it, if they know how. I'm guessing you know how."

"I'm no farrier, but I can put a shoe on a horse if I have to. Fortunately, I don't have to. We started out without any extra horses. I can take the saddle off of this one and turn it loose."

"Then we'll just have one extra mount, and since there's two of us, we might as well not have any. If it comes down to a long chase, one spare horse won't do us a damned bit of good."

Unfortunately, Tyler was right about that, and Luke knew it. Leaving Bent Creek with only the gray and the paint was at least understandable; at the time Luke hadn't been convinced at all that Tyler was telling the truth about hired killers trying to intercept them on their way to White Fork.

Now that Luke knew the real odds facing them, the idea of having spare mounts had been comforting. He decided he wasn't ready to give it up.

"Listen to me, Tyler," he said. The sharp tone of his voice made the young man look intently at him. "If I take those handcuffs off of you and we ride into Pettifer's place, I'm going to watch you the whole time we're there. If you show the least little sign of trying some trick, I'm going to pull a gun and kill you. No questions, no asking for explanations, no hesitation. Just a bullet and you're done."

"Killing me won't stop Axtell and his men from coming after you."

"Let them," Luke said. "I won't take your body to White Fork. I'll let you lay right where you fall. Then I'll turn around and ride away from here. I don't like missing out on a reward, but there are other bounties out there. I can leave this part of the country behind before Axtell's men even have a clue I've gone. Manfred Douglas may worry about me for a while, but after enough time passes without anything happening, he'll decide that I'm no threat to his son after all and call off his gun-wolves."

"Well, that's just about the most cold-blooded thing I've ever heard," Tyler said, staring at Luke. "After we've ridden together all this time, you'd just shoot me and ride away?"

"Damn straight I would. Plus, it hasn't been *that* long, and we're not actually riding together. You're my prisoner, remember?"

"All right, all right," Tyler said. "But if you kill me, then the truth about what happened to Rachel will never come out."

"That's a good reason for you not to give me any trouble." Luke reached in his pocket for the handcuff keys. "Twist around there and stick your hands out." He drew one of the Remingtons. "Remember, it only takes one hand to unlock those cuffs, and one hand to blow a hole through you if you try anything."

Full dark had fallen by the time Luke and Tyler reached the trading post. Tyler had spent the first few minutes of the ride swinging his arms around in circles.

"Man alive, that sure feels good!" he had said. "My muscles were really starting to cramp up with my arms pulled behind me that way. A fella's not meant to ride all bound up for hours at a time."

"I think maybe I'll buy myself a wagon," Luke had said in response to that.

"A wagon? What for?"

"I'll get some iron bars and build a cage in the back. Then when I have to deliver a prisoner like you, I'll just lock him up in there like an animal so he won't be complaining all the time about being handcuffed."

"Won't he just complain instead about being locked up in a cage?"

"Probably."

"I know I would, if it was me."

"I don't doubt it for a second," Luke had said.

He had to give Tyler a little credit, though. The ride to Malachi Pettifer's place had been about two miles, and Tyler hadn't tried anything so far. He had ridden calmly alongside Luke, who was now mounted on the gray again and leading the horse that had thrown the shoe.

As they approached the low, rambling log building that housed the trading post, Tyler reined in and said, "Wait a minute. If we ride in there with these horses that belonged to Simms and Larrabee, and any of Axtell's men are there, they're liable to recognize the horses."

"Won't they recognize *you*?" Luke asked.

"Oh. Yeah, I guess that's true, isn't it? Well, we knew we were taking a chance by stopping here."

"We wouldn't be if circumstances were different. You're right, though, we need to get that shoe fixed."

"Nice to hear somebody say I was right about something. That didn't happen too often when I was growing up."

In the light from the moon and stars, Luke spotted a small, squat building set off a short distance from the trading post. An iron pipe stuck up from its roof.

"That must be the blacksmith shop," he said. "I'll fire up the forge first thing in the morning, get the job done, and we'll be on our way as quickly as possible."

On the other side of the trading post was a pole corral with a long, slope-roofed shed attached to it. Luke and Tyler rode in that direction.

As they came closer, Luke saw that six horses were already in the enclosure. Pettifer was doing a pretty good business, if those mounts were any indication.

The place was quiet, that lighted window they had spotted earlier the only sign of life other than the horses in the corral. Luke could hear the chuckling of the Powder River as it flowed between its banks about fifty yards away.

"Open that gate and ride on in," he told Tyler. The young man lifted the rope latch holding the corral gate closed and swung it back. After Tyler had ridden in, Luke followed, leading the other two horses. He nodded toward the gate, indicating that Tyler should close it.

Tyler hesitated, looking off into the darkness, and Luke wondered if he was pondering the odds of making a run for it.

If so, it didn't take him long to reach a

decision. He closed and fastened the gate.

"All right, you can unsaddle all these horses now," Luke told him. "Saddles go over there in the shed. Make sure there's grain in the feeder, too."

"What are you gonna do while I'm working?" Tyler wanted to know.

Luke swung down from the gray, pulled his rifle from its sheath, and said, "I've got my own job. It's called standing here, keeping an eye on you, and hoping you don't give me any reason to shoot you."

CHAPTER 16

Luke kept the Winchester's barrel pointed generally toward the ground as they walked around the trading post to the entrance, so it didn't actually look like he was holding a gun on Tyler.

Both of them knew, however, that he could raise the rifle and fire in the blink of an eye.

The door had a latch much like the one on the corral gate. Tyler lifted it and pushed the door in. The smell that wafted out was a mixture of stale beer, tobacco smoke, animal hides, some sort of spicy food, and unwashed human flesh. It reminded Luke of scores of other frontier trading posts he had visited during his bounty-hunting career.

The floor was split logs fitted closely together. Thick, roughly square beams that had been hacked out of other logs were set in two rows, four to each row, and supported the exposed ceiling joists.

The rows of beams also served to divide the big room into thirds. Straight ahead when Luke and Tyler came in were several sets of shelves filled with supplies and trade goods. At the back was a long counter with more supplies behind it, including racks that held rifles and shotguns. A stack of hides was piled to one side, showing that Pettifer traded with some of the trappers who still worked far back in the mountains as if it were fifty years earlier and the fur trade was still at its height.

The section to the right served as a saloon and eatery. A bar made of thick planks laid across barrels ran along that wall. There were four tables, as well, where customers could eat, drink, or play cards. At the back was a big fireplace with a stewpot hanging on an iron stand, staying warm over a blaze that had burned down almost to embers.

Curtains had been hung between the beams on the left to close off that section. Back there would be small, squalid rooms where men could sleep or consort with whores, if Pettifer had any working for him.

The only lamp burning at the moment was on the saloon side, which meant the rest of the trading post was dim and shadowy. Luke didn't like that very much, but on the other hand, it might work to his advantage. If any of the men in here were holding a grudge against him, they'd be less likely to recognize him in the bad light. He planned to keep his head down and let the brim of his black hat obscure his face as much as he could without drawing attention to himself.

Two men stood at the bar. Two more were seated at one of the tables, shoveling stew into their mouths from the wooden bowls in front of them. That left two unaccounted for . . . assuming six men had ridden in on those half-dozen horses in the corral and they didn't have any extra mounts with them.

The faces of the men turned toward the newcomers. At first glance, Luke didn't see anybody he recognized. But if the light was bad for them, it was hard for him to see, too, so he couldn't make out their features all that well.

A fat man with a long white beard that hung far down his chest stood behind the bar. He wore a canvas apron tied around his neck and behind his back, but he didn't appear to have a shirt on underneath it. Luke wondered if the man was wearing any trousers but then decided that maybe he didn't want to know.

"Come in, gentlemen, come in," the man

greeted them in a booming voice. "All are welcome at Pettifer's."

One of the men at the bar snickered and said, "Unless you're wearin' a damn law-dog's badge, ain't that right, Malachi?"

"It's perfectly fine for a peace officer to walk through that door," Pettifer said. "Walking out again . . ." The thick, bare shoulders rose and fell. "That might be a different story."

"No badges here," Luke said, talking past Tyler who was still in front of him. "Never wore one and never will."

"Step up and have a drink, then," Pettifer invited with a wave of a pudgy hand.

Luke and Tyler walked over to the bar, swinging wide around the table where the two men sat so that Luke could watch them from the corner of his eye. They probably knew exactly what he was doing, but in a place like this, such cautious behavior was to be expected. A man riding the owlhoot never knew when he would run into an enemy. For that reason, Luke watched the two men standing at the bar, as well.

"Got beer and whiskey, both fine libations made right here in Pettifer City," the fat, bearded man said.

Luke thought Pettifer City was a pretty grandiose title for a trading post in the middle of nowhere, but he didn't mention that, just asked, "What's the ratio of snake heads to gunpowder in the whiskey?"

"Eh?"

"Beer," Luke said. "One each for my friend and me."

"Comin' up."

Pettifer set two big tin cups on the bar, reached down to the floor and picked up a bucket, and poured amber liquid from the bucket into the cups. Luke tried not to shudder.

"Four bits apiece, so that'll be a dollar," Pettifer said.

Using his left hand, Luke took a coin from his pocket and slid it across the bar. He didn't like the fact that his back was turned to the curtained-off area on the other side of the trading post. There was no mirror hung behind the bar, either, so he couldn't watch for any signs of movement that way.

Once again, Tyler proved to be pretty quick-witted. As if he'd been reading Luke's mind, he picked up his cup of beer, half-turned so that he could lean on the bar with his other elbow, and took a drink. Positioned that way, he could watch Luke's back without being too obvious about it. He sighed in satisfaction and licked his lips after he downed the swallow of beer.

Luke tried his, found it at least palatable, and then let the cup sit on the bar while he said to Pettifer, "I saw what looked like a blacksmith shop out there."

"Well, it's not much more than a forge and a bellows, but it'll do in a pinch. You got a pinch, friend?"

"I have a horse that's thrown a shoe. How much for the use of the forge?"

"Two dollars," Pettifer answered without hesitation. "You stoke it and do all the work yourself. You're just payin' for the fact that I had the foresight to build it."

"Fair enough," Luke said. "I'll be using it first thing in the morning, if it's not already spoken for."

Pettifer shook his head and said, "We've got a deal. Why don't you go ahead and pay now, so we don't have to worry about it in the morning?"

As a rule, Luke didn't like paying for things in advance, but he wasn't going to argue and draw attention to him and Tyler. Instead he took a five-dollar gold piece from his pocket this time and said, "I assume this will buy us a couple of bowls of stew and a place to sleep tonight, along with the use of the forge?"

"As a matter of fact, I've got a special deal going on just that combination," Pettifer said. With practiced ease, he caught the coin as Luke tossed it to him and dropped it into a pocket on the apron. He took a couple of bowls from a shelf, set them on the bar with a pair of spoons, and told Luke and Tyler, "Help yourselves from the pot over yonder."

Luke nodded toward the bowls and spoons, indicating that Tyler should pick them up. Then, with the rifle in one hand and the cup of beer in the other, he went over to one of the empty tables.

He set the beer down and laid the rifle across the table. Tyler left his beer there, too, as they went over to the fireplace and the stewpot.

"I haven't seen anybody in here I know," Tyler said, pitching his voice low enough that Pettifer and the other men in the room couldn't hear it.

"Neither have I," Luke said, "and more importantly, none of them seem to recognize either of us."

They filled their bowls using the dipper that hung from the stand, then carried them back over to the table. The beer might not have been very good, but the stew was surprisingly tasty, Luke found when he dug in. It was filled with chunks of venison, wild onions, carrots, and potatoes. He hadn't noticed it in the twilight, but somewhere around the trading post had to be a garden.

Pettifer didn't strike Luke as the type to tend a garden, so that argued for the presence of a woman around the place. That hunch was confirmed a few minutes later when one of the curtains was thrust back and a man in the bullhide chaps of a Texan swaggered through, followed by a woman in a plain shirt and long skirt. Her blond hair was roughly cropped so that it fell just above her shoulders.

The pug-nosed, sunburned Texan joined the two men standing at the bar, who greeted him with ribald comments and good-natured slaps on the back. He was young, probably not even twenty yet, and Luke supposed this might have been his first time with a woman. One of the other men called out to Pettifer to pour a drink for the youngster.

Pettifer did that, then went down to the other end of the bar where the blonde was standing. He nodded toward the far side of the trading post and asked her, "Spotted Fawn still back there with the other one?"

"That's right," the blonde said as Pettifer filled a shot glass with whiskey for her.

"Didn't hear any sort of trouble going on, did you? It's been a while."

She shook her head and picked up the

glass. She threw back the drink and set the empty on the bar with a thump.

In a half-whisper, Tyler said to Luke, "Hard to believe a gal like her and one as sweet and innocent as Rachel are even the same species."

Luke chewed and swallowed and said, "We're all human beings, subject to the same frailties and magnificences."

"You quoting that Marcus fella again, or some other old Roman?"

"No. That one is my own."

The two men with the young Texan either lacked the funds for a whore or had already taken their turn, because they didn't show any interest in the blonde. After a few minutes she motioned for Pettifer to pour her another drink, then picked up the glass and sauntered over to the table where Luke and Tyler sat. Luke could tell that she was trying to put a seductive sway in her walk, but she wasn't having much success at that.

"Hello, boys," she said as she came up to the table. She put a well-worn smile on her face.

Luke didn't point out that he hadn't been a boy since before he had gone off to war, and that was a lot of years ago.

"My name's Millie," the blonde continued. "What do they call you fellas?"

"Tired and hungry," Luke said. He appreciated time spent with pleasant female company as much as any man, but this wasn't really the time or place.

"Which one are you?" she asked.

"Both."

Millie gave up on him and turned to Tyler, saying, "And that would make you . . . ?"

"Flat broke, ma'am, and I surely do regret to say it."

Millie sighed and said, "No more than I'm sorry to hear it."

She was younger than Luke had thought at first and reasonably pretty in an already faded way. With a foot, he pushed back one of the empty chairs at the table and said, "You look a mite tired yourself. Why don't you sit down for a while?"

Millie frowned.

"Sittin's not really how I earn my keep."

Luke took out another dollar and laid it on the table.

"Sit," he told her again. "I've been on the trail now for several days with nothing nice to look at. You're a welcome change from that, Millie."

She glanced at the bar, where Pettifer stood watching her. Making sure that he could see what she was doing, she picked up the coin and dropped it down the front of her shirt, then sat down between Luke and Tyler.

"You can tell me your names if you want," she said. "I know better than to shoot my mouth off to any badge-toters who come sniffin' around."

"I'm Judd, he's Luke," Tyler said before Luke could respond. Luke would have preferred that Tyler hadn't admitted even that much, but he supposed it wouldn't hurt anything. After all, the men who were hunting Tyler already knew his name and what he looked like.

"I'm happy to meet both of you," Millie said. "And happy to sit down and do nothin' for a few minutes. You wouldn't think whorin' would wear a body out so much, but it sure does."

"Anything keeping you from going somewhere else and making a fresh start?" Luke asked.

"Everything in the world, mister," she said with a weary sigh. "Everything in the world."

"You should do like that old fella Emperor Marcus," Tyler said. "Do the best you can with what you got and let the rest move on past you."

She frowned at him and said, "What?"

Before they could continue this rather odd

discussion of stoic philosophy, the young Texan in the bullhide chaps strode over to the table. The three sitting there turned their heads to look at him as he hooked his thumbs in his belt and announced, "I'm ready to go again, Millie."

"Oh, I doubt that, kid," she said. "I know you're young, but you best wait a little while longer."

"I said I'm ready *now.*"

Over at the bar, his friends cackled. Luke figured they had prodded the youngster into approaching the table.

Luke had finished his stew. He pushed the empty bowl away and said, "The lady's time has been bought and paid for, friend, and I believe that dollar I laid down still has more time to run."

"He's right —" Millie began.

The Texan glared at Luke and said, "I didn't ask you, old man. I'm talkin' to this here dirty whore."

"Hey, there's no need for talk like that," Tyler said. The legs of his chair scraped on the rough floor as he slid it back a little.

The Texan tensed, his right hand moving quickly to hover over the wooden grips of what appeared to be an old cap-and-ball revolver holstered on his hip.

"You just stay out of it," he snapped. "I

193

don't need no advice from the likes o' you. You ain't even packin' a gun. What's the matter? You a damn yellow-bellied coward? Too scared to carry a gun?"

Luke tried not to roll his eyes in disgust. After the day they'd had, the last thing they needed to encounter was some obnoxious young buck who probably thought he was fast on the draw, that fantasy no doubt fueled by liquor and countless dime-novel scenarios pored over in bunkhouses and outhouses.

Tyler said, "I'm not scared. Just not looking for trouble. Why don't you go back to your friends, let us talk to the lady for a while, and then if she wants to do some more business with you, that'll be up to her."

"You keep callin' her a lady? Don't you know a dirty whore when you see one?" The Texan let out a raucous laugh. "Oh, I get it now! You're one o' them fellas who ain't interested in gals. That's why you ain't taken her over yonder to the rooms. You wouldn't know what to do with her if you did." He jabbed his left thumb against his chest. "Well, *I* sure as hell do!"

"Yeah," Millie said, "that's why we sat back there playin' cards for twenty minutes so you could lie to your friends about everything you done to me."

The Texan's eyes widened in outrage. He yelled, "You lyin' bitch!" His left arm swung out before Luke or Tyler could stop him, and the back of his hand cracked across Millie's face with enough force to knock her out of the chair to the floor.

Tyler exploded out of his chair with a shout and tackled the Texan, driving him off his feet.

Chapter 17

Luke was on his feet a split-second later with both Remingtons drawn and cocked.

One was aimed in the general direction of the two men sitting at a table. They had been sharing drinks from a bottle after finishing their supper. Both were middle-aged and tired-looking, and although they watched the fracas between Tyler and the Texan, neither of them seemed to have any inclination to join in.

The same wasn't true of the two men at the bar, the youngster's friends. They had looked startled when Tyler tackled the Texan, but then they'd scowled and started forward as if to help their partner.

Luke's other Remington, its long barrel pointed straight at them, stopped them in their tracks. They wore furious expressions, but staring down the barrel of the revolver had frozen their feet.

"Right there, boys," Luke said. "You'll do

just fine staying exactly where you are."

On the rough, sawdust-littered floor, Tyler and his opponent had rolled over several times, punching and kicking and gouging. There might have even been some biting going on; Luke couldn't tell. There were no rules in this fight, which the young Texan demonstrated by trying to ram his chaps-clad knee into Tyler's groin.

Tyler twisted away from that vicious blow and clapped a hand over the other man's face, digging for his eyes. The Texan jerked his head away and clipped Tyler on the chin with a wild punch. That rocked Tyler's head back. The Texan grabbed Tyler's shirt front and slung him to the side.

As Tyler rolled over again, the Texan scrambled to his feet and went after him. A boot toe thudded into Tyler's ribs.

Luke didn't like to see anybody being kicked while he was down, but he knew if he took his attention off of the Texan's friends, they would rush to join the fight.

Tyler was on his own in this battle.

The Texan tried to kick him again, but this time Tyler got his hands up and grabbed the young man's boot as it came at him. Tyler heaved, throwing the Texan off his feet and sending him crashing to the floor on his back. That knocked the breath out of the Texan and stunned him long enough for Tyler to make it to his feet. He had to grab the back of a chair and brace himself on it until his legs steadied.

The Texan rolled onto his side and then got his hands and knees under him. As he came up, he yelled, "I'm gonna blow your lights out, you bastard!"

Before he could reach for his gun, though, Pettifer leveled a shotgun at him from behind the counter and said, "Keep your hand away from that hogleg!"

The young Texan glared at him but didn't make a move for the Colt on his hip.

"I don't mind fights in my place," Pettifer went on, "but they're gonna be fair. You two can beat yourselves to death if you're of a mind to, but no gunplay!"

Luke didn't feel any admiration for Pettifer — the man harbored outlaws and was a whoremonger — but at least he still had a semblance of honor about him. That Western code of fair play could be found in most people who lived on the frontier, even its lowest denizens.

For a second the Texan looked like he was going to slap leather anyway, despite the threatening scattergun, but then he thought better of it. Instead he reached for the buckle of his gunbelt, unfastened it, and lowered the belt and holstered gun onto one of the tables.

Then he balled his fists and charged at Tyler, bellowing out his rage as he did so.

Tyler met the attack with hard fists of his own. He blocked some of the Texan's punches, absorbed the force of the ones that got through, and swung blow after blow of his own.

For a long moment, the two young men stood toe to toe, slugging away at each other, as stubborn and brutal as primordial beasts struggling in the dawn of time, Luke thought. Both faces were bloody now, and drops of crimson flew every time a fist crashed into flesh.

Then one of Tyler's feet slipped as he tried to shift to a different position, causing his guard to drop. The Texan's right flew in and slammed into Tyler's cheekbone with enough force to send him reeling back against the bar.

The Texan crowded against him, keeping him pinned there while hooking punch after punch into Tyler's midsection. Tyler was helpless and gasping for breath. His face had gone gray under the onslaught.

Luke didn't want to see Tyler beaten to death. That would assure that the truth about Rachel Montgomery's murder would never be revealed. He was about to step in when Tyler made a desperate grab and got hold of the Texan's left ear.

Tyler twisted as hard as he could, and more blood flew as skin ripped and separated. The Texan howled in pain and tried to jerk away, but Tyler kept twisting until the ear was torn halfway off his opponent's head.

He finally let go and swung his left in a wicked hook. The punch wasn't moving very fast, but the Texan was so concerned with his mutilated ear that he couldn't get out of the way in time. Tyler's fist caught him on the jaw and jerked his head to the side. Tyler hit him with a right. The Texan staggered back a couple of steps.

Now Tyler was the one crowding his opponent, keeping the Texan off balance with a flurry of punches. Luke could tell that Tyler was putting the last of his strength into this counterattack. If it failed to end the fight, Tyler was probably done for.

The Texan couldn't get his hands up anymore, though, so punch after punch thudded home. As the Texan began to sway, Tyler swung a roundhouse right that landed solidly and lifted the youngster completely off his feet.

This time when the Texan crashed down,

it was with a finality that said he wouldn't be getting up again anytime soon.

Millie had long since gotten to her feet after the Texan knocked her out of the chair. Luke had seen that from the corner of his eye. She had stood to one side, watching anxiously as the two young men battled.

Now, with the Texan out cold, she stepped up hurriedly to Tyler and caught hold of his arm to steady him as he swayed and looked like he might fall down, too.

"You didn't have to stand up for me like that," she told him, then smiled. "But I've got to admit, it was kind of nice."

Tyler managed to return the smile, although it looked like it hurt him to move his bruised, bloody face.

"Yes'm," he said as his breath rasped in his throat. "I can't abide . . . anybody hurtin' . . . a lady."

"Well, the kid was right about that part, I reckon. I ain't no ways a lady. But it's nice somebody might think so and act like it, whether it's true or not."

Luke motioned with the Remington's barrel to the Texan's two friends and said, "Get him up and out of here." He looked at Pettifer. "That is, if you have no objection."

Pettifer had lowered the shotgun but still held the double-barreled weapon. He shook his head and said, "They hadn't paid for rooms for the night, just booze and a poke for the kid. That gives you more of a say on who stays and who goes, as far as I'm concerned."

Luke nodded toward the Texan's senseless form again, and this time the other two men came forward to pick him up, although they wore surly frowns as they did so.

They got him to his feet, but it took both of them to keep him there. The Texan had started to make incoherent noises and move his head a little, but he was still a long way from having his wits about him.

As the other two started half carrying, half dragging him toward the entrance, one of the men who'd been sitting at the table stood, picked up the Texan's hat, and put it on the youngster's head. The Texan didn't seem to notice.

"Hell of a fight," the older man said to Tyler. "Wish it could have gone on longer."

"No offense," Tyler said, "but I sure as hell don't."

The Texan's two companions hauled him out of the trading post and into the night. When the door had swung closed behind them, Luke looked at the two older men and said, "You fellas didn't have any cards in that game, did you?"

The one still sitting at the table said, "Not hardly, mister. Mack and me are just passin' through. We don't know any of you folks and would just as soon keep it that way."

"Sounds good to me," Luke said. He holstered both guns. He would remain alert, of course, but his instincts told him the other two customers didn't represent any threat.

"Honey, let's get you set down," Millie said to Tyler as she helped him over to the table. "You look a little green."

"Yeah, I might not have . . . eaten that big bowl of stew . . . if I'd known I was gonna get punched in the belly so much."

Tyler didn't make it to the table. He turned and lurched toward the door instead, holding a hand to his mouth. Millie went with him, helping hold him up, and they made it outside before Tyler began losing his supper.

Pettifer put the shotgun somewhere back under the bar where he had gotten it and told Luke, "No refunds on the stew because it didn't stay down."

"Not your fault that it didn't," Luke said. "You might have stepped in, though, when that obnoxious Texan began to mistreat the young woman."

"I wouldn't have let him do any real harm to her," Pettifer said as his beefy shoulders

203

went up and down again. "A whore's got to be used to getting knocked around a little, though. That's just the way things are."

And that code of honor Luke had been thinking about earlier didn't run very deep in this place's proprietor, obviously.

Luke was turning back toward the table where his Winchester still lay when he spotted someone he hadn't seen before standing at the end of the bar. She was a short, stocky woman with long black hair done in two braids. Clearly an Indian, even though she wore white woman's clothing. Luke recalled Pettifer asking Millie about somebody called Spotted Fawn, and he knew that was who he was looking at now.

When the trouble broke out, she had been in one of the rooms on the other side of the building, servicing a customer. Luke figured she had come back into this part of the trading post while the fight was going on between Tyler and the Texan, and he hadn't noticed her because he'd been keeping his attention focused on the Texan's two friends and on the battle itself.

That thought put a frown on Luke's face. He didn't like the fact that someone had been able to move around in here without him noticing.

And there was no sign of Spotted Fawn's

customer, either. Was he still over there on the other side of the building, sleeping in one of the little rooms, or had he managed to get out of the trading post without Luke seeing him? The idea that someone could be drifting around out there, unaccounted for, his identity unknown, was pretty worrisome.

That thought had barely had time to form in Luke's brain before a gunshot suddenly blasted, somewhere outside.

CHAPTER 18

Luke lunged toward the door, cursing bitterly to himself because he knew that Tyler was outside and might be in danger. Of course, he would have needed eyes in the back of his head to see everything that had gone on in the trading post during the ruckus . . . but to Luke's way of thinking, that was exactly what he should have done.

Another shot roared. One of the Remingtons was in Luke's right hand as he used his left to throw the door open. Colt flame bloomed in the darkness to his right as a third shot split the night.

He didn't know who was behind the gun, so he couldn't target the muzzle flash. Instead he darted through the door and veered sharply left to look for some cover.

There was none to be found. A second later, his left foot struck something soft and yielding and he stumbled, going to a knee. Thinking he had just tripped on Tyler's body, he thrust out his left hand to touch the motionless figure sprawled on the ground in front of him.

The contours he discovered were definitely female. He didn't detect any signs of life, either.

Millie, he thought as he edged over next to the wall, into the shadows. He was counting on his dark clothing concealing him from the gunman, at least for a moment or two.

Tyler was still out here somewhere. Was it possible that was him with the gun? Could he have gotten his hands on a weapon somehow and shot Millie in order to lure Luke out here and gun him down, too?

The idea was so far-fetched that Luke discarded it almost at once. It was true that Tyler had been desperate to escape when Luke first captured him, but over the past few days he seemed to have accepted the fact that going back to White Fork and exposing Spence Douglas's guilt was the best course open to him.

Besides, Luke didn't believe for a second that Tyler would have shot the blonde, especially after fighting such a brutal battle to defend her the way he had done.

But that left Tyler's whereabouts a mystery, as was the identity of the would-be killer.

No more shots had sounded. Luke figured that meant the gunman couldn't see him and was watching for some sign, something for him to shoot at.

Luke couldn't stay where he was, even though moving was a risk. Hugging the wall, he slipped as quietly as possible toward the corner of the building. The gunman was over by the corral, so Luke thought he might be able to surprise the man by circling around behind the trading post.

He wasn't the only one who'd had that idea. An angry shout suddenly rang out, followed less than a heartbeat later by the explosion of another shot. Luke saw a tongue of orange flame spurt from a gun muzzle, then he heard the sounds of a struggle, punctuated by grunts of effort.

Luke abandoned the shadows and raced toward the fight. He had a feeling that Judd Tyler was in the thick of it, and he didn't know what the odds were. The would-be killer might be the man who had been with Spotted Fawn, in which case he was probably alone, but it was possible the young Texan and his friends had lingered outside, hoping to get revenge on Tyler.

Either way, Luke knew Tyler needed his

help. The young man was outnumbered, outgunned — or both.

Another shot shattered the night air. This time Luke was close enough to make out the two struggling figures in the glare from the muzzle flash. He heard one of them cry out as the shapes parted. The lean form stumbled backward.

"Tyler, hit the dirt!" Luke shouted.

The man who'd evidently been hit dropped to the ground while the other shape twisted back toward Luke. He still couldn't be absolutely certain which one was which, but when the gun went off yet again and Luke heard the slap of the slug just past his ear, he figured it didn't really matter.

Anybody trying to kill him was going to get a bullet — or several — in return.

The Remington roared and bucked in his fist. He triggered three swift shots, and with each blast the man who had lurked outside, waiting to kill, rocked back under the impact of the bullets. The man fell sideways to his knees, then crumpled forward.

Luke used his left hand to fish a lucifer out of his shirt pocket, then snapped the match to life with an iron-hard thumbnail. His eyes were slitted against the glare. He held the lucifer so that its light fell across the man on the ground.

Luke couldn't see the man's face because of the way he was lying, but his hat had fallen off and revealed a skull that was as bald as a billiard ball.

Definitely *not* Judd Tyler.

A moan came from the other man, then a gasped question: "Luke?"

"Yeah," Luke said. "How bad are you hit, Tyler?"

"I dunno . . . Not bad, I think. But what about Millie?"

"We'll have to check on her and see," Luke said, although from what he had found earlier, he wasn't very optimistic about the young woman's condition.

The match had burned down. Luke dropped it and lit another, and while it was burning brightly he used the toe of his boot to roll the man he'd shot onto his back. The blankly staring eyes and the shirt front sodden with blood that was black in the harsh light confirmed that the man was dead.

Tyler had gotten up, hurried over to Millie, and dropped to his knees beside her. He said, "Oh, damn. Damn it, damn it, damn it."

Luke shook out the second match before it could burn his fingers and swung away from the dead man.

"She didn't make it?"

"No." Tyler's voice was choked with emotion. "It looks like that first shot hit her right in the heart. It was meant for me. The bastard was aiming at *me,* Luke. She stepped in front of me just as the gun went off. Pure bad luck. Neither of us knew he was anywhere around."

"The workings of fate are often beyond our comprehension."

"Damn it, don't spew quotes at me! Not now."

"I'm not," Luke said. "It's just the truth . . . unpleasant though it may be sometimes."

"Didn't really know her at all," Tyler muttered. "Barely even met her. Just knew her name and that she was a . . . a whore. But she saved my life anyway."

"You know a man with a bald head, even though he's not very old? Maybe thirty."

Tyler looked up and repeated, "A bald head? Let me see."

He stood up and stumbled over while Luke lit another lucifer. Tyler stared down at the corpse with hate in his eyes and said, "That's Cue Ball Hennessy. He's one of Axtell's deputies, too. I told you they were probably closin' in on us."

"No badge pinned to his shirt," Luke said.

"It's probably in his pocket or his saddle-bags. I reckon he must've taken it off before he rode in here, knowing that he wouldn't get any cooperation from Pettifer or any of the place's customers if they knew he was a lawman . . . even the pitiful excuse for one that he was."

The mention of Pettifer made Luke glance toward the door. The trading post's owner and the other two men were still inside. None of them had even poked a head out, as far as Luke knew. Which wasn't surprising. The sort of *hombres* who would stop at a place like this knew how to mind their own business.

Luke was curious about something, though. He called, "Pettifer! Get out here!"

A moment later, Pettifer's bulky figure appeared in the open doorway. He had the shotgun in his hands again. Caution cloaked the trading post owner as he looked around.

"All the shooting over?" he asked.

"That's right," Luke said. "Fetch a lantern, Pettifer."

Pettifer cocked his head to the side and said, "Why do you want me to do that?"

"Something here I want you to take a look at. A couple of somethings, in fact." Luke's voice hardened. "Get that lantern."

Instead of doing what Luke told him, Pet-

212

tifer turned his head and shouted over his shoulder, "Spotted Fawn! Light a lantern and bring it out here!"

The Indian woman appeared a minute later, holding the burning lantern in front of her. She stepped out and lifted it higher, so that the circle of yellow light it cast washed over Millie's body.

A choked sound came from Pettifer's throat. He said, "Aw . . . aw, hell. She's dead, isn't she?"

"Indeed she is," Luke said. "This man fired the shot that killed her."

Spotted Fawn turned, throwing the light over Luke, Tyler — who had moved to stand beside him — and the body of Cue Ball Hennessy.

"Recognize him?" Luke asked. His voice was still flat and hard.

"He's the, uh, fella who was with Spotted Fawn when you gents came in," Pettifer said.

"Are you in the habit of helping lawmen now?"

The two older men who had been in the trading post had come out to stand just in front of the door. Both stiffened when they heard Luke's question.

"He's a lawman?" Pettifer's response was practically an alarmed yelp. "He's not wearing a badge!"

"Yeah, but I recognize him," Tyler said. "He's one of Sheriff Gus Axtell's deputies from White Fork, across the line in Montana Territory."

"Well, how in blazes could I be expected to know that?" Pettifer's voice became more blustery as he regained some of his confidence. "I can't recognize every lawman on the whole damn frontier. If a fella comes into my place and he's not wearing a badge, and he doesn't *tell* me he's a lawman, I don't have any way of knowin' about it."

"What *did* he tell you?" Luke asked. "I'm betting he had a few questions, didn't he?"

"Well, uh . . ." Suddenly, Pettifer was more uncertain again. "He might've said he was looking for a couple of friends of his."

"Did he describe them?"

"One of them." Pettifer nodded toward Tyler. "Description sounded sort of like this young fella here. I told him I hadn't seen anybody lately who looked like that."

"What did he do then?"

"Had a drink and decided to take Spotted Fawn over to the other side of the building for a poke. Nothing out of the ordinary as far as I could tell."

"But when we came in," Luke said, "you didn't think to let us know that a man who might be looking for us was only a few feet away?"

"Hell, it was none of my business! I figured the fella would come out sooner or later and see you, and if you were the ones he was looking for, he'd recognize you. If you weren't, what the hell did it matter?"

"But he came out while that fight was going on and no one noticed him. Then he waited out here to bushwhack my friend. And because of that, Millie is dead."

"But it's not my fault! I couldn't have known any of that was gonna happen."

"Actions have consequences, intended or not," Luke said. "Tomorrow morning, one of those consequences will be a burial."

CHAPTER 19

Spotted Fawn brought a blanket outside and wrapped Millie's body in it. The two middle-aged outlaws carried the shrouded shape inside and placed it gently on the counter at the rear of the trading post.

Then one of the men said, "Reckon we'll be driftin'. Time was, folks knew it was safe for *hombres* on the dodge like us to stop here. Now, with Pettifer caterin' to star packers, I ain't sure that it is anymore."

"We'll make sure that word gets around, too," the other man said.

Pettifer had set his shotgun on the bar. Now, as the two men walked out, he clapped both hands to his head and groaned.

"Ruined," he said. "My business is ruined, and none of it is my fault!"

"You'll survive," Luke told him. "Men like you always find a way."

Pettifer glared at him and demanded, "What do you mean by that?"

"I mean you provide women and liquor, and there'll always be a market for those things."

"Well . . . yeah, I suppose you're right about that. But it'll take a while, once word about this gets around, for fellas to start trusting me again."

Luke couldn't muster up any sympathy for the man. He went back outside to drag Hennessy's body away from the front of the place. If Pettifer wanted the deputy buried, he could damned well dig the grave himself . . . although it was more likely he'd make Spotted Fawn do it.

When Luke came back in, he found Tyler sitting at the table where they had been earlier, staring gloomily toward the back of the building where Millie's body lay.

"She's dead because of me," he said as Luke sat down. "Just like Rachel."

"You didn't kill either of them," Luke pointed out.

"But if I'd walked Rachel home that night the way I wanted to, Spence couldn't have gotten her in the woods and killed her. And if *that* hadn't happened, I wouldn't have been on the run, you wouldn't have caught me, and we wouldn't have been here tonight for Millie to get killed."

"There was a big prairie fire over east of

here a while back," Luke said. "Was that your fault, too? Any time anything happens, you can find some sort of convoluted reasoning to make it your fault, if you want to waste time doing that. It makes more sense to do something about it if you can, though."

"What can I do about this? They're both dead."

"You can make sure Spence Douglas doesn't get away with what he did. You can see that justice is served." Luke shrugged. "As for Millie, we can see to it that she gets a proper burial in the morning. Sometimes that's all you can do."

"I reckon," Tyler said, although he didn't sound like he really believed it.

"In the meantime, we'd better see how badly you're hurt. Hennessy shot you, remember?"

Tyler dismissed that with a wave of his hand and said, "The bullet just grazed my side. It hurts some, but I don't care."

"You'd better care. You don't want to get blood poisoning or have the wound fester. Let me take a look at it."

Grudgingly, Tyler pulled up his shirt, which had a bullet rip and a bloodstain on the left side. He was right about the injury. The bullet fired by Hennessy had barely struck him, leaving a crimson streak along his ribs.

"Does it hurt any when you take a deep breath?" Luke asked.

Tyler tried it, drawing in air and then blowing it back out again. He shook his head and said, "Nope."

"That slug didn't break any ribs, then. Probably didn't even bruise them. It ought to be cleaned with a rag and some whiskey, though."

"That rotgut that Pettifer sells might do more harm than good."

"I can sprinkle some gunpowder on the wound and light it, if you'd prefer," Luke said.

Tyler shuddered and shook his head. He called over to the bar, "Pettifer, bring us a bottle and a clean rag, if you can find one in this hellhole."

"You don't have any call to talk to me like that," Pettifer said, "no matter what you may think about me." He sighed. "But I guess I don't have much choice, do I? I'm not likely to get any more customers to-night."

Pettifer brought the rag and the whiskey. Spotted Fawn walked over from the other part of the building and took the items from him. She poured the liquor onto the rag and cleaned the wound with surprising gentleness.

Luke had a hunch this wasn't the first bullet wound she had patched up. Working at a place like Pettifer's, the Indian woman probably had experience at all sorts of things.

She wasn't talkative, though. Luke hadn't heard a word come out of her mouth so far, and she gave no sign of speaking up any time soon. When she finished cleaning the wound, she cut a strip off a bolt of cloth she took from one of the shelves in the trading post and bound it around Tyler's torso as a bandage.

Pettifer said, "I'll have to charge you for that cloth, you know."

"Consider it a barter," Luke said. "You'll be getting a grave dug out of the deal."

Since at this point Luke trusted Judd Tyler more than he did Pettifer, the two of them took turns standing guard during the night. Pettifer might decide that he could recoup some of his potential losses from this incident by robbing and murdering both of them in their sleep.

When Luke explained this reasoning to Tyler, the young man nodded and said, "Yeah, it's a good idea for one of us to stay awake the whole time we're here. You might ought to let me have a gun, though."

"I'm not that trusting just yet. If there's any trouble, you just give a shout. I'll be awake in a hurry."

"All right," Tyler said with a resigned sigh. "But I hope nobody has to bury *us* in the morning."

"That's not likely to happen," Luke said, then added, "Pettifer would just throw our bodies outside for the wolves and the buzzards."

The rest of the night passed peacefully enough, however, and Luke and Tyler were up early. A groggy, sullen Pettifer told them they could find a shovel in the shed next to the corral. Spotted Fawn had coffee brewing. When it was ready, she gave cups to Luke and Tyler, still without saying anything.

Fortified by the strong, black brew, they went out into the cool morning air and walked to the shed. As they did, buzzards lifted from the other side of the trading post, and Luke knew they'd been at Cue Ball Hennessy's body already.

When they had the shovel, they walked to the top of a little knoll about fifty yards from the trading post. The view wasn't bad, with the Powder River flowing below them and sage-covered flats stretching off into the distance beyond the stream. Tyler looked around and nodded.

"I reckon this isn't a bad place. As pretty as anywhere we'll find around here, I expect."

"I think Millie will rest comfortably here," Luke agreed.

Tyler had the shovel, so he started digging, but he hadn't been at it for very long when Luke could tell that the young man was stiff and sore from the bullet graze on his side. He took the shovel from Tyler and said, "I'll finish up."

"I feel like I ought to —"

"Just keep an eye out for more visitors. Some of Axtell's other deputies could come drifting in."

While Tyler did that, Luke dug. The sun was up, sparkling on the river, and the temperature rose with it until sweat covered Luke's face and dampened his shirt. The ground up here on top of the knoll wasn't *too* hard and rocky, though, so it didn't take him very long before he had the grave ready.

Leaving the shovel beside the pile of dirt so they could fill in the hole later, the two of them went back down to the trading post.

Spotted Fawn had cleaned Millie's face and body and clothed her in a dark blue dress that went well with her blond hair. A corner of the blanket was turned back so that her face was visible.

"She looks peaceful," Tyler said with a solemn expression on his face as he stood in front of the counter where the body lay. He held his hat in his hands.

"She is at peace," Luke said, "probably more so than she's been for quite some time." His hat was off, too. "Maybe for her entire life."

Spotted Fawn wore the buckskins of her people now. With an equally solemn expression on her face, she covered Millie and tucked the blanket in.

Over at the bar, Pettifer leaned on the planks and belched.

"Lot of fuss to go to for a whore," he said. His voice and the deep flush on his face were evidence that he'd been drinking quite a bit.

"You'd better keep your mouth shut, mister," Tyler told him. "Nobody's in any mood to listen to it."

"This is my place," Pettifer said. "I'll talk if I want to, by God, and I'll say whatever I please!"

Tyler took a step toward the bar, but Luke put a hand on his arm to stop him.

"He's just blowing hot air," Luke said. "It's not worth the trouble. Let's go, Judd.

We've got something more important to do."

"Yeah, you're right." Tyler clapped his hat on and stood there glaring at Pettifer for a second before he turned and helped Luke pick up Millie's body.

They carried her to the waiting grave at the top of the knoll, followed by Spotted Fawn. After placing the body carefully in the grave, they removed their hats again and Luke recited The Lord's Prayer.

When he was finished, Spotted Fawn began to chant softly. Luke recognized it as a death song, although he couldn't make out the words. He had begun to wonder if the woman was mute, but clearly she just hadn't had anything she wanted to say until now.

Pettifer never came out of the trading post, not that Luke had expected him to.

Once Spotted Fawn fell silent, Luke picked up the shovel and began the grim task of filling in the grave.

It was midmorning before he made it to the blacksmith shop and fired up the forge, and the sun was at its zenith before he had replaced the horse's shoe and they were ready to go.

As they were saddling up, Spotted Fawn came out of the trading post carrying an oilcloth-wrapped bundle.

"Food for the trail," she said in perfectly good English. "It's just roast beef and biscuits."

"And it's much appreciated," Luke told her as he took the bundle and tied it to his saddle. "Are you going to be all right here, Spotted Fawn?"

"I will be fine," she said. Then she added, "But Pettifer would be wise to sleep with one eye open. He will not, though."

She turned and walked back into the trading post.

As they were riding away, Tyler looked back and said, "That old boy's gonna wake up some morning with his throat cut."

"No doubt," Luke agreed. "And it couldn't happen to a more deserving fellow."

CHAPTER 20

They followed the east bank of the Powder River until they came to a place where the stream shallowed out over its rocky bed, making it easy to ford. Blue sky arched overhead, seemingly endless, and a breeze stirred the air, carrying with it the clean tang of the evergreens that covered the hills to the west. Imposing, snowcapped peaks rose behind those hills.

"Mighty pretty country," Tyler said as they rode. "Too bad there's so much death in it."

"You'll find death wherever you go," Luke said. "So you might as well enjoy the good things when you come across them, like this beautiful day."

"This so-called beautiful day of yours started with a burial, remember?"

"And who knows how it'll end? But right now, that sky is magnificent, the air is invigorating, and we have good horses underneath us and a purpose in life. *Carpe diem,* my young friend, *carpe diem.*"

"What?" Tyler asked with a frown.

"It's Latin for *seize the day.*"

Tyler looked at him for several seconds, then said, "I haven't run into all that many bounty hunters, but I reckon if I'd met a thousand of them, you'd still be the oddest of the bunch, Luke Jensen."

"And I'll take that as a compliment, thank you," Luke said, grinning.

By late afternoon they had covered quite a few miles from the trading post and hadn't seen any other travelers along the way, but Luke knew they had to be fairly close to one of the old immigrant trails that ran through this part of the country.

In recent years, with the railroads spreading out to more and more places, those trails weren't used as much as they had been in earlier times, when tens of thousands of settlers had come west in covered wagons drawn by mules or oxen. That exodus had gone on for decades, and a tumultuous era it had been, as the pioneers battled the elements, outlaws, and Indians to find and keep their new homes.

Luke had seen some of those wagon trains and even traveled briefly with a few of them, but since he'd never had any interest in settling down they held no real appeal for him. Those immigrants were a whole different breed than he was.

If he and Tyler spotted any wagons, it would be wise to steer clear of them, he decided. The two of them were being hunted. They were *quarry.*

He didn't want to bring down trouble on a bunch of pilgrims who would be facing enough problems of their own.

Luke didn't mention any of what he'd been mulling over to his companion. Tyler was easily distracted, and Luke wanted to keep him focused on returning to White Fork and revealing the truth about what had happened to Rachel Montgomery.

As evening began to settle over the landscape, Luke led Tyler away from the river in search of a campsite. The stream attracted wildlife, some of which would be predators.

It might attract human predators, too. Luke figured it would be better to put some distance between the two of them and anybody else who might come along.

They found a spot at the base of a hill with enough boulders scattered around to shield their fire. As they dismounted, Luke told Tyler, "You take care of the horses."

"Be glad to. I'm just happy you decided not to handcuff me again after we left Pettifer's place."

"You should've reminded me," Luke said, although actually it hadn't been an oversight. He had decided to risk leaving the handcuffs off of Tyler.

"Not hardly! It was painful enough riding all day with this bullet graze on my side and all the bruises I've got from the tussle with that son of a bitch. If I'd had my hands cuffed behind my back, too, it would've been pure misery. So I wasn't just about to say anything."

"Just don't make me regret the decision. Anyway, I may still cuff you tonight and tie you to one of those trees."

"You don't have to do that," Tyler said. "I'm not going anywhere. I swear it, Luke."

"Well, if I'd known you longer, your word might mean something to me. On the other hand, since you're a self-confessed rustler, stagecoach robber, and all-around shady character, I probably still wouldn't trust you."

"A man can change, you know."

Luke might have argued about that, but he remembered the way his own life had taken a different trail in recent years. Sure, he was still a bounty hunter, but after spending a lot of time using a false name, claiming no family, and making no friends, he found himself with a brother in Smoke and some friends in the old mountain man Preacher and those two youngsters, Ace and Chance Jensen, who shared the same last name but as far as any of them knew were no blood relation.

He might see those folks only every so often, but in all the ways that counted, they were his family now . . . a family he had believed he would never have again.

So he didn't argue with Tyler. He just said, "I'll get a fire going while you tend to those animals."

"Sounds good to me," Tyler said with a smile and a nod.

Luke kept the fire small and used it only to boil coffee since they had the food Spotted Fawn had given them for their supper. He extinguished the flames as soon as they had eaten. They sat in the dark, nursing cups of coffee and listening to the night.

"You think it might be a good idea for us to take turns standing guard again?" Tyler asked.

"It won't hurt anything."

"But you still don't want to give me a gun."

"That's right. I don't believe in leading anybody into temptation."

"So you've read the Bible, too, and not just those old Roman fellas."

"Of course."

"Being the son of a saloonkeeper, I never made it to church much. And when I did, all the things the preachers talked about sort of went in one ear and out the other. I might've paid more attention if they'd all had daughters who looked like Rachel. But none of 'em did until the Reverend Mr. Montgomery."

"I don't really consider myself a religious man," Luke said. "My mother was a church-going woman, but it never seemed to take with me and my brother. I think Smoke and I finally came to terms with a sort of spirituality that suits us, though. It's just not the organized kind."

"What about your sister?"

Luke shook his head and said, "I haven't seen Janey in almost twenty years. Don't know where she is. My brother saw her a few times after we all left home, but the last time was some years back. Actually, I don't even know if she's still alive."

"That's a shame, I reckon."

Luke nodded and dashed the dregs of his coffee into the campfire's ashes.

"It is, but it's another of those things I can't really do anything about, so I try not to let it worry me." He stood up. "Why don't you go ahead and turn in? Get a few hours' sleep and then I'll wake you to spell me."

"All right."

Luke tucked his Winchester under his arm and walked slowly around the camp, peering through the shadows and listening intently for anything that might indicate trouble was brewing. The night was quiet and peaceful. The only sounds he heard were the horses moving around a little, now and then.

Tyler crawled into his bedroll and was soon snoring.

Luke sat down with his back against a rock and the rifle across his lap. He knew he could stay awake because he had done so in similar situations many times in the past. When a man's life often depended on staying alert when he needed to be, he either acquired that skill — or died.

Luke was still here and intended to be around for a long time to come.

Time passed slowly. The stars wheeled through the ebony sky overhead. Luke sat there, awake but not actually thinking about much of anything, just a bundle of muscles, nerves, and bones.

But he was fully alert in less than a

heartbeat when the distant popping of gunfire drifted through the night air.

He came to his feet like a snake uncoiling. His hands tightened instinctively on the rifle even though he could tell from the sound of the shots that they weren't close. A mile to the north, he judged. Maybe more.

But that was still close enough to bother him. He snapped, "Tyler."

The young man snorted and mumbled but didn't wake up. Luke said his name again, sharper and louder this time. Tyler sat up, looked around wildly, and said, "What? What? Is it Axtell's deputies? Are they after us?"

"Take it easy," Luke said. "Listen."

"Listen to what?"

"Something other than the sound of your own flapping gums. Be quiet, damn it."

Tyler was quiet, but only for a moment. Then he stood up and said, "Sounds like a war going on."

Not quite a war, Luke thought . . . but at least a pretty good-size skirmish. The rapid and continuous *pop-pop-pop* told him numerous guns were going off. Nobody could shoot and reload a single weapon, or even a few weapons, that fast.

"Saddle up," he told Tyler. "We're going to see what all the commotion's about."

"Wait just a minute. Whatever it is, it doesn't have anything to do with us. I don't know anybody in this part of the country except you and Axtell's deputies, and I sure as hell don't want to ride right up to them!"

"You're probably right about it not having anything to do with us, but somebody's in a lot of trouble over there, and I wouldn't be able to sleep well knowing that I just ignored it."

"Well, that's mighty noble of you, especially coming from a bounty hunter."

Anger boiled up inside Luke. He said, "I thought we'd gotten past some of that."

"I haven't forgotten how you had to make a deal with me for that loot before you'd agree to help me."

"I agreed to help you so that justice would be done," Luke said. "But I don't see any reason not to make a profit on it as well."

"Well, then, where's the profit in getting mixed up in whatever that ruckus is?"

"Like I said, being able to sleep at night. Now shut up and get your saddle on one of those horses. Unless you'd rather I handcuff you again and do it for you. Then I'll throw you on the horse and you can ride in where there's a bunch of lead flying around with your hands fastened behind your back."

"No, no, no need to do that," Tyler muttered. "But I still think you're loco!"

"You're hardly the first to believe that," Luke said.

CHAPTER 21

The gunfire continued, making it easy for Luke and Tyler to follow it to its source. It didn't take them long, either, to find the battle.

Luke spotted an orange glow over the trees along the river, and a few minutes later he and Tyler came in sight of a wagon camp in a large meadow beside the stream. A couple of dozen vehicles were arranged in the traditional circle with the livestock and the campfires inside.

Two of the big immigrant wagons were burning, flames shooting high from the blazing canvas covers over their beds.

In the open space between the river and wagons, a couple of men lay crumpled and unmoving with buckets lying beside them. In the light from the burning wagons, Luke could see arrows sticking up from the bodies.

It was easy enough to tell what had happened. The men had tried to reach the river so they could fetch water and throw it on the wagons to keep the flames from spreading. They had reacted just like the attackers expected. Arrows fired from the nearby trees had skewered the helpless men.

"Indians?" Tyler said with a gulp in his voice.

"That's right. They're mostly peaceful around here these days, but from time to time one of the tribes goes on a rampage. It's only been a few years, you know, since George Custer ran into a few of them up on the Little Bighorn."

As Luke spoke, a pair of flaming arrows arched out of the trees. One of them fell short of the wagons, but the other thudded into the sideboards of one of the vehicles.

A man vaulted over the wagon tongue and dashed around to yank the burning arrow loose, but as he ripped it out of the board and cast it away from the wagon, a regular arrow drove into the back of his thigh. He yelled in pain, grabbed at the injury, and fell as the leg folded up beneath him.

Despite being wounded, the man seemed to realize that he was in mortal danger. He used his hands, elbows, and the knee on his good leg to pull himself under the wagon. Another arrow dug its head into the ground beside him, missing him by only inches.

Men waiting on the other side of the wagon reached out, grabbed the wounded man's arms, and quickly hauled him to safety.

"I didn't think Indians were supposed to attack at night," Tyler said.

"Indians attack when it suits them to attack," Luke said. "By and large, they're superb strategists. You can't predict what they'll do, and that gives them an advantage right there. If they had the same numbers and weapons we do . . ." Luke shook his head. "We wouldn't be here. We'd be back in Europe somewhere, waiting for the Indians to come across the Atlantic and conquer *us*."

Trees surrounded the wagon camp on three sides, with the river on the fourth side. The immigrants kept up a steady fire into the woods, but Luke knew that had to be mostly futile. The attackers would stay safely behind the trees, stepping out only long enough to launch another arrow or fire a shot if they had any rifles. If the defenders hit any of them, it would be pure luck.

"What are we gonna do?" Tyler asked.

"I don't know about you, but I can't ride away and leave those folks to their fate."

"We don't know how many Indians are in

those trees. There could be a thousand!"

"More like a hundred, I imagine. Maybe less. The tribes can't muster the same sort of war parties they used to. After the Custer massacre, a lot of them went north into Canada and haven't come back yet."

"A hundred bloodthirsty savages is still too many for us to take on."

"We won't be doing it by ourselves. We'll be joining forces with those immigrants."

"You expect me to ride into the thick of a fight like that without a gun?"

Luke considered, then grunted and reached for the butt of his Winchester. He pulled the rifle from its sheath and held it out to Tyler.

"Don't make me regret doing this," he said.

"Don't worry. We're on the same side."

Luke wished he could believe that completely. But for now all he could do was hope that Tyler was telling the truth. He drew one of the Remingtons and dug his heels into the gray's flanks. As the horse leaped forward, Luke shouted, "Come on!"

He expected Tyler to follow his lead and didn't look back to make sure that he was. They galloped along the river bank for a hundred yards, then Luke veered into the trees.

He put the reins between his teeth, drew the other revolver, and guided the horse with his knees. It was dangerous, riding swiftly through the shadows this way. He risked being swept out of the saddle by a low-hanging branch. But it was also the best way to take the Indians by surprise.

One of the attackers must have heard them coming. A figure leaped in front of Luke. The light from the burning wagons penetrated into the woods, but it was unreliable, flickering and dancing and causing shadows to leap this way and that. Luke caught a glimpse of a painted face twisted in hate and an arrow drawn back on a bowstring. The next instant he fired the Remington in his left hand and that face disappeared in a red spray as the slug tore into it.

An arrow hummed past his ear. He fired both guns, alternating right and left, and the muzzle flashes revealed buckskin-clad forms toppling off their feet. Behind Luke, the Winchester cracked. Tyler was getting in on the fight as well.

Luke had no idea how many Indians he and Tyler killed or wounded in that wild charge, but he knew they did considerable damage to the war party and that had been his intention. He broke out of the trees again and glanced back over his shoulder to make sure Tyler had made it.

The young man was still there, wide-eyed but apparently unharmed. He leaned forward in his saddle and urged the paint pony up next to Luke's gray.

"We hit 'em hard!" he shouted. "Reckon they'll give up now?"

"Not likely," Luke replied. "But at least we whittled down the odds some!"

Arrows fell around them as they rode hard for the wagon camp. Luke spotted a man standing between two of the vehicles, waving them on, and he headed for that spot. He didn't know how good a jumper the gray was, but they were about to find out.

Luke hauled back on the reins, lifting the horse's head, and the gray soared over the wagon tongue. Tyler's pony made the leap as well, even more nimble in its brief flight. Luke pulled the gray in a tight turn and dropped from the saddle to the ground.

The man who had waved them into the camp stood there holding a rifle. The broad, floppy brim of a felt hat hung over his angular face. The man reminded Luke of pictures he'd seen of Abraham Lincoln without the famous beard.

"I never saw the likes of that!" the man said. "The two of you charged through those savages like a couple of knights on horseback!"

"If we're knights, our armor is tarnished, I assure you," Luke said. "But we heard the commotion and figured you folks could use a hand."

"We sure can. I'm Jonathan Howard, the captain of this wagon train."

"Luke Jensen," Luke introduced himself. "This young fellow is Judd Tyler."

He didn't offer any more details than that.

"It's a pleasure, although I wish we'd met under better circumstances. Grab yourself a spot, gentlemen. There's plenty to go around!"

Luke waved Tyler over to one of the wagons where there weren't any defenders. He positioned Tyler at the back of the vehicle and told him, "Make your shots count. We have a good supply of ammunition, but there's no point in wasting bullets. In other words, don't just blaze away blindly at the trees. Wait until you can see something to shoot at."

"I've been in tight spots before," Tyler said. "I'm not gonna panic, if that's what you're worried about."

Luke just nodded and went to the front of the wagon where he could use the driver's box as cover. He reloaded both Remingtons.

The range to the trees was a little far for handguns, but Luke was an excellent shot and the long-barreled guns were powerful enough to cover that distance. He thought he could give a good account of himself with them.

And if the Indians rushed the wagons, as Luke figured they would sooner or later, then the revolvers would come in mighty handy for the close work.

He spotted muzzle flashes here and there in the trees. As he'd suspected, some of the Indians had rifles, more than likely stolen from soldiers or homesteaders they had massacred. Although it was possible the weapons had been supplied by gunrunners who didn't mind doing business with the Indians as long as the price was right.

Either way, those flashes gave Luke something to aim at. He holstered the left-hand Remington and waited with the right-hand gun ready until he saw another spurt of orange flame.

As soon as he did, he reacted instantly, aiming the revolver and squeezing the trigger with one smooth contraction of his finger. Unfortunately, he couldn't see what his bullet hit, if anything, but he noticed that no more muzzle flashes came from that spot.

The Indian who had fired the rifle might have shifted to another tree. It was even possible he had run out of ammunition and that was his last bullet.

But it was also possible he was lying out there with Luke's slug in him, too, so Luke was going to assume the latter.

He crouched there at the front of the wagon and waited for another target.

As he did, he heard the Winchester's sharp crack at the other end of the vehicle as Tyler continued firing. Luke thought maybe it was time to go ahead and start trusting the young man, although it was difficult for him to fully trust any fugitive from the law, no matter what the circumstances.

Jonathan Howard, the wagon train captain, had hurried over to one of the other wagons after introducing himself to Luke and Tyler. After firing several shots at the Indians, he trotted back to the wagon they were defending, stooping low and moving fast when he crossed the gaps between the vehicles.

"I don't suppose you fellas are scouts for the army or anything," Howard said. "There's not a whole company of cavalry in the area that's going to show up any minute now."

"No such luck," Luke said. "We're just

passing through these parts." He looked around the circle of wagons, realizing something he had noticed earlier without the significance of it really sinking in on him. "Your camp is pretty lightly defended. Seems like there ought to be more men."

With a gloomy expression on his face, Howard nodded and said, "That's because a dozen of our men, including my son, are off hunting fresh meat for us. We hadn't run into any trouble at all, so we figured it was safe to split up. They headed upriver earlier today, and we're not expecting them back until tomorrow."

"The Indians have probably been watching you for days, just waiting for you to do something like that."

"I know it was foolish, but we honestly didn't think it would do any harm."

"Maybe the hunters will hear the shooting and hurry back," Luke said.

Howard shook his head.

"They left early enough in the day that they're probably out of earshot. Reckon there's a good chance they'll ride in tomorrow and find the wagons burned and all of us slaughtered."

"We'll just have to hold out until they return," Luke said.

"I reckon it won't hurt anything to hope —"

Howard's feeble attempt at optimism was interrupted by a cry from Judd Tyler at the other end of the wagon.

"Here they come!" the young man yelled.

CHAPTER 22

Somewhere off to Luke's right, a woman screamed in sheer terror. He wheeled in that direction and saw the same thing Tyler had.

Indians on horseback had burst out of the trees on the opposite side of the camp from the river. They charged toward the wagons, riding flat out.

At the same time, the warriors on the two flanks stepped up their attack even more, pouring arrows and rifle fire at the wagons in a deadly barrage designed to keep the defenders occupied and take a toll on them as well, so they wouldn't be able to stop the mounted attackers from overrunning the camp.

Howard turned and dashed toward the area where the charging Indians were headed. Luke was right behind him, but as Tyler started to abandon his post, Luke called to him, "Stay there! This could be a feint!"

Tyler seemed to understand. He jerked his head in a nod, swung around, and resumed peppering the woods with slugs from the Winchester.

Other men were converging on the spot where the Indians were going to try to breach the circle. Gunshots roared in a thunderous barrage, but the mounted warriors were moving fast and had almost reached the wagons by the time Luke and Howard reached one of the gaps between vehicles. A couple of ponies were riderless, showing that the defenders' fire had done a little good, but not enough.

The first of the attackers leaped his pony over a wagon tongue and soared into the circle. He yipped shrilly as he fired the rifle he held and one of the immigrants went down, drilled through the head.

An instant later, both of Luke's Remingtons roared. The impact of two slugs crashing into the warrior's buckskin-clad body lifted him off his pony. He hit the ground in a limp sprawl.

One Indian was down, but three more were already inside the camp. A man shrieked in agony as one of the mounted warriors ran him through with a lance. A second later, Jonathan Howard brought that Indian down with a rifle shot, but not in time to save the man who had been mortally wounded with the lance.

It was a whirlwind of action inside the circle of wagons, and if Luke Jensen had not been there, the immigrants might well have been overwhelmed and slaughtered, just as Jonathan Howard had said.

But Luke seemed to be everywhere at once, spinning, darting, and most of all shooting. Flame lanced from each of the revolvers in turn, and every time one of the Remingtons blasted, an Indian fell, shot through the head or the body.

Luke knew the situation was desperate. He called on every bit of fighting skill he had amassed over the long and perilous years, first in the war, and then during his career as a bounty hunter.

When his revolvers ran dry, he jammed them back in their holsters and snatched up a fallen Winchester from the ground to continue battling. He emptied the rifle as well, and just as the hammer fell on an empty chamber, the surviving warriors leaped their ponies back over the wagon tongues and fled, still yipping defiantly but no longer fighting.

Some of the immigrants started to emerge from cover as the Indians fled. Luke waved at them and called, "Get back down, you fools!"

They started to follow his order, but not in time to keep one man from being struck in the shoulder by an arrow that came streaking in from the darkness. Just because the frontal attack was over didn't mean that the wagon train was out of danger.

During the fighting, Luke had strayed quite a distance from the wagon where he had last seen Judd Tyler. He glanced in that direction as he reloaded his revolvers, then looked again as he realized he didn't see Tyler.

Ducking low, he hurried along the line of wagons to make sure the young man wasn't lying somewhere Luke couldn't see him, either wounded or dead.

Luke hoped Tyler hadn't been killed in the battle. Even though he had never met any of the people in White Fork, he already wanted the truth about Rachel Montgomery's murder to come out.

There was no sign of Tyler around the wagon. Luke looked underneath it. Still nothing.

He went in search of Jonathan Howard and found the man a couple of wagons away. A young woman had torn away the bloody sleeve of Howard's shirt and was wrapping a bandage around his upper left arm.

"Hurt bad?" Luke asked.

Howard shook his head and said, "An arrow scratched me, that's all." He nodded toward the young woman and added, "Mr. Jensen, this is my daughter Deborah."

"Pleased to meet you, miss, despite the circumstances."

Deborah Howard was in her late teens or early twenties, with long, straight hair so fair it was almost white. She was strikingly pretty, even though the strain of the attack had drawn her features tight.

"Thank you for helping us, Mr. Jensen," she said. "I never saw anybody who could handle guns like you do."

"I promise you, miss, if we'd had my brothers here, we would have had those savages outnumbered." He turned back to Howard and went on, "Have you seen Tyler, the young fellow I came in with?"

Howard frowned and shook his head.

"Isn't he over yonder at that wagon?"

"No. I can't find him."

"Well, let's look around," Howard said as Deborah finished bandaging his arm. "He's got to be here somewhere. I need to check on all the folks and make sure they know we need to keep fighting. Those Indians haven't given up, have they?"

"Not hardly," Luke said.

They went quickly around the circle. Three men had been killed in the battle, in addition to the two lost earlier, and several more were wounded but insisted that they could still fight.

The defenders' spirits seemed to be high, but Luke could sense that they were getting close to the breaking point. A person's nerves could only stand the constant fear of being killed by an arrow or a rifle shot for so long.

While Howard was assessing the state of the group, Luke was looking for Judd Tyler. By the time they got back to the wagon where Deborah was waiting with a rifle in her hands, Luke had been forced to accept a grim conclusion.

Tyler was gone.

Sometime during the chaos of battle, the young man had slipped away. He must have decided he would rather risk his life trying to get past the Indians than return to White Fork and face a trial.

Which meant that Luke was right back where he'd started . . . only now he was surrounded by bloodthirsty savages who wanted to kill him and lift his hair.

■ ■ ■ ■

Arrows still flew into the wagon camp occasionally, and the rifle fire from the trees continued as well, although at a more desultory pace now.

The relative lull in the fighting gave the immigrants a chance to patch up their wounds and to eat and drink a little.

Luke was angry that Judd Tyler had gotten away from him. The paint pony Tyler had ridden was still here in the camp, along with Luke's gray. They had left the two extra horses back at the spot where they had camped for the night before they heard the distant gunfire.

That meant either Tyler had fled on foot, or he had grabbed one of the Indian ponies and taken off on it. Clearly, he had been willing to run whatever risks he needed to in order to escape.

The Indians had left behind nine dead warriors, most of them killed by Luke. He and some of the other men dragged the bodies to the side, where they wouldn't be in the way.

Now that Luke was able to get a better look at the attackers, he could tell that they were Cheyenne. There was a good chance some of them had been at the Little Bighorn. The massive Indian army had been composed mostly of Sioux but had included Cheyenne warriors and members of several other tribes as well.

Luke had no great admiration for George Armstrong Custer, but he didn't mind thinking that maybe the deaths of some of the members of the Seventh Cavalry had been avenged here tonight.

The two wagons that had been ablaze when Luke and Tyler arrived had burned on down to ashes and rubble, but with a lot of hard, dangerous work, the immigrants had been able to keep the flames from spreading to the other vehicles.

Still, that left two gaps in the circle that would have to be defended heavily, because Luke was sure that when the Indians attacked again, they would concentrate their charge on those weak spots.

He was standing next to one of the wagons, keeping an eye on the trees, when Deborah Howard came up to him with a cup in her hands.

"Would that happen to be coffee?" Luke asked the young woman with a smile.

She returned the smile and said, "It would be. Would you like it?"

"More than almost anything right now."

He took the cup from her and sipped from it. "Ah. Nectar of the gods." He took another sip and frowned in thought. "Is that a hint of . . . bourbon I taste?"

"We're from Kentucky," Deborah said. "My pa thinks a shot of bourbon improves almost anything, including coffee."

"Your father is a wise man." Luke drank again and sighed in satisfaction as he felt the bracing effects of the coffee and the whiskey go through him. "Earlier he mentioned that your brother is one of the men with the hunting party . . ."

"Nolan is his name. He's our chief scout. He's been out here in the West before, working as a scout on several wagon trains. When Pa and I decided to pull up stakes and start fresh in Montana, Pa wrote to Nolan and asked him to sign on with this group."

"It's none of my business," Luke said, "but I've been to Kentucky and it strikes me as fine country. Some of the finest farming land I've ever seen, in fact."

"You're wondering why we'd want to leave there and go some place like White Fork, Montana, aren't you?"

Luke raised an eyebrow and said, "You're headed for White Fork?"

"That's right. I know that's ranching country, but there's a valley near there that's government land, just opened up for home-steading."

"Some of the cattlemen in the area may not appreciate farmers moving in."

Luke was thinking primarily of Manfred Douglas, who was used to ruling the area around White Fork with an iron fist. The conflicts between ranchers and homestead-ers were a bloody and ongoing problem on the frontier.

"Pa got a letter from the local judge as-suring him it would be all right."

"Judge Keller?"

Deborah brightened and asked, "Do you know him?"

"Only by reputation. I'm told that he's a decent, honest man."

Of course, he had been told that by Judd Tyler, Luke reminded himself, and Tyler had run off at the earliest possible op-portunity, so he wasn't sure how much he could rely on the information.

"I hope that's right," Deborah said. "As for why we left Kentucky . . . my pa was a businessman there, not a farmer. He did all right, but he's always moved around some, started stores in different places, and he got the urge again. I guess some men are just like that, not able to stay in one place forever. You know what I mean?"

"I understand completely," Luke said. That sort of restlessness seemed to be a Jensen trait as well. Smoke was the only man he knew carrying that name who had been able to put down roots . . . and it wasn't like Smoke spent all his time on his vast ranch in Colorado called the Sugarloaf. He traipsed off to other places on a fairly regular basis and usually wound up in a heap of trouble.

That seemed to be a Jensen trait as well.

"Well, I need to take coffee to some of the other men," Deborah said.

Luke raised the cup to her in a salute and told her, "I'm much obliged to you for this. It'll help me get through the night, that's for sure."

Deborah started to turn away, then paused.

"When you rode in earlier, there was a young man with you . . ." she said.

The interest in her voice and eyes was unmistakable. Luke figured he would be doing her a favor by quashing it immediately, in case they did survive this siege.

"He's gone," Luke said in a flat, hard voice. "And I don't reckon we'll ever see him again."

"He was . . . killed in the fighting?"

"No. I don't know where he is. He appears to have gotten out while the getting was good." Luke couldn't keep a bitter edge out of his voice.

"Oh. He didn't really seem like that sort to me . . ."

"I guess you can never really tell about people. But if I ever *do* run into him again, I plan to have some pretty choice words for him, I can tell you that."

And that was one more reason he wanted to make it through this stand-off, he thought.

He had a score to settle with Judd Tyler.

CHAPTER 23

By the time several hours had gone by, Luke had figured out what the Cheyenne were doing. He went looking for Jonathan Howard, and when he found the wagon train captain, he said, "The Indians aren't going to launch another full-scale attack until dawn."

"You're sure about that?" Howard asked.

"Like I said before, you can never be completely sure what Indians will do, but I think that's likely their plan. They're going to sit out there all night, firing an arrow into the camp from time to time or taking the occasional potshot, just to keep you on edge and wear you out. They'll wait until the strain has you exhausted, and then they'll attack when they believe their enemy is at his lowest ebb."

Howard rubbed his jaw and frowned in thought.

"What you say makes a lot of sense, Mr.

Jensen. But won't they be worn out by then, too?"

Luke shook his head and said, "No, they're out there right now taking turns sleeping. They're not nervous. They know they have the upper hand."

"So what should we do?"

"Spread the word that your folks should get some shut-eye as well. They can sleep in hourlong shifts, so you'll still have plenty of defenders awake all the time. I know it won't be easy for them to relax, and an hour or two of sleep won't do them *that* much good, but it's better than nothing."

"You seem to have a lot of experience at this sort of thing, like you've been an Indian fighter for a long time."

Luke shook his head again and said, "No, not really. I've been in more than my share of bad scrapes, with white men and Indians alike, but mostly it's just common sense."

"All right. I'm not too proud to take advice from a man who knows what he's talking about, that's for sure."

Luke might have some words of advice for him about how to deal with potential trouble once they got to White Fork, too, but that could wait until after they had survived this particular peril.

Howard hurried off to tell the defenders

to get some rest if they could. Deborah, who had been standing nearby while Luke was talking to her father, came over to Luke and said, "What about you, Mr. Jensen? Are you going to try to sleep?"

"No, I reckon I'll stay awake and keep an eye on the situation," Luke said with a faint smile. "I might be wrong about what the Cheyenne are planning, you know, and I wouldn't want to be taken by surprise."

"The Cheyenne," she repeated. She cast a glance toward the other side of the camp, where the corpses of the dead warriors were lying, and shuddered. "Is that the tribe they belong to?"

"That's right. I can tell by their war paint and the decorations on their clothes and the way they wear their hair."

"They're all savages to me."

Luke shrugged and said, "They have a different way of life from you and me, there's no doubt about that. Whether it's good or bad depends entirely on a person's perspective. I've never been able to hate the Indians for doing what they see as defending their homeland . . . but I can certainly hate them for some of the atrocities they've carried out in that effort."

"I don't see why they can't just leave us

alone. There's plenty of room for everybody."

"You'd think so," Luke said. "But history teaches us that civilization always expands to fill the available space . . . and often space that *isn't* available until it's taken away from whoever has it. Did you ever know the government to give anything back once it's taken whatever it is away from the people?"

"Well . . . no."

"There's the history of the world in a nutshell. Civilization seizes more and more power for itself until it's too fat and bloated to move . . . then the barbarians come in, cleanse everything in blood, and the whole process starts over."

She frowned at him and asked, "If that's true, then what's the point in trying to make things better?"

"Hope," Luke said. "The only thing that keeps the world in balance."

Deborah sighed and said, "Well, I just hope we make it out of this alive, and somebody else can write the history later on."

"That's the only sensible course," Luke agreed.

"And I hope we find out what happened to your young friend," she added.

"So do I," Luke said. "If we get out of

here, that's the first chore on my list."

Luke remained alert for the rest of the night, fortified by the bourbon-laced cups of coffee that Deborah Howard brought to him from time to time. As expected, the Cheyenne didn't launch another attack. They taunted the immigrants just enough to keep them nervous and on edge. Luke wasn't sure how many of the would-be homesteaders were able to follow his counsel and get some sleep.

But as a gray tinge appeared in the eastern sky to herald the approach of dawn, he knew the time for sleep was over. He found Jonathan Howard again and told the man to pass the word that everyone should be ready for trouble.

The men stood tensely behind the wagons, opening and closing their hands on the rifles they gripped. Some of the women and older children stood with them, ready to reload or if necessary take up arms themselves. The rest of the women and children were huddled under a large sheet of canvas that had been stretched on poles to serve as protection from the arrows dropping out of the sky.

Luke's Remingtons were fully loaded, as was the borrowed Winchester he held. He

263

watched the sky grow lighter and lighter, shading from black to gray. When the first streaks of rose and pale blue and gold began to appear, he leaned forward and rested the rifle barrel across the driver's seat of the wagon as he aimed at the trees.

Like fiery stars ascending to the heavens instead of falling, flaming arrows suddenly streaked upward and then arced down, more than a dozen of them this time.

Mounted warriors burst from the trees right behind them.

The Cheyenne weren't taking the defenders by surprise as they had hoped, however. A volley of rifle fire rang out, sweeping several of the Indians from their ponies. Some of the mounts were hit, too, and went down, throwing their riders. The warriors fell in a welter of flailing hooves, and some of them didn't get back up again.

But there were too many of the Cheyenne raiders, and once again they were moving too fast for the immigrants to blunt their charge. Luke's repeater cracked again and again with deadly accuracy, but there were only so many of the attackers he could bring down before they reached the wagons.

Screams and shouts filled the camp. Some of the flaming arrows had struck the canvas protecting the women and children and set it on fire, so they had to scramble out from underneath it. More wagons began to burn as well. The women and older children tried to put out those fires, throwing buckets of dirt that had been prepared earlier onto the flames. That worked for the most part, but a couple of the blazes got out of control and began to consume those two wagons.

Luke emptied the Winchester, spraying lead through the ranks of the Indians as quickly as he could work the rifle's lever. Then he threw it down, yanked out the revolvers, and went to work with them. He shot a couple of the warriors off their horses as they leaped into the camp.

This time they weren't going to be able to repel the attack, he sensed. The odds were too high against him and his fellow defenders.

But they would fight to the end, knowing they could expect no mercy from the savages.

In the pale light of dawn, Luke spotted more of the Indians charging out of the trees all around the camp, most of these on foot. But with warriors already inside the circle of wagons and the desperate struggle going on there, no one had a chance to shoot at these war-painted reinforcements. In moments they would swarm in, adding to the already overwhelming odds, and the battle would be almost over.

That was when Luke heard more hoof-beats and the swift rataplan of gunfire growing louder and louder. He jerked his head around and saw another group of riders entering the fray, this one composed of white men with blazing guns in their hands.

The newcomers swept through the Indians on foot like a wildfire racing across the prairie, gunning down some of the attackers and trampling others with steel-shod hooves. They pounded around the wagons, wiping out the warriors caught in front of them.

Then the two men leading them angled their horses through one of the gaps where a burned-out wagon had stood and the rescuers smashed into the Indians who had penetrated the circle. Guns flashed in the dawn. Men shouted and died.

Luke stalked through the chaos like an avenging angel, flame spouting from the muzzles of his revolvers as he fired, right, left, right, left. He battled his way toward the two men who had led the newcomers into the wagon camp. One of them was a tall, dark-haired young man in a buckskin shirt and flat-crowned hat.

The other was Judd Tyler.

Luke had never expected to see Tyler again, but here the fugitive was, fighting side by side with the other young man as they drove the Cheyenne out of the camp. The unexpected arrival of help for the immigrants had turned the tide of battle and swung the odds toward the white men. The Indians were just trying to fight their way out of what had become a trap for them.

A few of them made it. Most didn't.

No defiant yips came from the ones who escaped this time. They ran and galloped for their lives without looking back. As Luke watched them go, he thought that they wouldn't be back. They would return to their village, lick their wounds, and decide that maybe preying on wagon trains wasn't a good idea after all. Better to go off to Canada or else make peace.

Tyler was riding an Indian pony, one of the possibilities that Luke had considered earlier. As he approached, Tyler slid down from the horse and greeted him with a grin and an exuberant whoop.

"Luke! Damn it, I was hoping you could hold out until I got back with these fellas! I knew if anybody could rally those folks to hold on, it'd be you."

Deborah Howard was embracing the other young man while her father slapped him on the back. Luke nodded toward them and said to Tyler, "That's Nolan Howard?"

"Yeah, and the rest of the hunting party from the wagon train," Tyler said. "I heard what Mr. Howard told you about where they'd gone, and I thought maybe if I could find them, I could get back here with them by daybreak."

"You weren't trying to escape?"

Tyler's eyes widened. He said, "Escape? Hell, no! I had to make it out through those Indians, and let me tell you, that was no picnic." He held up his arm, showing a rip in the shirt sleeve, and then pointed to a couple of similar rips on the shirt's sides. "Arrows did that. That's how close they came to me. Luckily, I'm one hell of a rider and managed to grab a fast pony — again — so I was able to get out and go looking for Nolan and those other fellas."

"He saved our lives, too," Jonathan Howard said as he came up to Luke and Tyler. "Nolan just told me about your courageous effort, young man." He grabbed Tyler's hand and pumped it. "We owe you a debt we'll never be able to repay."

"No, sir, you don't owe me a thing," Tyler said, with what Luke suspected was a display of false modesty. "I just did what anybody else would have done."

"Anybody with more guts than common sense," Nolan Howard said as he came up with an arm around his sister's shoulders. "I reckon that describes you pretty good, Judd."

Tyler chuckled and said, "Sometimes, maybe."

It looked like he and Nolan Howard were friends already, Luke thought.

Deborah had something like that in mind, too. She stepped forward and said, "We never got introduced earlier, Mr. Tyler, but I'm Deborah Howard."

"Why, sure you are," Tyler said. "Nolan told me all about his sister. Said she was the prettiest gal in camp, so I knew as soon as I laid eyes on you, that had to be you."

"Oh." Deborah's face turned as rosy as the dawn, but she forged on. "I want to thank you for saving us, too."

"It was my pleasure, ma'am."

"You should call me Deborah."

Nolan said, "Yeah, because you're going to be traveling with us the rest of the way to White Fork, aren't you?"

Deborah looked at Tyler in surprise and said, "You're going to White Fork?"

Luke was the one who answered, saying, "We sure are." He paused, then added, more for Tyler's benefit than anyone else's, "This doesn't change a thing."

CHAPTER 24

Three more wagons had been lost to fire. Four men had died in the attack, as well as one woman and two children. At least a dozen of the immigrants were wounded, some seriously.

So it was a very sober, even sorrowful group of pilgrims that started north along the Powder River later that day, after those who had been killed were given proper burials. Everyone who had survived was glad to be alive, but they felt their losses keenly.

Luke and Tyler returned to their camp to pick up the two extra horses they had left there, with Tyler promising that they would catch up to the wagons later.

However, Luke had been thinking about that, and as they switched their saddles from the gray and the paint to the other two mounts, he said, "We're going to swing wide around that wagon train and get ahead of them."

"So that we can do some scouting for them?" Tyler said as he tightened one of his cinches.

"So that we can avoid bringing more trouble down on their heads."

Tyler frowned as he shook his head and said, "I don't understand."

"Think about it. How many deputies does Axtell have?"

"Close to a dozen."

"And there's no telling how many men Manfred Douglas may have hired on his own. That's a lot of guns out there, Tyler . . . all of them looking for you."

"What are you saying? That it's too dangerous for those folks from the wagon train if we travel with them?"

"That's exactly what I'm saying. Let's say half a dozen of those hired killers ride in some night. They'll want to take you with them, and me, too. Do you believe the Howards and the rest of those pilgrims will just stand aside and let them take us?" Luke didn't wait for Tyler's answer. He went on, "No, they won't, and you know it."

"Yeah, they'd probably try to put up a fight to protect us, wouldn't they?" Tyler looked like he didn't care for the conclusion, but it was obvious.

"And when that happens . . . when the

bullets start flying around . . . innocent people will be killed," Luke said. "I'd just as soon avoid that if possible. You remember what happened to Millie."

Tyler sighed and said, "Yeah, I remember. I'm not likely to forget any time soon. Damn it, there's been too many graves had to be dug since all this mess started!"

"So let's not cause any more to be dug if we can help it. We can move a lot faster than that wagon train. We'll ride around it and go on to White Fork."

"I'm sure gonna miss getting to know that gal Deborah better. I think she might've been a little sweet on me."

"Maybe by the time the wagons reach White Fork, the trial will be over and your name will be cleared," Luke said. "Then you can explain the whole thing to her. I'm sure she'll forgive you for not rejoining the wagon train like you promised."

"I hope so. But we've still got to make it to White Fork and get the truth about Rachel's murder out there, don't we?"

"Yes, there is still that little detail to take care of," Luke said.

They rode into a line of small hills that ran parallel to the river on its east side. Keeping to that higher ground, Luke and Tyler maintained a brisk pace.

Around the middle of the morning, Luke reined in and motioned for Tyler to follow suit. He leveled an arm and pointed west.

"Down there," he said. "You can see where the river is because of the trees."

"I know," Tyler said. "But I'm not sure what you're — Oh. I reckon I see them now. Those are the wagons, aren't they?"

The white canvas covers on the backs of the wagons were visible as the vehicles rolled slowly but steadily along the trail that followed the river. At this distance they weren't much more than white specks, but they were there.

Luke knew he could have made out a lot more detail if he'd used the pair of field glasses in his saddlebags, but there was really no need.

"Reckon they've started to wonder by now why we haven't caught up?" Tyler asked.

"Probably."

"They're gonna worry about us." Tyler frowned. "What if Mr. Howard sends Nolan or somebody else back to look for us? That's liable to slow 'em down. The longer they're out here, the more dangerous it is for them, isn't that right?"

"Not necessarily. You heard what Howard said. They hadn't run into any trouble at all on the journey until that Cheyenne war party attacked them. I think those Indians were so soundly defeated that they won't come back, and as for any other threats . . . well, a trip by wagon train is not without its risks to start with. Those people had to know that when they started out."

"I suppose you're right. But I still wish there had been some way to let them know what we were doing."

"If we had gone back to the wagons and told them we were heading on alone, Howard and the others would have argued with us and tried to change our minds." Luke chuckled. "What do you think you would have done, Tyler, if Deborah Howard had begged you to stay with her?"

"Yeah, yeah, you're right. Let's just go on. The sooner we get to White Fork and put all this behind us, the better."

"My sentiments exactly," Luke said.

They camped the next three nights in the hills without any trouble. Luke knew the wagon train was well behind them by now. The immigrants would have figured out that Luke and Tyler weren't coming back.

He estimated that two more days would put them across the border into Montana Territory. Another day after that ought to bring them to White Fork. Considering everything that had happened, actually they had made pretty good time.

He was ready for the journey to be over, too. The lingering doubts he'd had about Judd Tyler had been dispelled by what had happened at the wagon camp beside the Powder River. In the past, Tyler had fought and risked his life for himself, but back there he had fought to save others, and that counted for quite a bit in Luke's book.

Not only that, once he had made his escape from the camp, he could have just kept going instead of searching for the hunting party, finding them, and bringing them back in time to save the rest of the immigrants.

So Luke was confident that Tyler had told him the truth about what happened to Rachel Montgomery. It would be nice if the young man shared the evidence in his possession that pointed to Spence Douglas as the girl's killer, but Luke supposed he couldn't blame Tyler for wanting to play everything close to the vest.

Because of all that, Luke was eager to reach White Fork and contact Judge Clarence Keller. His plan was to stash Tyler somewhere nearby, out of sight, while he slipped into town and hunted up the judge.

Axtell's deputies and Douglas's other hired guns knew to kill anybody they found with Tyler, but it was likely none of them would recognize Luke if they saw him without Tyler being around.

That was the general plan Luke had formulated. He knew there was no point in trying to figure out all the details, because unforeseen circumstances nearly always caused plans to change. There came a point in any dangerous scheme when a man had to be quick to adapt and just do the best he could.

The next morning they put their saddles on the gray and the paint. Having the extra mounts had helped them cover the ground a little faster than Luke had anticipated.

An hour after riding out, they reached the end of the hills and went down a long, gentle slope into another broad basin. Tyler pointed to a blue line along the horizon to the northwest and said, "See those mountains up yonder? They're over the border in Montana. White Fork lies at the base of them. The town gets its name from a creek that flows out of the mountains there."

"So there actually is a creek, unlike Bent Creek."

Tyler chuckled.

"Yeah. It runs east and joins the Powder

several miles away. Manfred Douglas's range lies along both sides of the Powder for more than fifty miles."

"A big spread."

"From what I've heard, he came to Montana without much to his name except a powerful hunger for land and power. He's got plenty of both now."

Luke wasn't surprised that they could see the mountains marking White Fork's location, even though that destination was still almost three days away. He was well aware that distances were very deceptive, especially in this dry, clear air. Even though he knew they still had a long way to go, he was starting to feel better about the situation.

That was before the horse whose shoe he had replaced back at Pettifer's trading post began limping again that afternoon.

"Damn it!" Luke said after he had swung down from the saddle and examined the animal's hooves.

"He throw that same shoe?" Tyler asked.

"No, the other one on the front. Whoever shod this horse did a mighty poor job of it."

"Maybe you can whack it back into place with a gun butt."

"Maybe . . . but I don't think it's going to stay. Not unless we take it really slow and easy, anyway."

"And the longer we're out here, the more time that gives Douglas's gun-wolves to find us."

"That's right," Luke said. "They probably cast the net pretty far and wide, but by now, since they haven't found us, they will have started working their way back in this direction, thinking that we must have slipped past them. Which, of course, is what we did."

"Maybe we need to leave the extra horses here and make a run for it, get to White Fork just as fast as we can."

Luke considered the idea for a moment, then shook his head.

"We're still too far away for that. We'd run our mounts into the ground if we tried, and then we'd really be in trouble. No, the best we can do is for me to repair this shoe as well as I can, and then we'll keep going. Maybe we'll be lucky and none of those killers will come across us."

"And if we're not?"

"*Then* we make a run for it," Luke said.

CHAPTER 25

Luke spent some time reattaching the loose shoe, which hadn't come off completely, as best he could, and then he and Tyler resumed their journey. He had moved his saddle back to the gray so the horse having trouble wouldn't have to carry his weight. That seemed to help, as did the slow pace Luke set. The delay chafed at him, though.

And it didn't even seem to help that much, because by nightfall the shoe was loose and the horse was limping again.

"This is ridiculous," Luke said as they sat and made a cold supper from jerky and stale biscuits. Out in the open in the basin like this, with killers searching for them, he didn't want to risk having a fire. "At this rate it's going to take us another week to get to White Fork."

"You're sure in a hurry to turn me over to the law, is that it?" Tyler said.

"I'm in a hurry to resolve this situation so

we can clear your name."

"So you can get your hands on that cache of loot I promised you."

"I've put a considerable amount of time and effort into this, not to mention risking my neck on numerous occasions," Luke said. "As I've told you before, I don't think it's unreasonable to expect to make a little profit on the deal."

"And if I turn over all my money to you, what do I get out of it?"

"You don't have to dance at the end of a rope," Luke pointed out. "Or have your carcass left to rot out here before you ever get back to White Fork, which is what will happen if Sheriff Axtell's deputies catch us."

Tyler shrugged and said, "Yeah, well, I guess you're right about all that. And don't think I'm ungrateful for everything you've done for me so far, Luke. I just wish there was some way to settle this without waltzin' right back into that nest of rattlesnakes."

"It usually takes daring to snatch victory from the jaws of defeat."

"Is that another quote?"

"Nope. Just common sense."

With no coffee and nothing to do, Tyler turned in early, rolling up in his blankets and going to sleep. Luke would let him rest for a few hours, then wake him to stand guard during the middle of the night.

Luke sat there listening, but there was nothing to hear except the faint sounds of the horses grazing on the clumps of grass stubborn enough to grow in this semiarid basin. Time passed slowly.

Luke didn't doze off, but he drifted into a state where his senses were all alert but his brain was cloaked in a state of peaceful mindlessness.

That condition evaporated instantly when he heard something in the distance. He lifted his head and peered into the surrounding darkness while at the same time honing his ears to an ever sharper keenness.

Somewhere far off, hoofbeats sounded. That was what he had heard.

Riders were abroad in the night.

That didn't have to mean anything. Wandering cowpokes, an Indian hunting party, a cavalry patrol . . . all of those were possibilities, although none of them were exactly likely, either, Luke thought. Still, he couldn't just assume that the riders were searching for him and Tyler.

But he couldn't assume that they weren't.

The hoofbeats didn't come any closer. Luke listened to them for a while, until they finally faded away. Even so, he didn't relax again until he reached over and shook Tyler awake for his turn on guard duty.

Luke waited until the young man was good and alert, then said, "I heard some riders a while ago. They were a long way off to the east, and as far as I could tell they didn't come in this direction."

"Axtell's men," Tyler said. "Bound to be."

"We don't know that, but I'd say there's a good chance of it. After a while I couldn't hear them anymore. I don't know if they went the other direction or if they stopped and camped for the night."

Tyler ran his fingers through his hair and said, "I'm starting to understand what you tried to tell me about being a fugitive, Luke. As long as I was running, they'd never stop hounding me, would they?"

"That's right. You'd always be looking over your shoulder, wondering if you were going to die in the next five minutes."

"That's no way to live."

"I wouldn't think so."

"So I reckon I ought to thank you for forcing me into doing the right thing," Tyler said. "Even though I sure wasn't happy about it for a while."

"Well . . . we'd better wait and see if it pans out, I suppose."

"Even if it doesn't, I'm trying to do right by Rachel. That's got to be worth something, doesn't it?"

"It does," Luke agreed. "Right now, just keep your eyes and ears open while I get some shut-eye."

Nobody tried to sneak up on their camp during the night. In the morning, Luke banged the loose horseshoe back into place even though he knew it wasn't likely to hold. They rode north, taking it easy.

"If that shoe comes off again, we'll have no choice but to abandon the horse," Luke said. "I don't like it, but there it is. We've done all we can reasonably do."

"It's because of those riders you heard last night, isn't it?" Tyler said. "They've got you spooked."

"Not really. I knew all along there was a good chance we might run into more of Axtell's and Douglas's men as long as we were out here." Luke shrugged. "But hearing those riders didn't help matters any, I suppose."

They made slow but steady progress during the morning. The basin wasn't as flat as it looked from a distance, which wasn't surprising. It rose and fell in places, and an occasional rocky knoll thrust up from the ground.

Luke aimed toward one of those knolls,

thinking it might provide a little shade while they stopped for a midday meal and to let the horses rest. They hadn't gone very far in that direction when Tyler hipped around in the saddle to check their backtrail, which he did every so often.

This time he exclaimed, "Hell!"

Luke reined in and turned to look, too. Right away, he saw the column of dust rising into the brassy sky behind them.

"Whoever it is, they picked up our trail, and they're comin' on fast!" Tyler said.

"I think we know who it is," Luke said. "Nobody would be moving that fast out here without a purpose."

"And that purpose is bound to be filling me full of lead!" Tyler looked around with an air of desperation about him. "We've got to find some cover —"

"Up there," Luke said, pointing to the rocky knoll he had seen earlier. He hadn't mentioned it to Tyler at the time, just headed in that direction without explanation, knowing that Tyler would follow him.

Tyler squinted and said, "Looks like the best place to fort up that we're gonna find. Can we get there in time, before they catch up to us?"

"Only one way to find out," Luke said. He had been leading the horse with the bad shoe. Now he dropped the reins and heeled the gray into a run. The extra horse would just have to fend for itself.

Tyler let go of the other spare mount's reins and pounded after Luke on the paint. They were banking their lives on the horses with which they had started this journey.

This wasn't the first time Luke had been in a race for his life. As he rode, he looked back over his shoulder occasionally to see if the pursuit was gaining on them.

He was pleased to see that, judging by the dust cloud, it didn't seem to be. The killers had probably been riding long and hard over the past couple of weeks, and their horses weren't any fresher than Luke's and Tyler's were.

They drew closer to the rocky knoll. Over the pounding hoofbeats, Luke called, "We'll get up there and hold the high ground!"

"But there's nowhere to go from there," Tyler protested, "no other cover for miles around here! They'll have us trapped as sure as if we were up a tree!"

"Maybe," Luke said, "but it's the only chance we've got."

Tyler couldn't argue with that.

Even mounts as gallant as the gray and the paint had proven to be had to falter sooner or later, and they began to slow when the knoll was still half a mile away. Luke looked back again and judged that the column of dust was a little closer than it had been the last time he checked.

It was going to be a near thing, whether he and Tyler reached the higher ground in time for it to do any good.

They had come too far to give up now, though, and besides, both of them knew good and well that they couldn't expect any mercy if the men behind them worked for Gus Axtell or Manfred Douglas. The horses galloped on, giving it all they had even though that supply of strength was fading with every lunging stride.

The next time Luke looked back, he could make out the dark shapes of individual riders at the base of that dust column. If he could see the pursuers, that meant the pursuers could see him and Tyler, so he wasn't surprised when bullets began kicking up dirt behind them.

Tyler happened to be looking back and saw one of the spurts of earth and gravel as a slug plowed into the ground. He said, "They're shooting at us!"

"That pretty well answers the question of who they are, doesn't it?"

"Did you ever have any doubt?"

"Not really," Luke said.

The knoll was less than a quarter of a mile away now, but the riders in pursuit were only a couple of hundred yards behind. That was still too far for anything except a very lucky shot to find its target, especially when the shots came from the saddles of running horses.

Anything was possible, though, when the bullets started to fly. Luke knew all he and Tyler could do was keep moving.

Then the knoll was right in front of them, and they put their horses up the slope in frantic, plunging leaps.

"Go! Go!" Luke shouted to Tyler. He let the gray fall behind a little and twisted in the saddle to fire one of the revolvers back at the riders. Again, the odds of actually hitting any of them were tiny, but he wanted to let the men know they were in for a fight.

Tyler and the paint pony disappeared over the top of the knoll. Luke was glad they had reached safety, even though it was probably only temporary.

That thought had just flashed through his brain when the gray stumbled and went down. Luke reacted just fast enough to kick his feet loose from the stirrups, and the next instant he flew from the back of the fallen horse and crashed into the rocky ground with stunning force.

CHAPTER 26

For long seconds, the only thing Luke was capable of doing was lying there gasping for air while the world spun crazily around him. Up was down, down was up, and although he knew he needed to be doing something, for the life of him, he couldn't figure out what it was.

Then a bullet struck close by him, throwing dirt and gravel in his face, and the stinging impacts brought him back to his senses. He raised his head and pushed himself up with one hand. Another bullet whined past his ear. He looked down the slope and saw that the men on horseback had almost reached the knoll.

A rifle cracked somewhere close to him. Once, twice, and then again the sharp reports filled the air. Then a hand grabbed hold of Luke's upper left arm and tried to haul him to his feet.

"C'mon, Luke!" Tyler shouted. "We've

gotta get out of here!"

Luke looked up and saw Tyler standing there, the Winchester in his left hand while he used his right to try to lift Luke. Realizing that the young man had come back to help him, Luke called on his stunned nerves and muscles to work again and forced himself up.

He looked at his right hand and was shocked to see that the Remington was still in it. Somehow, instinct had kept him from dropping the gun when he slammed into the ground.

Since he was starting to see straight again, he raised the gun and blasted a couple of rounds toward the pursuers. Then he and Tyler backed toward the top of the knoll, still firing as they retreated.

The pursuers couldn't charge straight up the slope into the face of all the lead that Luke and Tyler were throwing at them. The riders spread out as they reached the knoll, throwing themselves from their saddles and continuing to fire as they hunted for cover. Although the bullets flew fast and furiously for several moments, none of them did any damage.

Then Luke and Tyler sprawled backward over the crest and rolled into the shelter of the boulders perched there.

"Man, that was close!" Tyler said as he lay there trying to catch his breath.

"Why'd you come down after me?" Luke said. "You were safe up here."

"Yeah, but safe for how long? I can't fight that bunch off all by myself." Tyler grinned. "Besides, I reckon I've gotten used to having your ugly face around, Luke. I didn't want to see you filled full of lead."

"I'm obliged to you. Without that covering fire you gave me, I probably wouldn't have made it the rest of the way up this hill."

Tyler looked around and said, "Yeah, and now that we're here . . . what next?"

Luke took stock of their situation as well. The knoll was mostly flat on top, an irregular circle about fifty feet in diameter. Grass grew here and there, along with a few scrubby bushes. Large rocks were scattered around. They had been here, unmoving, ever since geologic forces had thrust this knoll up from the surrounding flats in some unknown past era.

His horse must have scrambled to its feet after falling and joined Tyler's paint, because both animals were standing several yards away, cropping at the grass, apparently unhurt. The gray seemed to have a charmed life when it came to falling, but Luke wasn't going to complain about that bit of good fortune.

A few more shots had rung out after Luke and Tyler reached the top, but by now all the guns had fallen silent. Since the pursuers couldn't see them from down below, shooting was just a waste of bullets.

Luke figured the men had spread out even more. If they had the instincts of the predators they obviously were, they would be circling the knoll to insure that their prey stayed trapped up here until they figured out their next move.

"We'd better make sure they don't sneak up on us," Luke said. "You take one side and I'll take the other."

Tyler nodded in agreement and got to his feet to move in a crouching run toward the north side of the knoll. Luke took the south side, toward the direction they had come from. He edged up to one of the rocks, took his hat off, and risked a glance around the boulder.

Some sharp-eyed son of a bitch down below was watching. A gun blasted, and as Luke jerked his head back, a slug hammered into the rock and threw dust and stone chips into the air. The shot had missed by inches.

He heard another gun go off on the far side of the knoll. Tyler yelped.

"You hit?" Luke called to him.

"Nope," Tyler answered. "But I took a gander over here and it looks like the back door's nailed shut good and tight, too."

That came as no surprise to Luke. He would have employed the same tactic if he had been leading a posse after a couple of fugitives.

"As long as they don't try to make it up the hill, hold your fire," he told Tyler. "No sense in wasting our bullets taking potshots at them."

"They don't have very good cover," Tyler said. "Not as good as we do."

"No, but there are at least five times as many of them. Every time we expose ourselves to shoot at them, we increase the chances that one of them will wing one of us."

"Yeah, I suppose so," Tyler said, but he didn't sound like he cared for the idea of being cautious. "It'll be dark in six or seven hours, though, and then they can sneak up on us."

Luke couldn't argue with that, but his reply to Tyler was true as well.

"A lot can happen in six or seven hours."

What happened was that boredom set in on both sides. The deputies — if that's what they were — couldn't get a good shot, and Luke and Tyler didn't want to take a chance and step out from behind the boulders so they could draw a bead on the pursuers.

At the same time, nobody could actually relax in a standoff like this. The tension drew a man's nerves tighter and tighter, until it seemed like they would snap at any second.

By late afternoon, Tyler was as wild-eyed as a spooked horse. He took off his hat, raked his fingers through his hair until it stood up on end, and called across to Luke, "I'm not sure how much longer I can take this."

"You'll take it as long as you have to," Luke said. "That's the only way to stay alive in a situation like this. You have to wait for the breaks to come your way."

"Yeah? What if they don't? What if your luck stays bad and in the end you lose?"

"Then you go down fighting," Luke said with a shrug. "You make sure that you die as well — or better — than you lived."

"I'm not sure I'm that damn stoic," Tyler muttered.

Luke didn't reply, because something had caught his eye. A flicker of movement to the south. He saw it again, then stood up and went over to the gray, being careful not to give the gun-wolves below a clear shot at him.

He took his field glasses from one of his saddlebags, then returned to the boulder where he'd been crouching. He lifted the glasses to his eyes and peered through them. It took him a moment to locate and focus on what he had seen a moment earlier.

Then he lowered the glasses, smiled faintly, and told Tyler, "Make some noise over there, Judd."

"What?"

"Open fire on those men down there. Get them shooting back at you. It doesn't matter much if you hit them. Just be careful and don't let them hit you."

"Well, that's always the general idea, I reckon, the not getting hit part, I mean. What's this about, Luke? Why are we putting up a fight now?"

"Because help may be on the way," Luke said as he set the field glasses aside and drew his Remingtons.

He wheeled around the rock and began triggering both revolvers as fast as he could, raining lead down on the hunters who had chased them up here. A few slugs whined off the boulders near him, but Luke's unexpected barrage made most of the men duck their heads and hunker down.

On the other side of the knoll, Judd Tyler was following Luke's example and emptying the Winchester as fast as he could, swinging the barrel from side to side so that the bullets sprayed all around the enemy. When the hammer clicked on an empty chamber, he ducked back behind the rock just in time to avoid a hailstorm of lead.

The men on Luke's side launched a furious response of their own and fired at least a hundred rounds toward the top of the knoll in the next couple of minutes. None of the bullets did any damage except to the boulders, but the shooting created a wave of gun-thunder that spread out across the basin.

That was exactly what Luke was counting on.

He reloaded the Remingtons, waited until the firing from the bottom of the slope died down a little, and then blazed away again at the pursuers. That prompted another heavy round of return fire. To anyone listening, it would sound like a battle royal was going on, even though none of the shots were actually hitting much of anything.

"I thought you said not to burn up ammunition without a good reason," Tyler called across to him.

"There's a good reason," Luke said. He

reloaded again, then holstered the revolvers and picked up the field glasses. He looked through them to the south and saw the half-dozen men on horseback he had spotted earlier. The riders must have heard all the shooting, just as Luke intended, because they were coming toward the knoll and moving fast.

Nolan Howard was in the lead.

Luke had wanted to protect everyone connected to the wagon train from getting mixed up in his and Tyler's troubles, and that included Nolan and the rest of the scouts. That was why he and Tyler had gone around the wagons and moved on ahead of the immigrants.

The delays they had encountered along the way had given the scouts the chance to catch up, though, as Nolan and the others ranged far ahead of the wagons. Luke hadn't counted on that happening, but he knew there was a chance it might. That was one of the possibilities he'd been holding out for during the long, tense afternoon on the knoll.

Now Nolan and his fellow scouts were riding hard in this direction, obviously intent on finding out what all the commotion was about.

Luke moved back far enough that the

hired killers couldn't see him but the riders out on the flats still could. He took off his hat and waved it back and forth over his head, hoping to attract Nolan's attention.

The move seemed to work. The riders reined in and slowed to a stop. Luke saw sunlight wink off of something shiny. One of the men had a telescope or a pair of field glasses trained on the top of the knoll.

A moment later, the riders galloped toward the site of the standoff. Luke had a hunch that he'd been recognized, and that would be a warning to Nolan that the men around the base of the knoll were enemies.

"What in blue blazes is going on?" Tyler demanded.

"Help is on the way," Luke said. "In fact, it's almost here. Make sure that rifle is loaded, because in a few minutes we'll need to go down there and lend a hand." He smiled. "The hunters are about to become the hunted."

CHAPTER 27

Luke kept an eye on Nolan Howard and the other scouts from the top of the knoll. He was glad to see that they didn't just gallop up recklessly and throw themselves into the battle. They were outnumbered, and they needed the element of surprise on their side.

Instead they stopped when they were still a quarter of a mile away and dismounted to approach on foot. The hired killers were concentrating on the quarry they thought they had trapped, and with all the shooting going on, they wouldn't have been able to hear the hoofbeats as Nolan and his companions rode toward them.

The guns were so loud it would have taken a buffalo stampede to get their attention.

The men on the other side of the knoll had the rocky prominence between them and the newcomers, so they had to be completely unaware that the balance of power in this fight had shifted.

The men to the south of the knoll were hidden behind rocks and in shallow gullies. The wagon train scouts split up and crept toward them, as stealthily as Indians. When they reached a certain point, Luke couldn't see them anymore. All he could do was wait to see what happened.

That didn't take long. A few moments later, he heard startled shouts from below, followed instantly by rapid bursts of gunfire.

"Come on!" he shouted to Tyler as he waved a gun for the young man to join him. They lunged out from behind the rocks and started bounding down the slope.

Luke saw Nolan and the other scouts trading shots with the hired guns. Several men were sprawled on the ground already, but the others were putting up a fierce fight. Luke stopped and triggered the Remingtons. Tyler did likewise with the Winchester. Their shots scythed into the men who had pursued them here.

From the corner of his eye, Luke caught a glimpse of motion and pivoted to his left to see that the men who had been around on the other side of the knoll had mounted and were charging around to this side in response to the increase in firing.

"This way!" he said to Tyler as he moved

to cut off the reinforcements. Nolan and the others already had their hands full. It was up to Luke and Tyler to cover their flank from the higher ground.

Luke hammered shot after shot at the men on horseback as he slid and jumped down the slope. That didn't make for the most accurate shooting, but his efforts were rewarded by the sight of two men flinging their arms in the air and pitching from their saddles. A horse screamed and went down, throwing its rider over its head. Another man swayed violently to the side but managed to remain mounted. He turned his horse and raced away, hunched over in apparent pain.

The wounded man wasn't the only one fleeing. The other men who were still on horseback gave up the fight and pounded after him, throwing wild, futile shots over their shoulders. Luke lowered his revolvers as they rode out of range of his guns. Tyler sped them on their way with a few more rounds from the Winchester.

Then the two of them turned back to the battle between the wagon train scouts and the rest of the group of hired killers.

That conflict seemed to be over. The guns had fallen silent. Nolan Howard was climbing the slope toward Luke and Tyler while his companions checked the bodies of the men who'd been killed in the fight.

Nolan raised a hand in greeting and asked, "Are you fellas all right?" He didn't appear to be hurt.

"We're fine, thanks to you and your friends," Luke said. "You pulled us out of a mighty bad spot."

Nolan thumbed his hat back and smiled.

"Couldn't hardly believe my eyes when I saw it was you up there on that knob, Mr. Jensen," he said. "We figured we'd seen the last of the two of you." He looked at Tyler and added, "My sister wasn't very happy about that, either."

Tyler said, "Well, I, uh, it wasn't really my idea —"

"I'm the one who insisted that we not rejoin the wagon train," Luke said. "I knew that might bother some people, but it seemed like the best idea for you folks." He nodded toward the dead men. "And now you can see the reason why."

"You knew those fellas would be coming after you," Nolan said. "You didn't want my pa and Deborah and all the others getting mixed up in your trouble."

"That's exactly right." Luke added, "I wouldn't have involved you in this battle today if we'd had any choice in the matter."

"Hey, Nolan!" one of the scouts called with a note of alarm in his voice. "These men are wearing badges!"

Nolan's eyes widened. He looked around at Luke and Tyler with anger in his gaze.

"Badges?" he repeated. "We just killed a bunch of lawmen?"

"Well . . . in a manner of speaking. There's more to the story than that, though."

"There had damned well better be," Nolan said. "I'd hate to think that my friends and I just got crosswise with the law by rescuing a pair of owlhoots from a posse!"

Tyler said, "We can explain everything —"

"You'll have to." Nolan put his hand on the butt of his gun. His attitude had changed completely in the blink of an eye, the friendliness vanishing and angry suspicion taking its place. "Back at the wagon train. You're coming with us."

Luke wasn't sure the scouts could have stopped him if he wanted to take Tyler and ride away from here, but innocent men would be hurt if it came down to that.

Besides, it was possible he had made a mistake by avoiding the wagon train. At this point in the journey, with a horse that kept suffering from loose shoes, it might be better to go ahead and throw in with the

Howards and the rest of the immigrants. They weren't that far from White Fork, after all.

"You won't need that gun, Nolan," Luke said. "We'll come with you, and when we get to the wagons, we'll tell you the whole story. I'd just as soon wait until then, though, so we'll only have to tell it once."

Nolan frowned in thought for a second and then nodded.

"All right. Get your horses. But I'm coming with you. I don't want the two of you disappearing on us again."

"You didn't say anything to Nolan about Miss Montgomery or Spence Douglas when you found the hunting party after riding off from the wagon train that other time?" Luke asked Tyler in a quiet voice as they were fetching their horses. Nolan stood a short distance away, watching them.

"Not a word about any of that," Tyler said. "I just told him you and I were passing through the area and came on the wagon camp while it was under attack." He shrugged. "That was true as far as it went."

"Yes, it was." Luke tightened the cinches on the gray, which he had loosened earlier. He took the horse's reins and led it back over to where Nolan waited. "You fellows didn't happen to see a couple of saddled but riderless horses out there in the basin, did you?"

Nolan shook his head and said, "Nope. Those are your spare mounts you're talking about?"

"That's right. We had to let them go when those killers started chasing us."

"You mean those deputies."

"You'll see what I mean," Luke said.

Nolan just grunted as if he found that difficult to believe.

They joined the others, mounted up, and rode south. Behind them, buzzards had already begun to wheel in circles in the late afternoon sky.

He and Tyler certainly were littering this part of Wyoming with carcasses, Luke thought as he glanced back. Lucky for them there were plenty of winged and four-footed scavengers to clean up after them.

It was a short time after dark when the group of riders reached the spot beside the river where the wagon train had camped for the night. They had the two extra horses with them. The animals had trotted up while they were riding back to the wagons, seeking out the company of their fellows as horses were prone to do.

The men hadn't run into any more trouble along the way, but the atmosphere among the scouts was grim. They were all worried they would be branded murderers for killing lawmen.

Jonathan Howard had posted guards around the camp. They challenged Nolan and the others when they rode up out of the shadows. Nolan called to them, "It's just us . . . and we've brought a couple of visitors with us."

Some of the sentries started to call out friendly greetings to Luke and Tyler, but the bleak, angry expressions on the faces of Nolan and the other scouts made them fall silent. Puzzled frowns creased the guards' foreheads as the newcomers rode past them.

Jonathan Howard stepped over a wagon tongue and out of the circle of wagons to come out and meet them. He had a rifle tucked under his arm.

He began, "Expected you back before now, son —" and then stopped short as he caught sight of Luke and Tyler. "Well, now! Where did you two come from? We figured you didn't like our company after all." Howard looked back and forth between them and Nolan, and he frowned, too. "Say, what's going on here? Is there some sort of trouble?"

"Damn right there is," Nolan said. "Or at least there may be. I can't seem to get a straight story out of these two, but they've promised to explain the whole thing."

"What whole thing?"

"Earlier today we rescued them from a bunch of men who were trying to kill them."

"That seems fair enough," Howard said. "Mr. Jensen and Mr. Tyler may well have saved us from those Indians."

"Yeah . . . but the men who were after them wore badges."

Howard looked as shocked as Nolan had earlier. He even said the same thing, exclaiming, "Badges! They were lawmen?"

Luke said, "Deputies from White Fork."

"That's where we're going."

"I know."

"I . . . I don't understand. Does this mean the two of you are outlaws?"

Instead of answering the question, Luke said, "You'd better call a meeting of your entire company, Mr. Howard. Judd and I will be glad to explain, but everyone should hear the story, since whatever happens next could affect all of them."

"Yes . . . Yes, I suppose you're right —"

"Mr. Tyler! Mr. Jensen!"

The pleased exclamation made the men turn their heads toward the wagons. Deborah Howard had come out of the circle, and now she hurried toward them with a smile on her pretty face.

Nolan moved his horse so that he got between her and Luke and Tyler. She stopped short, clearly surprised by his action.

"Better go back to the wagons, Deborah," he said. "You don't want anything to do with these two."

"What in the world? What's wrong with you, Nolan? Why wouldn't I want to say hello to Mr. Tyler and Mr. Jensen?"

"Because they're a couple of dirty outlaws!" Nolan said bitterly.

"What? No! I don't believe that!"

Jonathan Howard took hold of his daughter's arm and said, "Come on, Deborah. They want a meeting of the company, and that's what they're going to get. The sooner we get to the bottom of this, the better!"

CHAPTER 28

Nolan Howard hadn't asked for their guns, but Luke knew he and Tyler couldn't try anything, surrounded as they were.

Besides, they didn't want to cause any trouble for the immigrants. They *wanted* these people on their side.

Tyler looked nervous, but as Jonathan Howard gathered the entire group in the center of the big circle, he said quietly to Luke, "Do you think they'll believe me?"

"There's only one way to find out," Luke said. "I believe you, and that ought to carry some weight."

"Yeah." Tyler managed to smile. "You being a mercenary bounty hunter and all. No finer, more upstanding citizen than that, is there?"

Luke wasn't sure whether to be annoyed or amused. He settled for a chuckle and a shake of his head.

Some of the men built up the main campfire until its garish light filled the circle of wagons. Then Howard motioned for Luke and Tyler to come forward and face the group of slightly more than a hundred men, women, and children. Nolan and Deborah stood with their father.

Howard said, "I'm sure all of you remember Luke Jensen and Judd Tyler and all the help they gave us when we were being attacked by those Indians. More than likely, the news of what happened earlier today has gotten around the camp already, but if there are any of you who haven't heard, my son Nolan and the rest of our scouts saved Mr. Jensen and Mr. Tyler from a group of men who were trying to kill them." Howard paused, then added in an ominous tone, "Unfortunately, those men were deputies from White Fork."

Mutters of surprise came from some of the immigrants. Whether they had heard the rumors or not, having their leader put the situation so bluntly into words carried a disturbing impact.

A man asked, "Are you sure they were really lawmen, Jonathan?"

Nolan answered the question, saying, "They were wearing badges. And Jensen and Tyler haven't denied it."

"That's because it's the truth," Luke said,

causing more murmurs. "Those men who tried their best to kill Judd and myself were indeed deputies working for Sheriff Gus Axtell of White Fork. But that doesn't mean the errand they were on was a lawful one!"

Nolan glared at him and said, "What are you talking about?"

Luke reached to his pocket and said, "Bear with me here. This is going to make things look even worse, but it's important if you're going to know and understand the whole story."

"Luke, what are you —" Tyler began. He stopped short and caught his breath as Luke took a folded piece of paper from his pocket, unfolded it, and handed it to Jonathan Howard.

"This is a wanted poster!" Howard said after scanning what was printed on the paper. "It says . . . it says Judd Tyler is wanted for murder!"

"I knew it!" Nolan said. "Nothing but a dirty outlaw!"

Deborah shook her head and said, "I don't believe it. Mr. Tyler . . . Judd . . . it's not true, is it?"

Tyler looked uncomfortable and didn't answer, so Luke stepped up and said, "It's true that Judd was charged with the crime, but that doesn't mean he's guilty of it."

Jonathan Howard frowned and said to Tyler, "You claim you didn't kill this young woman, this . . . Rachel Montgomery?"

"I sure didn't, Mr. Howard," Tyler said, and his voice rang with sincerity. "Rachel was my friend. I never would have hurt her. I'd have died myself before I'd ever do that."

Howard thrust the wanted poster toward him and demanded, "Then why were you charged with her murder?"

"Because I know who the real killer is, and his pa — who's the richest and most powerful man around White Fork — doesn't want me to have a chance to tell anybody about it. But I will. I'll tell all of *you,* if you'll let me."

"You mean you'll spin some pack of lies —" Nolan began. His father held up a hand to stop him.

"We'll listen to you," Jonathan Howard said. He looked at Luke. "But first I'd like to know what part you play in all of this, Mr. Jensen."

"That's simple enough," Luke said. "I'm a bounty hunter. All I wanted was to collect the thousand dollars' reward on this young fellow's head. That was before I heard his story and decided I believed it."

Howard shook his head and said, "I don't understand. If you believe he didn't kill that girl, why are you taking him to White Fork?"

"So he can stand trial and get up in front of a judge and everybody else to tell the truth about what happened to Rachel Montgomery. That's the only way the real story will ever get out . . . and the only way Judd can clear his name and not have to live the rest of his life as a fugitive."

It was quiet in the camp as Luke stopped talking. The immigrants stood watching and listening intently. The crackling of the fire was the loudest sound in the night.

Then Jonathan Howard nodded and said, "All right, Mr. Tyler. Tell us your story. And if you want us to believe you, I'd advise you to start at the beginning."

That was what Tyler did for the next quarter-hour, telling the tale as he had told it to Luke so many days earlier. Nolan Howard folded his arms and glared while Tyler was talking and made a few skeptical noises along the way.

His sister Deborah, on the other hand, listened raptly, her eyes growing wide and shining with tears when Tyler described how he had found Rachel Montgomery's body.

The next time Nolan let out a disbelieving "Huh!" Deborah turned and swatted him on the arm.

"Stop that," she told her brother. "Can't you see how much the tragedy affected poor Mr. Tyler?"

"You're just stuck on him because you think he's good-looking," Nolan said.

Deborah's face turned a bright red. She said, "That's not true." She looked at Tyler and added, "You just go right ahead, Mr. Tyler. I'm sorry we interrupted."

When Tyler was finished with his story, Jonathan Howard turned to Luke and asked, "Do you believe all this, Mr. Jensen, even though you hoped to collect the bounty for Mr. Tyler's capture?"

"I do," Luke said. "I was just as skeptical as any of you at first. Even you, Nolan. I don't know how many outlaws and killers over the years have told me they're innocent. I can't count that high. But Tyler's got some things to back up his story."

"Like what?" Nolan asked.

"Like the fact we both heard two of Sheriff Axtell's deputies admit the sheriff ordered them to find us and kill us. That doesn't sound like what an honest peace officer would do if he wanted a prisoner brought in for trial. The man who tried to kill Judd at Pettifer's place never said anything to us, but he didn't act like a normal deputy would, either. He hid in the darkness and tried to ambush Judd, but he missed and killed an innocent woman instead."

One of the women in the group said with a dour look of disapproval on her face, "I thought you said she was a harlot."

Jonathan Howard waved her down and said, "That's not really important right now, Martha." He turned back to Luke and Tyler. "What you're saying makes sense, Mr. Jensen, but you don't have anything to back it up except your word. None of us heard what those deputies said."

"That's right," Nolan said. "The only thing we've got to go by is what we saw today. Sure, those men had you outnumbered, and it looked like they wanted to kill you, true enough, but wouldn't they have acted the same way if they were a posse of honest deputies trying to round up some wanted fugitives?"

"*I'm* not wanted," Luke pointed out.

"You weren't . . . until you started trying to help a man who's on the run from the law. Doesn't that make you guilty of a crime, too?"

Nolan had a point there, Luke supposed. In the eyes of the law, he *was* guilty. The mitigating circumstance of Tyler's innocence wouldn't come into play unless it was proven in court that he hadn't killed Rachel Montgomery.

So Luke had a lot riding on this, too. Unless Tyler's name was cleared, his wouldn't be, either, and he could easily find himself with murder charges hanging over his own head because of the deputies he'd killed.

It was a mess, plain and simple.

Luke didn't answer Nolan's accusation directly. Instead, he said in a clear, powerful tone, "There's one way to settle all of this, and that's for Judd Tyler to stand trial in White Fork and prove his innocence. That's what we've been after all along. So take us there, and you'll see for yourselves that we've been telling the truth."

Jonathan Howard said, "You mean take you there and turn you over to this Sheriff Axtell?"

"You do that and you'll never see us alive again," Tyler said with a gloomy shake of his head. "We'll be shot trying to escape before Axtell even gets us locked up good. That's what he'll claim, anyway."

"I have a plan," Luke said, "but it involves reaching Judge Clarence Keller and letting him know what's going on."

Howard rubbed his chin and said, "I've corresponded with Judge Keller about the range that's been opened up for homesteading. It's hard to tell from letters, but he struck me as an honest, upstanding man."

"He is," Tyler said. "He'll do everything he can to conduct a fair trial . . . if he gets a chance to."

Nolan Howard still wore a dubious frown on his face, but he didn't seem quite as hostile as he had been a few minutes earlier. He said, "Are the two of you willing to turn your guns over to us until we get to White Fork?"

Tyler looked like he was going to argue about that, but Luke held up a hand to forestall his protest.

"I don't like being disarmed," Luke said. "But maybe it'll show you how much I believe in Judd's story if we agree to that suggestion." He put his hands on the Remingtons but didn't pull them from their holsters. "I want your word, though, that if there's any sort of trouble, you'll give us our guns so we can defend ourselves."

Nolan started to shake his head, but his father said, "I'll give you my word on that, Mr. Jensen."

"Very well." Luke drew the revolvers, turned them around with a deft flip of his wrists, and offered the ivory-handled butts to Howard. "We're literally putting our lives in your hands, Mr. Howard."

"Well, I don't know about turning over this Winchester —" Tyler began.

"It's *my* Winchester," Luke said. "Give it to Nolan."

With obvious reluctance, Tyler held out the rifle so Nolan Howard could take it.

Jonathan Howard said, "How many more days will it take us to reach White Fork?"

"Two, maybe three," Luke told him.

"Do you think we'll run into any more of this Sheriff Axtell's deputies along the way?"

"It's possible." Luke shrugged. "If we do, Judd and I will lie low and stay out of sight. Maybe they won't insist on searching the wagons."

"And if they do?"

"Then you'll probably have a chance to see for yourself that they're nothing but a pack of cold-blooded killers," Luke said.

CHAPTER 29

Later, after things had settled down some-
what and the immigrants had gone back to
their normal evening activities, Luke told
Jonathan Howard that the sentries around
the wagon camp should stay as alert as possible that night.

"Do you think there's liable to be trouble?" Howard asked.

"A few of Axtell's deputies got away,"
Luke said. "It's possible they might run into
some of the other men searching for Judd
and me and then try to track us. I don't
think they'd attack the wagon train on their
own, though. The odds would be too high
against them. Hired guns generally like to
have all the advantage on their side if they
can get it."

Howard nodded and said, "What about
that sheriff? Do you think they'll go back to
him and tell him that it was some of our
men who helped you and killed the other

deputies?"

"They wouldn't have any way of knowing who Nolan and the other scouts were," Luke pointed out. "So they couldn't warn Axtell to look out for you folks."

"Well, that's a relief," Howard said, but then he frowned. "What about when we reach White Fork, though? If the men who got away see Nolan and the others, isn't there a chance they'll recognize them?"

"It could happen," Luke said with a nod. "But maybe by then things will have changed. When we get close to town, I intend for Judd and I to leave the wagon train. I'm going to try to get Judd into Judge Keller's custody before Axtell or Manfred Douglas even know we're there."

"Does the judge hold enough sway to protect the two of you?"

Luke smiled and said, "We sort of have to hope so."

Howard nodded and went to talk to the sentries, leaving Luke to sit on a crate near one of the fires and sip from a cup of coffee a woman had given him. She had smiled and been pleasant enough when she offered him the coffee, and Luke thought it was good that at least some of the pilgrims were giving him and Tyler the benefit of the doubt.

Not all of them, though, by any means. He saw plenty of hostile, sidewise glances directed his way.

The one person who had accepted Tyler's story, beyond a doubt, was Deborah Howard. The pretty young blonde was sitting with him now on the lowered tailgate of the Howard wagon. Tyler had a cup of coffee, too, but he was too busy talking to Deborah to do more than take an occasional sip. She smiled and nodded as she listened to Tyler.

Luke couldn't hear what Tyler was saying, but he knew the young man had the gift of gab. It was natural for him to try to impress a pretty girl.

Luke looked the other way and saw that he wasn't the only one watching Tyler and Deborah. Nolan Howard stood beside one of the other wagons with his arms crossed over his chest and an angry glare on his face. Clearly, he didn't like the attention his sister and Tyler were paying to each other.

Maybe that was just an older brother's protective instincts and he would have felt that way about any young man Deborah showed an interest in. But Luke didn't think so. Nolan had decided Tyler was guilty, and it would take hard evidence to convince him otherwise.

Luke wondered again about the proof Tyler claimed to have, the proof that pointed to Spence Douglas as Rachel's killer. A lot was riding on that, and Luke still would have liked to know what it was.

He would find out, he supposed, at the trial.

If they both lived that long.

One of the immigrants was a farrier, and the next morning he did a better job of reattaching the loose shoe on the extra horse Luke and Tyler had brought along.

"Shouldn't give you any more trouble," the broad-shouldered man told Luke when he was finished with the task. "Looks to be a good horse. He deserves a better shoein' next time."

"I couldn't agree more," Luke said. "I'm not the one who had him shod. In fact, he doesn't even belong to me. I plan to return him to whoever has a legitimate claim to him, once we settle all our other issues in White Fork."

"You mean about whether the youngster killed that preacher's girl." The man scowled. "I'd hate to think I'm maybe helpin' a killer to go free."

"You're not," Luke assured him. "We're going to see that justice is done, one way or the other. I believe that in the end, Judd Tyler will be proven to be an innocent man."

Innocent of murder, anyway, Luke added to himself. Tyler still had some rustling and stagecoach robberies to answer for. But first things first.

And the first thing on the list was reaching White Fork safely.

The wagons lined up and rolled out before the sun had risen very high in the sky. They stayed close to the river, since the going was easier there. Luke and Tyler rode alongside the Howard wagon. Jonathan Howard had the reins, although he mentioned that Deborah, who sat beside him, was perfectly capable of handling the team of oxen and driving the wagon.

"She's a fine shot with a rifle, too," Howard added.

Deborah blushed and said, "Pa, you don't have to go around singing my praises."

"I'm just proud of you, that's all. Any father would be."

Tyler looked like he was about to make some glib comment. Luke silenced him with a stern look. Jonathan Howard was a reluctant ally at best. There was no need to risk angering him by throwing a budding romance between his daughter and a wanted fugitive in his face.

Even though the miles rolled steadily

behind the wagons over the course of that long day, it didn't seem like they were making much progress toward the mountains. Luke knew that was an illusion. Judging how far away something was could be difficult out here in this big, lonely country. Landmarks seemed like they were as distant as ever, and then suddenly, there they were, right in front of you.

By the time they made camp that evening, some of the members of the wagon train seemed to have gotten used to having Luke and Tyler around. There weren't as many dark, ominous looks directed at them.

Nolan and the other scouts had been out all day, ranging ahead of the wagons as usual. When they came back in, Luke was close enough to overhear the conversation when the young man reported to his father.

"There's a creek up ahead we'll get to about midday tomorrow," Nolan said. "It runs into the Powder from the west, so we'll have to cross it."

"Is there a good ford?" Jonathan Howard asked.

"That's just it. There's not, at least not one that we were able to find. And the creek is flowing pretty good, probably from snow melt up in those mountains to the west."

"We've crossed plenty of streams during

324

the journey," Howard said. "Is this one deep enough to float the wagons?"

Nolan thought about it for a second and then nodded.

"I reckon it is."

"Then we'll do it that way, just as we have before. As long as the current's not too strong, we shouldn't have much trouble."

"I just wanted to let you know what we'll be facing tomorrow," Nolan said.

Howard nodded.

"One more obstacle," he said, "and then our way should be clear all the way to White Fork, right?"

"As far as I know, Pa. This route's as new to me as it is to you. There hasn't been any homesteading in these parts until now, so our train is the first one over this trail."

Howard smiled and said, "We're pioneers. I like that."

Luke hoped he felt the same way after this group of immigrants had dealt with the harsh Montana winters, cattlemen who didn't particularly want them there, the chance of hostile Indians, and all the other hardships that were a farmer's lot in life. As a young man, Luke had seen his father trying to scratch a living out of the hardscrabble hills in the Missouri Ozarks and had experienced that for himself before he went off to war.

Even if things had happened differently, he never would have returned to that sort of life. He had already been thinking about heading west when the war was over . . .

All that was years in the past, Luke thought with a shake of his head. His trail had been much different from those of his father Emmett and his brother Kirby, now called Smoke, but all three of them had wound up on the frontier, their farming days over and done with.

When it came time to turn in, Luke went to look for Judd Tyler. He hadn't seen the young man for a while, but he wasn't particularly worried that Tyler had run off again. Tyler knew his only chance for a real future lay in a trial and an acquittal. Luke was convinced he wasn't going to risk that.

As Luke walked around the camp, however, he didn't see any sign of Tyler. Suspicion started to nag at the back of his mind. He didn't think he had misjudged the young man, but anything was possible, he supposed.

Then he heard a faint noise from nearby and stepped around the back of one of the wagons to peer into the thick shadows on the side away from the campfires. He spotted movement there from a dark, oddly shaped figure that turned into two as Luke watched, then one again. He heard a soft gasp, then a whispered, "Oh, Judd . . . !"

Luke said, "Don't you think you ought to wait until you're not a fugitive from the law before you start sparking the young woman, Tyler?"

The harsh words made both people on the other side of the wagon exclaim in surprise and spring apart.

"Damn it, Luke!" Tyler said. "You shouldn't ought to sneak up on a fella like that, especially when he's . . . when he's . . ."

"Kissing a pretty girl?" Luke asked. "You'd better hope that's all you were doing."

Deborah Howard moved close enough for him to see her in the light that came through the gaps between the wagons. She looked a little disheveled and embarrassed, but all her buttons appeared to be buttoned and her hair wasn't *too* tangled.

"That's all we were doing, Mr. Jensen, I swear it," she said. The words tumbled out of her mouth. "Please don't tell my pa or Nolan. And don't blame Judd. It was my idea —"

Tyler stepped up behind her and rested a hand on her shoulder.

"Now that's just not true," he said. "I'm the one who talked Deborah into comin' around here with me, and I'm the one who started the kissin'."

"But I didn't try to stop you," she said. "I didn't even tell you to stop."

"Well . . . as good as I am at kissing, it would have taken a heap of willpower for you to do that," Tyler said. He smirked a little, which caused Luke to roll his eyes.

"It's late," he said. "Miss Howard, you'd better get back to your wagon before your father starts wondering where you are. And Tyler, you need to get some sleep. We both do."

"All right, I reckon." Tyler's hand was still resting on Deborah's shoulder. He used it to turn her slightly toward him as he added, "I didn't mean to do anything to offend you —"

"Oh, you didn't," she assured him, her voice a little breathless now.

"I'll see you in the morning —"

Luke was about to tell Tyler to quit stalling, when Nolan Howard stepped around the front end of the wagon. He said, "Deborah, I thought I heard you talking to somebody around here. Pa sent me to look for — What the hell! Get your hand off my sister, you son of a bitch!"

He lunged toward Tyler and swung his right fist in a roundhouse punch.

Chapter 30

"Nolan, no!" Deborah cried as she tried to throw herself between Tyler and her brother.

Since Tyler already had his hand on her shoulder, he was able to push her out of the way. But that left him wide open for Nolan's punch, which crashed into his jaw and sent him flying back toward Luke.

Luke caught Tyler under the arms and kept him from falling. Nolan was so angry he would have rushed in and tried to hit Tyler again, but Deborah was able to grab him this time.

"Nolan, stop it!" she said as she hung on to his arm. "What do you think you're doing?"

"What any good brother would," Nolan said. "I'm trying to keep my sister from gettin' mixed up with a no-good murderer and outlaw!"

Tyler straightened up and pulled loose from Luke's grip. He raised a hand to his jaw where Nolan had hit him and rubbed it for a second, then said, "I never denied that I've broken the law a few times, but I didn't murder Rachel Montgomery or anybody else! What's it gonna take to convince you of that, Howard?"

"A hell of a lot more than I've seen so far."

Deborah said, "Nolan, you don't have any right to interfere in my life —"

"Like blazes I don't! I'm your big brother. It's my job to protect you, especially when it looks like Pa won't —"

Jonathan Howard's voice, taut with anger, came from the front of the wagon.

"Won't what, Nolan? Won't jump to conclusions and refuse to give a man the benefit of the doubt? Because it seems like that's what you're doing when you accuse Mr. Tyler that way."

Nolan turned to his father and said, "He's an outlaw! You saw the wanted poster with your own eyes, Pa. Why should I give him the benefit of any doubt?"

"Because you've heard his story, just like the rest of us. A wanted poster isn't enough, Nolan. A man should be considered innocent until proven guilty in a court of law, remember?"

"Yeah, but he was pawing Deborah!"

330

Howard looked at his daughter, but before he could ask the question, she said, "Judd and I were back here talking, Pa. And we . . . we kissed a little, I reckon. But he didn't do anything improper, I swear it."

Jonathan Howard didn't look pleased by what Deborah had just told him, but Luke could tell he was making an effort to keep his temper under control.

"There was a time when that would have been enough to demand a proposal of marriage and a wedding," Howard said after a moment. "I suppose that people are more . . . enlightened . . . now." He frowned at Tyler. "Mr. Tyler, we've extended our protection and our hospitality to you and Mr. Jensen, in return for all the assistance you've given us. But it would be wise of you not to try to take advantage of the gratitude this company feels toward you."

"Yes, sir," Tyler said. "I mean, no, sir. I won't. I give you my word on that."

Howard looked like he wasn't sure just how much Tyler's word actually meant, but he nodded and said, "We understand each other, then." He turned to his children. "Nolan, Deborah, get on back to the wagon."

"This is all Nolan's fault —" Deborah began.

"I won't have the two of you squabbling like you're little children again. You're adults. Try acting like it."

Howard stalked off, past the small group of immigrants who had been drawn by the commotion. Deborah and Nolan followed him, although they hesitated and eyed each other suspiciously before they started after their father. Each of them probably thought the other might try to linger, Luke supposed, and they weren't going to allow that.

After the Howards were gone and the crowd, such as it was, had scattered, Tyler picked up his hat and slapped it against his leg a couple of times in a frustrated gesture. He took hold of his jaw with his other hand and moved it back and forth.

"Checking to see if it's broken?" Luke said.

"I don't think it is."

"Not for lack of trying on young Mr. Howard's part, though."

"I don't know why the hell he had to do that. I'd never do anything to hurt Deborah. She's about the sweetest girl I've ever known."

"Sweeter than Rachel Montgomery?"

"Well . . . Hell, it's different, Luke! Rachel was like . . . a dream. Something you always know you're never gonna have in real life, no matter how much you might believe you want it. But Deborah . . . she's the sort of gal you can think about maybe settling down with one day, and it could really happen. I'm not sure I could ever deserve somebody like that, though. Not after some of the things I've done."

"Like stealing cattle and holding up stage-coaches."

"Yeah." Tyler sighed. "I probably ought to just forget about her and stop thinking about how things might be one of these days."

"We have to deal with that murder charge first, and keep Axtell and the Douglases from killing you while we're at it. I think that's a full enough plate for anybody, don't you?"

"Yeah, it sure is," Tyler said.

Luke had a hunch that no matter what the young man said, though, thoughts of Deborah Howard and the life they might have together would still be lurking in the back of his head.

Nolan Howard was right in his estimation of when the wagon train would reach the stream that had to be crossed. The sun was almost directly overhead when the lead wagon rolled up to the edge of the creek bank and stopped.

The other scouts had gone on ahead, but Nolan was riding with the train today. Luke didn't know if that was because the young man wanted to be on hand for the crossing, or because Nolan was keeping an eye on his sister and Tyler to make sure they stayed apart.

There had certainly been plenty of unfriendly frowns passing back and forth between Tyler and Nolan today, but they had kept their distance, not even saying anything to each other.

The wagon in the lead today belonged to a rawboned man in late middle age named Clint Haskins. He was a bachelor, so he hadn't objected to having company when Luke suggested that he and Tyler ride with him.

The wagon train was close enough to White Fork now that there was a good chance they might encounter some of Axtell's deputies or Manfred Douglas's gunwolves scouring the countryside for the men they wanted to kill. Luke figured it would be a good idea for him and Tyler to ride inside one of the wagons, out of sight, so that anyone who studied the wagon train through field glasses wouldn't spot them.

Haskins was the garrulous sort. He had

been talking all morning, giving Luke and Tyler his life history as the wagon jolted along.

The Howard wagon was fourth in line. Instead of having the wagons in the same order every day, one of Jonathan Howard's ideas had been to let them switch around, so that no one had to take the lead or bring up the rear all the time. That seemed to have been good for morale, because the company was in decent spirits despite the recent troubles.

Jonathan Howard climbed down from his wagon and walked forward to look out over the creek. Nolan sat on horseback nearby. Luke and Tyler watched from inside Clint Haskins's wagon.

As Nolan had said, the stream was flowing swiftly, with a strong current. It was only about twenty yards wide, though, so the wagons would be able to cross without being pushed too far downstream. The banks were fairly steep, but the oxen were sturdy enough to haul the wagons down and then up again.

Jonathan Howard turned toward the lead wagon and asked, "Do you want to lead the way, Clint, or would you rather swing aside so someone else can do it?"

"You're joshin', ain't you?" Haskins said.

"I never turned aside from nothin' in my life, and I ain't figurin' on startin' now."

Howard smiled and said, "That's exactly the answer I expected from you, my friend. Go ahead whenever you're ready. Once all the wagons are on the other side, we'll stop for a meal and to let the teams rest."

"I'll ride on across," Nolan said. He nudged his horse into motion.

The horse entered the creek with some reluctance but didn't take long to start swimming. Nolan slipped off the saddle but held tight to the horn so his mount wouldn't have to carry his weight. He let the horse pull him along. In a matter of minutes, both of them were standing on the opposite bank with creek water running off of them.

Nolan took his hat off and waved Haskins on.

"Come ahead, Clint!" he called. "Just stay as straight as you can!"

Haskins popped his whip, yelled at the oxen, and slapped the reins against their rumps until the huge, stolid beasts lurched forward. The wagon started to roll.

Inside the wagon bed, as they sat on crates of supplies under the arching canvas cover, Tyler looked uneasy as he said to Luke, "I've never been on a boat in my life. This is as close as I've ever come. I don't think

I'm gonna like it."

"You'll be fine," Luke told him. "These wagons float, and the seams between the boards are sealed with pitch so they're not supposed to leak."

"Yeah, well, all sorts of things in life wind up doing what they're not supposed to."

Luke couldn't argue with that statement, so he didn't say anything. The oxen plodded out into the water, and a few moments later he could tell from the slight bobbing motion that the wagon was floating.

Instinct kept the oxen swimming forward. There wasn't much Haskins could do now to control anything. He, Luke, and Tyler were at the mercy of the stream and the heavy-shouldered beasts of burden churning through the water.

Then, sooner really than Luke expected, he felt the crunch of gravel as the wagon wheels hit bottom again and sought purchase. Finding it with no trouble, the wagon rolled out of the creek and up the bank, drawn on inexorably by the team hitched to it.

"Well, shoot, that was easy!" Haskins said.

"I hope it'll be like that for all the others," Luke said.

The other wagons had to have room to pull up out of the creek as they crossed.

Haskins drove ahead until Nolan rode alongside and told him he had gone far enough. Luke and Tyler moved to the back of the vehicle so they could watch over the tailgate while the rest of the wagon train crossed the creek.

The next two wagons made it without any problems, each driver waiting until the one in front was completely across before starting into the stream. That brought the Howard wagon to the edge of the bank, where Jonathan Howard started his team forward as soon as the third wagon was clear.

At first it appeared that this crossing would go as smoothly as the others had. The current pushed the wagon a little farther downstream than the others, but that didn't seem to be a problem.

Then, with no warning, the wagon stopped. The oxen continued swimming, but they couldn't pull the wagon free from whatever obstruction had brought it to a halt.

"We hit some sort of snag!" Jonathan Howard shouted.

Nolan was sitting on his horse beside Clint Haskins's wagon. He said, "Hell!" and urged the animal into a run, heading back toward the creek.

338

"Maybe we'd better go and help," Tyler suggested as he leaned forward with an anxious expression on his face.

"We need to stay out of sight if we can," Luke said. He knew what Tyler was worried about. Deborah Howard was perched on the wagon seat beside her father, and for the moment they seemed to be stranded in the middle of the stream. The situation wasn't all that dangerous right now, Luke thought . . . but it could turn that way.

They watched as Nolan rode out into the creek. He stayed in the saddle this time, even though his horse had to struggle more. Luke and Tyler were close enough to hear him call to his father and sister, "Must be a rock or an old log or something sticking up from the creek bed! The team can pull you loose! Just keep them going!"

Howard nodded, then popped his whip and shouted at the oxen. Nolan leaned over from his saddle and caught hold of the harness. He tugged on it, urging the team to keep pulling.

Whatever the obstruction was, it gave way suddenly, with no warning. The wagon lurched forward, and the extra force made it slew sideways a little. Deborah cried out in alarm as she started to topple off the seat. Her father made a grab for her arm.

At the same time, the lead ox where Nolan had been crowding in on the team slammed into the young scout's horse. The collision drove the horse over at an angle, and as water splashed in its face, the animal panicked. Horse and rider both disappeared under the swift water in a welter of flailing hooves.

CHAPTER 31

"Deborah!" Tyler cried. He was halfway out the back of the wagon before Luke caught hold of his shirt collar.

"Wait a minute! Her father's got her."

It was true. Jonathan Howard had clamped his hand around Deborah's arm and pulled her back onto the seat. The oxen were swimming hard again toward the opposite bank, dragging the wagon behind them.

Water flew high in the air as Nolan's horse surfaced, kicking and thrashing. Jonathan Howard looked around wildly and bellowed, "Nolan! Nolan!"

There was no sign of the young scout.

"Nolan didn't come up!" Tyler said as his hands clenched on the tailgate of Haskins's wagon.

"He could have hit his head on something when he went under," Luke said. "Or his horse might have clipped him with a hoof."

Tyler looked over at him, eyes wide with urgency, and said, "Luke —"

"Go," Luke said with a nod.

Tyler put a hand on the tailgate and vaulted over it. He hit the ground running. It wasn't far to the creek, and Tyler covered the distance in a hurry. He splashed out into the stream and started swimming toward the spot where Nolan had gone under.

While Tyler was doing that, Jonathan Howard drove the team on relentlessly until the oxen reached the bank and pulled the wagon out. Howard stopped the vehicle as soon as it reached level ground and leaped down from the seat to run back toward the creek. Deborah was right behind him.

Luke had abandoned Haskins's wagon as well. He trotted toward the stream, as did other immigrants on both sides of the creek. As he reached the bank, Tyler's head burst up out of the water. The young man splashed for a second as he shook his head to get his soaked hair out of his eyes. Then Tyler gulped down another deep breath and went under again.

"Nolan's got to be all right," Deborah said. "He's just got to!"

"I can't understand why he didn't come up," Howard said as he put an arm around his daughter's shoulders and pulled her against his side. "He's a good swimmer. He always has been."

Luke came up beside them and said, "Something must have happened to knock Nolan out when he went under. If he's a good swimmer, as you say, that's the only explanation."

People gathered on both sides of the creek to watch with tense expectation. Luke thought about diving in the creek himself, but he realized if he did that, he might just get in Tyler's way or confuse the issue. As things stood now, if Tyler found anybody under the water, it had to be Nolan Howard.

Suddenly, with another big splash, Tyler broke the surface again. This time, he wasn't alone. He had one arm around Nolan's limp form, supporting the young scout as he tried to drive the two of them toward the bank with desperate kicks. He flailed at the water with his free arm.

"Somebody help them!" Jonathan Howard exclaimed.

Several men plunged into the water. They were able to wade out almost to where Tyler and Nolan were. One of them reached out, caught hold of Tyler's arm, and drew them closer. Then some of the other men grabbed Nolan and took the burden from Tyler. They carried him to shore, leaving

Tyler to trudge on in with one man beside him, holding his arm to help support him.

Luke was waiting as the men lowered Nolan to the ground. He said, "Roll him over on his belly and turn his head to one side." When that had been done, Luke planted a knee on either side of Nolan's torso, put his hands on the young man's back, and started pumping with both arms like a bellows.

He kept it up steadily for thirty seconds, feeling a bleakness growing inside him as he did so, but then Nolan suddenly coughed and spasmed. Creek water spewed from his mouth. Luke continued pumping for several seconds as Nolan coughed up the rest of the water he had swallowed.

Luke got to his feet and said, "Get him up and walk him around some. He was under longer than was good for him, but maybe not long enough to do any permanent damage."

Several of the men lifted Nolan, who was still coughing and retching. His steps were uncertain, but with their help he was able to stumble along.

"Is he going to be all right?" Deborah asked.

"There's an excellent chance of it," Luke told her. "It's a good thing Judd found him when he did, though. If Nolan had been under the water for another minute or two, it might have been too late."

Tyler walked up, soaked and breathing hard. Deborah didn't seem to care how wet he was. She threw her arms around him and hugged him tightly.

"Thank you," she said. "Thank you for saving my brother."

Tyler looked a little startled, but he clearly didn't mind being hugged like that. While Deborah was still embracing him, Jonathan Howard clasped his hand and wrung it with equal fervor.

"You saved my boy's life," Howard said. "I can never thank you enough for that, Mr. Tyler."

"Well," Tyler said, his voice a little hoarse because he had swallowed some water, too, "you can call me Judd. That'd be a start."

"Thank you, Judd. From the bottom of my heart."

"And mine, too," Deborah said. She followed that with a kiss, twining her arms around Tyler's neck as she pressed her mouth to his.

Howard let that go on for a moment, then cleared his throat and said, "Uh, Deborah, you might want to let the boy breathe. He's been underwater, you know."

Deborah broke the kiss, stepped back, and blushed furiously. Luke wanted to laugh at her expression, but he managed to hold it to a chuckle.

Nolan walked up, still with a man on either side of him to steady him, but he looked a lot better than he had a few minutes earlier. He thrust out a hand toward Tyler and said in an even hoarser voice, "They tell me . . . you pulled me out of there. Reckon you . . . saved my life. I'm obliged . . . to you."

Tyler clasped his hand and said, "I'm just glad I found you in time. I was getting a mite worried."

"Don't know . . . what happened to me." Nolan let go of Tyler's hand and raised his fingers to a lump on his head. "Got some kind of wallop . . . when I went under. That's the last thing . . . I remember."

Luke said, "We'll probably never know for sure how you got knocked out, but the important thing is that Judd was able to pull you before you drowned."

"And you were able to pump that creek water out of him, Luke," Jonathan Howard added. "We owe you a debt, too."

"I'd say we're all square. Nolan and the other scouts saved our bacon a couple of days ago."

Deborah said, "And the two of you saved the whole wagon train a few days before that."

Luke smiled and shrugged.

"Like I said, let's call it square. Judd and I will get out of sight again, and the rest of you can get back to what you were doing. There are still quite a few wagons to get across this creek, you know."

"I just hope we don't have any more trouble like that!" Howard said. "There are only so many times folks can push their luck."

Luke hoped that didn't apply to him and Tyler having to come out into the open like they had, but only time would tell.

After near-tragedy had been averted, the rest of the wagons crossed without incident. They stood in a long line while men built fires and women boiled coffee and heated salt pork, beans, and biscuits left from breakfast.

Luke and Tyler changed into dry clothing in the back of Clint Haskins's wagon. The farmer brought them plates of food and cups of coffee.

"The little Howard gal wanted to bring the vittles, but I told her you rannihans

347

might not be decent," Haskins said with a grin.

"How's Nolan doing?" Luke asked.

"Seems to be all right. Still hackin' and coughin' a mite, like it's gonna take him a while to get all the water outta his innards, but I reckon he'll be fine. He's got ever' unmarried gal in the whole train fussin' over him, 'cept for his sister. She's too busy moonin' over this young fella."

Haskins nodded toward Tyler.

"No sign of any strangers around, is there?" Luke said.

"Nope." Haskins eyed him shrewdly. "You're thinkin' some o' them gunslingin' deputies might've been somewhere close by and spotted the two o' you?"

"It's not likely, but we can't rule it out."

"Right now, if any of those varmints showed up and tried to take you boys away, I reckon pert' near everybody in the bunch would rise up and stop 'em. Even the ones who've been suspicious o' this young scoundrel here" — Haskins jerked his chin toward Tyler — "figure we owe him a debt on account o' what he did for Nolan. *Especially* after the way Nolan clouted him the night before."

Tyler laughed and said, "Yeah, and I've got the bruise on my jaw to prove it. But hell, he's a good *hombre.* Can't blame a fella for wanting to look after his sister and protect her from a reprobate like me."

"I figure you're overestimatin' what a desperado you are, son. I've known some pretty bad varmints. I'm thinkin' you ain't one of them."

Luke had come around to that way of thinking himself over the past couple of weeks.

But there was still a matter of convincing a jury in White Fork . . . assuming they could stay alive that long.

The wagons rolled out again after the meal. Jonathan Howard urged his son to ride on their wagon for a while, but Nolan insisted on mounting up and riding out to resume his job as scout. Howard couldn't talk him out of it, so Nolan galloped ahead of the wagons, soon vanishing into the distance.

He had only been gone an hour or so, though, when a dust cloud up ahead indicated that several riders were coming fast from the north. Haskins spoke over his shoulder to Luke and Tyler, warning them of the approaching riders.

"Maybe you boys ought to get your guns back," the farmer suggested.

"Let's wait a little longer," Luke said. He

didn't like the looks of the way things were developing, though.

When the riders came in sight, he recognized Nolan and the other scouts from the wagon train. So did Haskins. He hauled back on the reins and brought his team to a halt, forcing the other wagons to stop as well. Jonathan Howard jumped down from his wagon and hurried forward.

"What's wrong?" he asked as he put a hand on the driver's box of Haskins's wagon.

"Riders comin'. Looks like your boy and the other scouts."

A few moments later, Nolan reined in, along with the other men. In a voice still hoarse from the earlier dunking, Nolan reported, "There's a bunch of men headed this way, Pa. Looks like they're heavily armed, and I'm pretty sure I saw sunlight reflecting from the badges on their chests."

"Deputies from White Fork," Howard said.

"And I think we all know who they're looking for," Luke added from inside the wagon.

CHAPTER 32

Grim-faced, Jonathan Howard said, "I'll pass the word to all the men in the company to check their guns and get ready for trouble. We won't let those fellas take you away from us, Luke. Not after everything you've done."

"We're obliged to you for the sentiment, Mr. Howard, but Judd and I can't allow you to put your lives at risk that way," Luke said. "The time has come for us to leave."

"We're lightin' a shuck?" Tyler asked.

Luke nodded and said, "I think that would be best."

"So do I." Tyler looked at Howard, Nolan, and Haskins and added, "No offense, but you folks don't need to get mixed up in a shooting scrape with Gus Axtell's men. They're cold-blooded killers, the lot of them. You wouldn't stand a chance."

"We've got them outnumbered," Nolan said.

"Wouldn't matter," Tyler replied with a shake of his head. "Those boys are too slick. Every one of them could gun down three or four of you before you could even lift a rifle."

"But it's just not right!" Jonathan Howard said. "We can't abandon you fellows."

"You won't be," Luke said. "We're the ones taking our leave of you. If we can have our horses . . . and our guns back . . ."

"Of course, of course. I'll see to it right away." Howard started to turn, then paused. "Deborah's not going to like this."

"She'll have to accept it for now," Tyler said. "Maybe later on, things will be different."

"I'll be counting on that," Howard said with an emphatic nod. "We all will. Your weapons are in my wagon. I'll get them."

"Judd, see to the horses," Luke said. "There's no point in us hiding now."

When Howard came back with Luke's revolvers, rifle, and knife, Luke told him, "When those deputies stop your wagons, they won't be happy to discover that we're not here. You need to tell them that we spotted their dust up ahead and took off on our own. You don't have any idea why, since we never told you anything except our names when we drifted up and threw in with your wagon train. If they accuse you of harboring fugitives, just plead ignorance and stick to that story."

"I don't like lying," Howard said, "or turning my back on friends, either."

"You and your people have to live in this area, Mr. Howard. Manford Douglas might forgive you for not realizing who Judd and I were, but if he knew that you took our side against him, there's a good chance he'd make life difficult for you. You need to make sure all your people understand what I'm telling you."

"Yeah, I guess what you're saying makes sense, but I don't have to like it." Howard frowned. "You're talking like this fellow Douglas is going to win, though. Like Judd won't be able to clear his name."

"Life is unpredictable. Hope for the best but prepare for the worst."

Luke checked the loads in his Remingtons and slid the long-barreled revolvers into their holsters.

Too many times that was the best preparation of all.

Judd Tyler came up leading Luke's gray and the paint he had ridden away from White Fork in the first place. They would leave the other two horses with the wagon train. As close as they were to their destination, they no longer needed the extra mounts, which had never been more than a mixed blessing anyway.

Deborah appeared right behind Tyler, hurrying along the line of wagons. She put a hand on his arm and said, "Judd, is what I hear true? You're leaving the wagon train?"

"We've got to," he told her. "Nolan and the other scouts spotted a bunch of Axtell's deputies heading this way. Only reason they'd be doing that is if one of the men looking for us caught a glimpse of Luke and me earlier and went to fetch a posse."

"Somebody saw you while you were saving my brother's life, that's what you mean. So in return for that good deed, you have to run for your own life again."

"Damn it, Tyler, she's right," Nolan said. "That has to be the explanation."

"That's the way it happens sometimes," Tyler said with a shrug. "We need to be riding, before they have a chance to get any closer."

"Take me with you."

It was a toss-up who looked more surprised by that suggestion: Deborah's father, her brother . . . or Tyler.

Nolan said, "Deborah, you can't —"

"I absolutely —" Jonathan Howard began at the same time.

Both of them fell silent as Tyler took hold of Deborah's shoulders and shook his head. He said, "I can't do that, and you know it, Deborah. I'm on the run. It's possible those deputies will spot us leaving the wagon train and come after us, and if they do, it'll mean a running fight if Luke and I are gonna get away. There's no way I'm gonna let you put yourself in that much danger."

"But I want to be with you," she said.

"You will be. Later, when this is all over."

"Can you guarantee that?"

"You know there's no way anybody can guarantee anything in this life . . . except for the way folks feel about each other."

Tyler demonstrated that sentiment by bringing his mouth down on Deborah's in a kiss. She clutched at him, and neither of them seemed to care — or even be aware — that quite a few people were around watching them, including her father and brother.

"Well, hell," Nolan muttered. "I want to punch him again, but I don't reckon that'd be a good idea. She's got her heart set on him, and once that little sis of mine makes her mind up, you're wasting time arguin' with her."

Luke smiled and said, "Yes, but Judd's right. We need to get out of here now, while there's still a chance that posse won't spot us." He raised his voice a little. "Did you hear me, Judd?"

"I heard you, I heard you," Tyler said as he broke the kiss. He gave Deborah a tight hug, then let go of her and stepped over to take up the reins of the paint pony. "If we're gonna light that shuck, let's set it on fire."

He and Luke swung up into their saddles and rode hard to the west, slowing only to half turn as each lifted an arm in farewell.

The terrain was rougher the farther they got from the river. Heavily wooded foothills rose in the distance, with gray mountains behind them, but another stretch of gullies and ridges ran along the edge of the basin separating Luke and Tyler from those heights.

"If we can make it to the hills, they'll have a hard time finding us," Tyler said. "I roamed and hunted all over 'em when I was a boy. There are even some caves up there we can use to hide out in if we need to."

"You make it sound like a good place for a desperado to cache the loot from his crooked jobs," Luke said.

Despite the perilous situation in which they found themselves, Tyler laughed.

"No, sir," he said. "You're not gonna trick me into spilling where that money's hidden.

If I did that, you might ride off and leave me to the tender mercies of those deputies."

Luke could tell the young man was joshing, but he said, "Surely you know me better than that by now."

"Maybe so, but I still don't aim to trust anybody too much until this is all said and done and everybody in White Fork knows the truth."

Luke agreed with that sentiment.

They were able to track the location of the posse by the dust cloud the deputies' horses kicked up. At first it continued almost due south toward the wagon train, but then without any warning the cloud split and some of the dust headed their way.

Tyler saw that and let out a curse.

"Somebody in that bunch must have eyes like a hawk!" he said. "They spotted us out here and some of 'em are coming after us, while the others go on and meet the wagons."

"At this distance, they couldn't have spotted us as anything except a couple of riders. We're too far away for them to recognize. Clearly, they don't want to take a chance on who we are, though, so they're going to come after us and see."

"Then it's time for us to fog it outta here," Tyler said. He leaned forward in the saddle and urged the paint into a gallop.

Luke did likewise on the gray, but he called over the pounding hoofbeats, "We can't push these horses too hard. We'll run them for a mile or so and then pull back."

Tyler nodded in understanding. He looked worried and Luke didn't blame him for feeling that way. Unless they were completely wrong about the identities of their pursuers, those men back there wanted both of them dead and would stop at nothing to achieve that goal.

They hadn't gone even a mile when the landscape got too rough for the horses to run flat-out anymore. Luke and Tyler had to pick their route through the broken land more carefully, sticking mostly to the gullies because they didn't want to be skylighted on any of the ridges. The ground was too hard and rocky to take very many tracks. Whether the posse would be able to follow them depended entirely on how skillful their trackers were.

"Dadgum it, they're not giving up!" Tyler said a half-hour later as he twisted in the saddle to check their backtrail. "That dust is still hanging back there."

"You didn't expect them to give up, did you?" Luke asked. "There's a decent bounty on your head to start with, and Douglas and

Axtell probably let their men know they can expect a bonus if you're dead. Now you're really talking about blood money."

"They're a couple of heartless bastards. And Spence is even worse."

"I hope we get a chance to prove that."

They rode on, cutting across the badlands as quickly as they dared in the hope of reaching the hills where they could hide out if necessary.

When Luke glanced over at Tyler a short time later, he saw the young man chewing his bottom lip, apparently in deep thought. After a moment, Tyler said, "Luke, if something happens to me but you make it, I'd like to think you'll see to it Spence Douglas gets what's coming to him."

"How can I do that? All I have to prove he killed Rachel Montgomery is your word."

"I know. I've been pondering about that. I think it's about time I let you in on that evidence against Spence I've got —"

Luke felt like saying it was about time, but before he could do that, the wicked crack of a rifle filled the air and a bullet whined off the boulder Tyler was riding past. Luke jerked his head up and spotted the rifleman standing on another slab of rock twenty yards away, levering the weapon in his hands and drawing a bead on them for another shot.

CHAPTER 33

One of the ivory-handled Remingtons flickered into Luke's hand so quickly it almost appeared like magic. Flame spouted from the revolver's long barrel at almost the same instant the rifleman fired again.

But not quite the same instant. Luke's shot blasted a shaved second of time ahead of the other man's. The rifle barrel jerked up and the bullet from it flew harmlessly far over the heads of Luke and Tyler. The round from Luke's gun had bored into the would-be killer's chest and disrupted his aim. He went over backward, falling off the rock and out of sight.

"Son of a gun!" Tyler said. "I never saw shooting like that!"

"You may have a chance to see it again if there are any more of them," Luke said. "None of that bunch could have gotten ahead of us. That man must have been here already, patrolling the edge of the hills and searching for you."

"If he was one of Axtell's men, he might've recognized this pony. If he wasn't . . ."

"Whether he was or wasn't," Luke said, his voice grim, "he fired the first shot. Can't blame a fellow for dancing if somebody else opens the ball."

He didn't holster the Remington until they had ridden another half a mile without encountering anyone else. He was convinced the rifleman had been a lone deputy on the hunt for Tyler.

They reached the edge of the badlands and started up the slope toward the trees. Now they were in the open again, but it couldn't be helped. The shelter of the wooded hills was right in front of them, and they had to try for it.

Rifles began to pop far behind them. At this range, it would be pure luck if one of the bullets found them, but Luke knew that was possible. Everybody had a certain amount of good luck — and bad — coming to him in his life.

But unless one of the deputies was armed with a Sharps buffalo gun and had the same skill with it as a legendary marksman such as Billy Dixon, Luke figured he and Tyler were safe.

For the moment. They still had to deal

with the dangers they would find waiting for them in White Fork.

They reached the trees without any trouble and disappeared into the thick growth. The members of the posse might still try to track them, but it would be more difficult now. Not only that, the deputies hadn't gotten close enough to be certain that the two men on horseback were the men they were looking for.

Luke wondered if they had found the man he'd killed down in the badlands. If so, that might be enough to convince them they were on the right trail. They wouldn't stop looking.

He and Tyler would just have to stay ahead of them.

"You know these hills, you said. How far is it to White Fork from here?"

Tyler pointed a little east of north and said, "About ten miles in that direction, I reckon. We can make it by nightfall, if we don't have to go to ground. And if we live that long."

"I plan on living that long," Luke said. "And *you're* not going to make it to town just yet. We need a place where I can leave you and you'll be safe until I've talked to Judge Keller. I assume you can tell me where to find him?"

"I know where his house is. He and his wife had me come to dinner there once, several years ago. I reckon they were trying to straighten me out after I started getting into trouble." A wry smile appeared on Tyler's face. "It didn't take."

"All right. We'll find a good hideout for you, then I'll slip into town and let the judge know what's going on." Luke paused. "He's not going to double-cross us and tip off Douglas and Axtell, is he?"

"I'd bet my life he won't."

"Good — because that's exactly what you'll be doing."

After they had ridden for a few more minutes, Tyler said, "I reckon I know a good place where I can hole up. It's just a little box canyon, but not many people know it's there. The brush grows so thick across the mouth of it you can't hardly see the entrance unless you know what you're looking for. I, uh, sort of made it even harder to see."

"Sounds like a good place to hold rustled stock until you were able to move it somewhere you could get rid of it."

"Yeah, I reckon it would be, but I'm not sayin' whether it was ever used for that."

Luke laughed and said, "Just lead the way,

Judd. We'll worry about your rehabilitation later."

The box canyon was as difficult to find as Tyler boasted it was. Without the young man to lead the way, Luke probably never would have known the place was there.

But once the young man moved aside some thick brush that was tied together to form a natural-looking barrier, the opening loomed in front of them, wide enough to drive a few cows through. Sheer rock walls rose fifty feet on either side of it.

"It widens out about a hundred feet in," Tyler said. "There's a little spring and some graze."

"A regular hole in the wall."

"Nothing that fancy. I never built a cabin or anything, just spread my bedroll when I needed to spend a night or two."

Luke glanced up at the late afternoon sky and said, "You shouldn't have to spend the night. I hope to be back to fetch you into town before morning. Does Judge Keller happen to have a barn?"

"More like a shed where he keeps his buggy and horse."

"That'll do, I imagine." Luke waved a hand at the narrow passage. "Lead on."

They rode along the cleft until it opened

up into the box canyon, as Tyler had promised. The canyon was less than a hundred yards long and about half that wide, big enough to hold a small jag of cattle but not much else.

The rocky wall bulged out on one side, enough to create an overhang. Tyler pointed to it and said, "A man can build a fire under there and it'll break up the smoke so nobody on the outside will ever see it."

"The voice of experience."

"Yeah, this place is almost like home to me. When I lit out from White Fork after Spence killed Rachel, I gave some thought to hiding out here. I wanted more distance between me and town, though. I knew once Manfred found out what happened, he'd have his gunnies out in force, scouring every foot of the countryside for me. Didn't want to take a chance on them finding me. I thought it'd be better to run as far and fast as I could." Tyler blew out a breath and shrugged his shoulders. "You can see how that worked out. Here I am anyway."

"Maybe one step closer to clearing your name and getting justice for Rachel. Just think of it that way."

"Squaring accounts for Rachel is the only thing keeping me going," Tyler said. "At least it was . . . until I met Deborah."

Luke wanted to wait until dark to set out for White Fork. Tyler stripped the saddle from his paint, gave the pony a rubdown, then built a fire and boiled a pot of coffee. Luke sipped a cup as he watched the dark blue of evening steal over the sky from east to west.

Tyler told him how to find the judge's house, then said, "You don't reckon Axtell's men hurt anybody with the wagon train, do you?"

"If Jonathan Howard and the others stuck to the story I told them to tell, the deputies wouldn't have had any reason to suspect them. They may have insisted on searching all the wagons, but once they did that and saw we weren't there, I think they'd leave those pilgrims alone. There's a limit to how far even crooked lawmen can push honest citizens without creating more trouble for themselves than it's worth."

Tyler said, "I hope you're right. If they hurt Deborah or anybody else . . ."

"It'll be one more score to settle, and we'll see that it is," Luke promised.

Stars had begun to twinkle into view in the cobalt sky overhead as Luke rode out of the canyon. Tyler replaced the brush behind him to conceal the opening. Tyler had told him the best route to White Fork, and Luke's instinctive sense of direction served him well, even at night.

He didn't rush as he headed in the direction of the settlement. It was possible some of his enemies were abroad in the night, and he wanted to be able to hear their horses if any of them came close to him.

However, by the time he spotted a cluster of lights in the distance and knew they had to come from White Fork, he hadn't run into anyone. He pushed the gray to a little faster pace, eager to reach his destination and talk to Judge Clarence Keller.

White Fork was a good-size town with a business district several blocks long and a number of residential streets around it. According to Tyler, the judge lived in a white, two-story frame house surrounded by cottonwoods, sitting at the western end of the primary cross street, three blocks from downtown. The courthouse, sheriff's office, and jail dominated the northern end of the settlement, while a couple of churches and the stagecoach station were at the southern end. The eastern side of the settlement was the red-light district, such as it was.

Luke aimed the gray toward the western fringes of town and looked for Judge Keller's house as he approached. The moon was up by now, and its light shone silvery on the whitewashed walls of the largest structure Luke could see. When he drew closer, he spotted the shed out back where Keller kept his horse and buggy.

Confident that he was in the right place, he reined in, swung down from the saddle, and went closer on foot. The gray and the horse in the shed whickered to each other, but they were fairly quiet about it. A dog barked in the night, but it wasn't close and didn't seem likely to alarm anyone in the house.

A light glowed in one of the windows on the back side of the house. Luke left the gray by the shed and catfooted toward the window. When he reached it, he took his hat off and ventured a look.

A man with white hair and an equally snowy mustache sat at a desk in a book-littered office. He wore a dressing gown and had what looked like a glass of whiskey at his elbow. A cigar smoldered in an ashtray. A thick, leather-bound volume was open on the desk in front of the man. A law book, perhaps, or just something the judge wanted to read. Luke was confident he was looking at Judge Clarence Keller.

He thought about tapping on the window to get Keller's attention, but he didn't want the judge to raise an alarm, so it might be wiser to get the drop on him until he had a chance to explain, Luke decided. He moved along the wall, trying the windows in the darkened rooms until he found one that slid up without making much noise. He threw a leg over the sill and climbed into what looked like a kitchen, judging by the furnishings he could make out in the dim light.

A moment later he was in a hallway, gliding toward the door of the judge's office, which stood open a couple of inches to allow light to spill into the hall. Luke eased one of the Remingtons out of its holster and held it ready as he used his other hand to swing the door open.

Judge Keller raised his head, his bushy white eyebrows climbing his forehead in surprise, as Luke stepped into the open doorway, leveled the Remington, and said in a quiet but forceful tone, "Please sit right where you are, Judge. I assure you, I mean you no harm. I just want to talk to you."

Before Keller could respond, Luke heard a whisper of sound behind him. An instant later something hard jabbed into the small of his back and a woman said, "You stand mighty still, young man, or I'll blow your spine in two."

CHAPTER 34

Instead of looking upset, the judge chuckled and said, "She'll do it, too, sir, let there be no doubt in your mind about that. She's a fierce one, my wife is."

Luke recognized the thing poking into his back as the muzzle of a gun, though he couldn't tell if it was a rifle or a pistol. He said, "Please be careful with that trigger, Mrs. Keller. I didn't come here to hurt anyone, and I'd hate to suffer a fate such as the one you describe."

"You talk fancy, like my husband," the woman said. "Educated man, are you?"

"Self-educated, for the most part."

"Well, you're smart enough to know that I mean what I say, aren't you?"

"I certainly am." Luke lifted both hands to elbow level, including the one holding the Remington, and held them out away from his body.

"Clarence, get his guns," the woman said.

"All right, Mildred," Keller said as he pushed his chair back and stood up. He came around the desk and approached Luke warily from the side. When he was close enough he reached up and took the revolver from Luke's hand, then circled back, out of reach, until he could hook the other Remington from its holster.

Luke could tell from the way Keller gripped the revolvers that the judge had handled guns before. That came as no surprise, since most men of Keller's age who had spent all or most of their lives on the frontier had seen their share of trouble and fought outlaws and Indians.

"Take your knife out and toss it on the desk," Keller said as he moved back. "Don't try anything funny with it."

"With a gun at my back and two more pointed at me from the front? I don't think I'm likely to try anything, Your Honor, funny or otherwise."

Luke slid the knife from its sheath and tossed it easily onto the desk, where it landed next to the open book the judge had been reading.

"Got a hideout gun anywhere?" Keller asked.

As a matter of fact, Luke had a two-shot, .41 caliber derringer concealed in a cunningly contrived holster inside his waist-band. He thought about denying it was there, then decided to tell the truth. He planned to put all his cards on the table for Keller, and he wanted the judge to believe him.

And the man's wife, as well. Luke had a hunch if he could convince Mrs. Keller he was telling the truth, that would carry a considerable amount of weight with the judge.

"I have a derringer," he said. "I'll take it out and place it on the desk as well, if you'll allow me to."

Keller hooked his thumbs over both gun hammers and nodded.

"Slow and easy," he said.

Luke took the derringer out and stepped forward to set it on the desk. Mrs. Keller came with him, keeping the gun barrel pressed into his back. Her steps told him she was far enough away that the weapon had to be a rifle.

"All right, I'm disarmed," he said. "You can lower your guns now."

"We'll be the judges of that, won't we, Mildred?"

"Are you making a joke, dear?"

Keller frowned and said, "I don't . . . Oh, of course. I said we'll be the judges of that, didn't I? And I'm a judge."

"And I'm perfectly happy for you to be the only one in the family. Should I do as this young man says and not poke this Henry rifle in his back anymore?"

"I think that would be safe," Keller said with a nod. "I plan to keep him covered, though, until I find out who he is and what he's doing here. If you're a thief, sir, I can assure you your stay in our jail won't be pleasant."

"I'm not a thief," Luke said. "Is it all right if I put my hands down now?"

Keller thought about it for a second, then nodded.

Luke lowered his arms, which he had raised again after putting the knife and the derringer on the desk. He looked over his shoulder, smiled, and said, "Ma'am, it's been a while since anyone referred to me as young. I'll take it as a compliment, especially coming from such a handsome woman."

"Don't try to charm me," Mrs. Keller said. "I may not look it now, but I *was* a bit of a belle in my youth, so I've heard plenty of false compliments."

"I assure you, I'm sincere."

Calling Mildred Keller a handsome woman wasn't much of a stretch. Her face and body might have softened and rounded some with middle age, but Luke could still see the belle she had been when she was young. Her thick brown hair had more than a few touches of gray in it, but they, along with the lines around her eyes, just gave her character.

Like her husband, she wore a dressing gown. She might have already retired for the evening, but something had alerted her to the presence of an intruder in the house.

"How did you know I was here?" Luke asked her.

"The floorboards in the kitchen make a little noise when someone walks on them, and my hearing is keen enough that I heard them. I knew Clarence wouldn't be in there — the kitchen is my domain, just as the courtroom is his — and he never hears anything when he's absorbed in his reading, so I thought I should see who was skulking around my house."

"And you armed yourself with a Henry rifle." Luke nodded toward the weapon she had tucked under her arm.

"My father made sure I knew how to shoot when I was just a little girl. We lived in Ohio at the time, when it was still the frontier, and those were bloody days."

"From what I've heard, they certainly were."

Judge Keller said, "Are you two going to stand there and palaver all night? You broke into my house, mister, and I want to know why."

Luke faced him again and said, "The best reason of all, Your Honor: a miscarriage of justice that needs to be addressed in the courtroom your wife spoke of."

"What are you talking about?" Keller asked, frowning.

"Judd Tyler."

Keller's frown deepened, and his wife said, "Oh, dear."

"Judd Tyler has been apprehended," Keller said. "He's being brought here to stand trial for the heinous murder of Miss Rachel Montgomery."

"Is that what Sheriff Axtell told you?" Luke asked.

"He informed me of the situation, yes. He told me it would probably be a good idea to conduct the trial as soon as possible after Tyler is brought in, since feelings about the case are running so high in the community."

"The sheriff wasn't being completely truthful with you, Your Honor," Luke said. "Tyler was caught down in Wyoming at a place called Bent Creek, and the man who caught him was supposed to bring him here to stand trial, but Axtell doesn't intend for

376

Judd Tyler to ever set foot inside a court-room."

Keller said, "That's an outrageous state-ment. How can you possibly know such a thing?"

"Because I'm the man who caught Tyler and was told to bring him here in order to collect the reward . . . and for the past week or so, deputies working for Sheriff Axtell have been trying to kill both of us."

Keller sputtered angrily for a couple of seconds, then managed to say, "You're the bounty hunter Sheriff Axtell mentioned? Jensen?"

"That's right. My name is Luke Jensen. Axtell's men have been trying to kill me, too. I can give you the names of three of them: Dave Simms, a man called Larrabee, and another known as Cue Ball Hennessy." Luke smiled faintly. "I'm afraid I don't know his actual given name. And there were others as well, more than a dozen, in fact. I suspect you're acquainted with Simms, Lar-rabee, and Hennessy?"

Before the judge could answer, Mrs. Kel-ler said, "They're animals. Most of the men who work for Gus Axtell are."

Keller said, "Now, Mildred, you shouldn't —"

"Don't try to deny it, Clarence. I've seen

377

you stomp around and heard you muttering about the heavy-handed way Axtell and his deputies enforce the law around here. Why, once you said they were little better than outlaws themselves!"

"Axtell was still duly elected —"

"By Manfred Douglas's money and influence, and you know it."

Luke had a hunch this wasn't the first time the Kellers had had a discussion such as this.

Mrs. Keller went on, "The sheriff is in Manfred's pocket. You should know, since he's tried to put you in that same pocket enough times."

"Nobody owns me!"

"Of course not, dear. You have too much integrity for that. But you're probably the only representative of the law around here who can honestly say that."

Keller glared at Luke and said, "There's got to be a lot more to this story."

"There is, Your Honor, and that's why I've come here. I wanted to be sure you knew the truth in this case. Judd Tyler didn't kill Miss Montgomery."

Mrs. Keller said, "I never believed he did. That boy may have done some . . . questionable . . . things, but he's no killer and he certainly never would have hurt Rachel. He adored her. Why, he followed her around like a puppy every chance he got!"

"Mildred, please," the judge said. "This is all very improper. Setting aside the fact that you broke into my house, Mr. Jensen, you shouldn't be discussing the case with me. It's prejudicial and highly irregular!"

"I wouldn't be here if all those hired guns working for Axtell and Douglas hadn't tried to kill Tyler and me," Luke said.

"The boy never should have run like he did. It just made him look guilty. If he's innocent, he should have stayed here and answered the charges against him."

"He couldn't do that, for the very same reason that Axtell and Douglas can't afford to allow him to stand trial. He knows who *really* killed Rachel Montgomery."

Judge Keller frowned at Luke for a long moment, then he drew in a deep breath and blew it out in a weary sigh. He turned and placed the Remingtons on the desk beside Luke's knife and derringer.

"All right, Jensen," he said. "Whatever it is you want to tell me, I'll listen . . . but that's all I'll promise!"

"That's all I'm asking, Your Honor," Luke said.

Chapter 35

"I believe there's still some coffee in the pot on the stove," Mrs. Keller said. "Would you like a cup, Mr. Jensen?"

"That would be much appreciated, ma'am," he told her.

"Have you had any supper?"

Luke had left the box canyon to ride to White Fork before Tyler rustled up any grub, so he said, "No, ma'am, I haven't. Things have been a little hectic."

"I have some leftover roast beef. I'll bring you a plate."

The judge said, "We're not running a hash house here, Mildred."

"No, but we're going to be hospitable to our guests," she said to him, then smiled at Luke. "I'll be right back, Mr. Jensen."

Luke took off his hat, returned the smile, and told her, "I'm much obliged to you, Mrs. Keller."

"Well, I feel like I owe you a little something. I *did* poke a rifle in your back, after all. I hope you don't have any hard feelings about that."

"None at all," he assured her.

She left the study, taking the Henry repeater with her. Judge Keller waved Luke into a leather chair in front of the desk and took his seat behind it again. He picked up the cigar, knocked the ash off the end of it, and stuck it in his mouth.

"Start talking," he said around the cylinder of tobacco. "If Judd Tyler didn't kill the preacher's girl, then who did?"

Luke sat down, looked across the desk at the judge, and said, "Spence Douglas."

Keller leaned back in the chair almost as if he'd been struck. His nostrils flared above the mustache as he drew in another deep breath. The cigar bobbed a little as his teeth clenched on it, and the coal on its end glowed red.

"Spence Douglas," he repeated as he set the cigar back in the ashtray. He reached for the glass of whiskey and downed it. As the empty glass thumped down on the desk, the judge went on, "You know Spence's father is the richest, most powerful man in this county."

"I'm well aware of that," Luke said.

"That's probably why Spence believes he's

381

above the law. His father feels the same way."

"No one is above the law in my jurisdiction, damn it!"

"That's what Judd Tyler told me. He says you're the most honest man in White Fork. That's why he's willing to stand trial in your court."

"He ran away."

"He was scared," Luke said. "He had just found the body of a young woman he greatly admired, who had been brutally choked to death. She was still warm, Your Honor. And Tyler already blamed himself for not being able to save her life."

"That didn't stop him from taking off for the tall and uncut like a frightened rabbit."

"That's because he knew no one would believe him if he tried to tell anybody what really happened. Then, some of Manfred Douglas's ranch hands found him and started yelling about how he was a killer and shooting at him." Luke leaned forward in the leather chair and clasped his hands together between his knees. "That's important, Your Honor. Those Circle M riders didn't find him with Miss Montgomery's body, yet they already knew she was dead and they immediately accused him of killing her . . . just like they had been told what to do and say."

The judge's bushy eyebrows lowered as he stared intently across the desk at Luke.

"I know what you're implying. You think Spence saw those men who work for his father and told them Tyler killed the girl . . . which means that if Tyler *didn't* do it, Spence must have."

"It stands to reason," Luke said. "He probably ran off into the woods when he heard someone coming and hung around long enough to see it was Tyler. It's the only explanation that makes any sense."

"Not necessarily. Many things *sound* logical but aren't true."

"Then throw in the fact that Spence argued with Miss Montgomery not long before she was killed, and the evidence against him begins to pile up."

Keller shook his head and said, "What you're talking about is a theory, Mr. Jensen. Pure speculation. A court of law requires *proof.* Lacking an eyewitness, it must be concrete, physical evidence indicating guilt."

"Tyler claims that he has proof of Spence's guilt."

"Oh? And what might that be?"

Luke didn't answer for a moment. Then he said, "I don't know. Tyler hasn't told me."

The judge blew out a scornful breath,

leaned back in his chair again, and shook his head.

"Then everything you've just told me, in addition to being irregular and improper, is worthless. Pure supposition, nothing more."

Before Luke could say anything else, the door opened and Mrs. Keller reappeared, carrying a tray into the study. The smells drifting from the coffee cup and the plate with several slices of roast beef and a couple of biscuits on it made Luke's stomach clench with hunger.

Mrs. Keller put the tray on the desk and said, "Here you go, Mr. Jensen. Have you and my husband worked out all the legal details of young Mr. Tyler's case yet?"

"We're still discussing it, ma'am."

"Well, don't let me interfere. Enjoy the food and coffee."

"I know I will. Thank you."

"I'm just glad you're trying to help Judd. Clarence and I tried to steer him onto the straight and narrow, you know." She sighed. "I'm afraid the effort wasn't successful, but I still don't believe he's as bad as he's been painted."

"Neither do I, Mrs. Keller. And for what it's worth, he told me that you and the judge tried to help him. He thinks kindly of you."

"I'm glad to hear that. Thank you for telling me, Mr. Jensen." She turned to her husband. "Clarence, do you need anything?"

"No, Mildred, you've done enough," Keller said. "You should go and get some rest. It's late."

"But not too late for Judd Tyler, I hope."

"We'll see," the judge said in a gruff voice.

Mrs. Keller had heated up the coffee. Luke was grateful for its bracing effect, and the roast beef and biscuits filled his belly and made him feel better, too.

Keller waited while Luke was eating. He puffed on his cigar and sat with his fingers steepled in front of his face, frowning in what appeared to be deep thought.

Finally he said, "Where is Judd Tyler now, Mr. Jensen?"

"I can't tell you that, Your Honor."

"I could send for the sheriff, you know. You're unarmed. I could hold you here and have you arrested, then compel you to answer my questions or be held in contempt of court."

"You could have me arrested . . . but you couldn't make me talk. You can't hold a dead man in contempt of court."

"What in blazes do you mean by that?"

"I mean the minute your back was turned, Axtell or one of his men would gun me down and then claim I was trying to escape. They have their orders from Manfred Douglas. He's already handed down a sentence of death for me and Tyler alike."

Keller shook his head and said, "I've never liked or trusted Gus Axtell, but you're making him out to be a cold-blooded murderer."

"If that's what Manfred Douglas wants, that's what he'll get."

"Tell me more about everything that's happened. You said there have been several attempts on your life?"

For the next few minutes, Luke went over all the trouble he and Tyler had run into on their way to White Fork, along with his growing conviction that Tyler was innocent, at least of Rachel Montgomery's murder.

"I was as skeptical as you starting out, Your Honor," he concluded, "but the more time went by and the more I saw for myself just how crooked Axtell's deputies are, the more I believed Tyler's story."

"Just what did you intend to accomplish by coming here and telling me all of this tonight?"

"I left Tyler in a safe place," Luke said, "because I wanted to talk to you and let you know he wants to give himself up. He wants to stand trial so he'll have a chance to tell his side of the story and produce whatever evidence he has. But he knows he can't do that if he surrenders to Sheriff Axtell. The only way is to keep him out of sight until the trial starts. Not even Axtell and Manfred Douglas would dare to kill him in open court."

"They'd have to kill me, too," Keller said. "And that would get the U.S. Marshals in here. Maybe even the army."

"Exactly. So what I'd like to do is slip Tyler into town and hide him out here, in your house."

"Good Lord, man!" Keller put his hands flat on the desk. "How would that look, a murder suspect spending the night in the judge's house?"

"Once the story gets out and everybody knows you were just trying to keep him safe so he could stand trial, I don't think it would reflect badly on you, Your Honor."

"Well . . . perhaps not."

The door swung open and Mildred Keller marched into the study again.

"I think it's a splendid idea," she said.

The judge came to his feet and said, "Mildred, I told you to go to bed, not to eavesdrop outside my door."

"Oh, and since when do I let you tell me what to do? You don't issue any judicial rulings from the bench in *this* house, Clarence

Keller!" While the judge stood there looking half-flabbergasted, Mrs. Keller turned to Luke and went on, "If you can bring Judd here, Mr. Jensen, I give you my word he'll be safe. No one has to know he's here until it's time for him to appear in court."

"Thank you, ma'am."

"No need to thank me. I'm just as devoted to the cause of justice in my own way as my husband is. Clarence knows that."

"It's true," Keller admitted with a shrug. "If Mildred does something, it's because she believes in her heart it's right. And since I've always trusted her heart . . ." He nodded. "All right, Jensen. If you can get Tyler here, he'll be safe."

"Thanks, Your Honor. How soon can you get a trial set up?"

"I can hold court tomorrow morning. There's nothing else on the docket. It'll take a while to empanel a jury, but not too long." A smile appeared on the judge's lips. "That won't give Manfred Douglas time to do anything except rattle his hocks into town when he hears what's going on."

"You think someone will get word to him?"

"Oh, he'll find out, sure enough," Keller said. "There are enough of his toadies here in White Fork that one of 'em is bound to

388

go racing out to the Circle M on horseback or in a buggy with the news as soon as the trial starts. But maybe it'll be over by the time he gets here. If Tyler is telling the truth about the evidence he has, there's a chance of it, anyway."

"Axtell may try to delay matters."

"Let him," Keller said with a dismissive wave. "I run my courtroom, not the sheriff."

"One thing you should remember, Your Honor . . . if things don't go their way, Douglas and Axtell are liable to decide to take the law into their own hands. Things might get ugly."

"I'm not afraid of them. Not with the law on my side."

Before Luke could say anything else, the sound of someone pounding on the front door of the house reached the study. Keller caught his breath, and his wife said, "Oh, my. Who could that be at this hour?"

"Nothing good, I'll wager," Keller said. "Mildred, do you mind finding out who our visitor is?"

"Not at all," she said. "Now, where did I put that rifle?"

CHAPTER 36

After Mrs. Keller had hurried out of the study, the judge said to Luke, "We'd better get you out of sight, just in case." He motioned to a door at the side of the room. "There's a storage closet through there. You can wait there until we find out what's going on."

Luke picked up his hat and settled it on his head. He asked, "What about my guns?"

Keller hesitated, then jerked his head in a nod.

"Go ahead and pick 'em up. I suppose at this point, I either trust you or I don't, Mr. Jensen."

"I'm glad you decided in favor of trusting me, Your Honor," Luke said as he picked up the Remingtons and slid them into their holsters. He sheathed the knife as well, tucked away the derringer, and continued, "I just want to see justice done."

He didn't add that finding out the location of all the loot Judd Tyler had hidden was riding on the outcome of this affair as well. Luke already had some ideas about that percolating in the back of his brain . . .

Keller opened the door and ushered Luke into the closet. Some boxes stacked on one side took up most of the space, but Luke still had enough room to squeeze in. The box on top of the stack was open. He saw books inside it and suspected the other boxes were filled with books as well.

Judge Keller was a man with a great love for the printed word, Luke thought, much like himself. Under different circumstances Luke would have enjoyed looking through the boxes and seeing what sort of volumes the judge owned.

"I'll leave the door open a crack," Keller said. "That way you'll know what's going on."

He turned away from the door as the swift patter of footsteps announced that Mrs. Keller had returned. She came into the study and whispered, "Clarence, it's Sheriff Axtell —"

Before Mrs. Keller could say anything else, a heavy footstep sounded and a man's voice said, "Sorry to bother you so late, Judge. I wouldn't have if I hadn't seen that your lamps are still burning."

Luke used his left hand to take off his hat, then leaned forward enough to peer through the inch-wide gap Keller had left when he pushed the door up.

"What is it, Sheriff?" the judge asked. "Some trouble, I expect, or else you wouldn't be here at this hour."

"I wanted to warn you. Judd Tyler has been spotted not far from town."

Axtell moved forward as he spoke, enough that Luke could see him through the narrow opening. The sheriff was a middle-aged man, tall and burly like a bear, with thinning fair hair and a face that looked like it had been hacked out from a slab of pale gray stone. He held his hat in one hand as a show of respect for the judge, but a mocking glitter lurked in his piggish eyes.

Keller stood beside the desk and asked, "Why would you feel the need to warn me about this matter, Sheriff? Tyler is no threat to me."

"He might be," Axtell said. "He knows you're the only judge in these parts. Maybe he figures if he was to kill you, he couldn't be put on trial for killing the Montgomery girl."

"I thought he was in custody."

"He was . . . but it was some no-account bounty hunter who was bringing him up here from Wyoming. The fella could have decided to work with Tyler instead of turning him in. There's no tellin' what Tyler might have promised him."

"That seems unlikely."

Axtell's brawny shoulders rose and fell.

"You can't tell what a bounty hunter will do. Most of 'em are just one step from being outlaws themselves."

Luke knew what Axtell was doing. The sheriff was laying the groundwork for killing both him and Tyler by establishing the suspicion that they were working together. That way Axtell and his deputies could gun them down with impunity. Adding that made-up threat to the judge just strengthened his case for killing Luke and Tyler.

For a long moment, Keller didn't say anything. Luke couldn't help but wonder what the judge was thinking. If Keller decided he didn't believe in Tyler's innocence after all, this would be a perfect opportunity for him to tell Axtell that Luke was right behind the door. That wouldn't land Tyler, but killing or capturing Luke would deprive Tyler of his only ally.

It would give Axtell a chance to put Luke out of the way, too. Knowing that, Luke wrapped the fingers of his right hand around an ivory-handled gun butt. He was ready to kick the door open and throw down on Axtell if he had to.

"Well, I'm not worried about Tyler or anyone who might be with him," Judge Keller said in a firm voice. "They wouldn't dare harm me."

"I sure hope you're right, Judge," Axtell said. "My deputies and I will do our best to make sure those varmints don't get anywhere close to you."

"Thank you, Sheriff," Keller said, playing along like he believed Axtell's lies.

"I'm gonna put a couple of deputies on guard outside your house, just in case."

"That's not necessary —"

"Better safe than sorry," Axtell said. "Good night, Judge. Ma'am."

"Good night, Sheriff," Mrs. Keller said. Her voice was a little frosty, but Axtell either didn't notice or more likely didn't care what the judge's wife thought of him.

Luke listened to the heavy steps fade as the crooked lawman left the house.

The closet door swung open. Keller stood there with a worried frown on his face.

"I suppose you heard everything the sheriff had to say."

"Yeah," Luke said. "None of it was good, or true, either."

"Except the part about putting deputies

outside the house." Keller stroked his chin. "That was true. He doesn't want Tyler reaching me, not out of any concern for my life, but because he's afraid of what Tyler might tell me. What you *already* told me, although Axtell doesn't know that."

"Yeah, that's the way I figure it, too."

Mrs. Keller said, "If no one else can get in, that means you can't get *out*, Mr. Jensen."

"I'll have to find a way, not only out, but back in again with Tyler."

"You'll be risking your life," the judge told him.

"Won't be the first time," Luke said.

Mrs. Keller turned to her husband and said, "Clarence, what about the cellar?"

The judge snapped his fingers and nodded.

"Of course. An excellent idea, my dear." He turned to Luke. "Twenty years ago, when we built this house, the Indians still represented quite a threat, considerably more than they do today. So I decided it would be a good idea for us to have a means of escape if we were ever trapped here in the house. There's a tunnel that runs from the cellar out to the shed."

"And that's where I left my horse," Luke said. "If any of Axtell's deputies start prowling around, they'll find it and know something's up. I need to get out of here as quickly as I can before that happens."

"I'll show you the tunnel," Keller said, nodding. "I just hope it hasn't fallen in. I haven't checked on it for a long time. There's been no need. The savages haven't bothered us." He grunted, then added, "Although I suppose savages will always be with us in one form or another. In this case most of them are wearing badges, or the veneer of wealth and power."

The judge held up a lantern as he led Luke down a flight of wooden stairs into a cellar with earthen walls. A door in the kitchen opened onto the stairs. When they reached the bottom, Luke looked around and saw shelves where glass jars full of preserved vegetables sat.

"My wife enjoys having a garden and putting up food," Keller said. "We don't eat most of it, but it gives her something to do. There's a bin over there full of potatoes, and another of corn. And there's the tunnel."

It was a dark, cobweb-draped opening with no door, definitely uninviting as it loomed on the other side of the cellar. As Keller approached with the lantern, though, the light spread into the tunnel, which was shored up with beams much like a mine shaft. It wasn't very long, since it only had to reach the shed behind the house. Luke could see all the way to the other end and was relieved the tunnel seemed to be intact.

"I appreciate all your help, Your Honor," he told Keller.

"If it clears the name of an innocent man and is responsible for the guilty party being brought to justice, the risk is well worth it. I'll stay here with the lantern, Mr. Jensen, so you can see where you're going."

"Where does the tunnel come up in the shed?"

"There's a trapdoor in the tack room. It has some empty grain sacks thrown on top of it so the door isn't visible, but they won't be any trouble to move aside."

"I'll bring Tyler back this way."

"I'll be waiting for you in the kitchen," Keller said. "With that Henry rifle, just in case someone else comes out of the tunnel."

Luke shook hands with the older man, then brushed the cobwebs aside and stepped through the opening. He had never been fond of being underground, although it didn't bother him enough to keep him from going wherever he needed to go, as in this case. He strode quickly along the tunnel until he reached a ladder built into the wall.

The judge was right: it wasn't difficult to raise the trapdoor at the top of the ladder. The grain sacks concealed it but didn't weigh much. Luke climbed out and then lowered the trapdoor carefully enough it didn't make a sound as he closed it. He kicked the burlap sacks back over it.

The inside of the tack room was so dark he had to fumble around for a moment before he found the door and stepped out into the shed. Enough light from the moon and stars came in for him to see the stall to his right where the buggy horse stood swishing its tail. The judge's buggy was parked to Luke's left. The shed was open across the front.

Luke stood beside one of the beams holding up the roof and drew a revolver. The last thing he wanted right now was gunplay, but he would shoot his way out of here if he had to. He didn't know if Sheriff Axtell had already posted deputies around the judge's house or if the lawman was just getting to that now. Either way, there was no time to waste.

He listened intently for several seconds. Not hearing anything, Luke knew he had to risk moving. He stepped out and swung around to the side of the shed, quickly enough that he was only out in the open for a heartbeat before plunging back into shadow.

He heard a horse move around. This was where he had left the gray, and from the sound of it, the animal was still there. Luke eased along the wall until he saw the horse's dark bulk. The gray was calm, which meant no one had come poking around. At least, Luke hoped that was the case.

He holstered the Remington, found the reins where he had tied them to a small bush, and was about to step up into the saddle when a figure stepped around the corner of the shed. A man's suspicious voice said, "Hey, is somebody back here? Whoever's there, don't move, or I'll blow holes in you!"

CHAPTER 37

Luke's brain worked with lightning speed. He stepped away from the horse and moved toward the man who had just accosted him, saying in an angry growl, "Damn it, what are you doing back here? The sheriff told *me* to stand guard out here by the shed."

Moonlight reflected on the gun in the man's hand. Luke's quick reaction confused him, though, so he lowered the gun and stepped forward.

"Who's that? That you, Charlie?"

Luke grunted and took a step, too, which brought him within reach of the man. The silvery light shone on the badge pinned to the deputy's vest, as well as glinting from the gun barrel.

"I swear," the man went on, "the right hand never knows what the left —"

Before he could finish the old saying, Luke's right fist came up and shot out to crash into the man's jaw. The blow had all of Luke's considerable strength behind it and landed solidly. The deputy's chin snapped to the side, and his knees unhinged.

He dropped like a rock, already out cold when he hit the ground.

For a second, Luke massaged his right hand with his left. He hated to hit anybody like that with his primary gun hand, but he hadn't had time to do anything except strike swiftly, with enough force to knock his enemy unconscious.

Luke stooped, picked up the gun the man had dropped, and stuck it behind his belt. He got hold of the deputy under the arms and dragged his limp body into the shed. When he reached the tack room, he kicked the grain sacks aside, lifted the trapdoor, and lowered the deputy feet-first through the opening before dropping him.

The man landed with a dull thud at the bottom of the ladder and collapsed into a senseless heap.

Luke descended quickly, taking one of the burlap bags with him. He took out his knife to cut the bag into strips, then used them to tie the deputy's hands and feet and gag him. The man was showing signs of coming around, but there was nothing he could do now. Trussed up like that, he was helpless.

Luke dragged him to the side of the tunnel and left him there. Chances were, the deputy wouldn't be missed for a while, and even if he was, it was unlikely any of Axtell's men knew about this old tunnel from the judge's house to the shed. The fellow would be uncomfortable but all right until Luke came back to free him or sent someone to do the job.

And if nobody ever came back, Luke figured the deputy could work his way loose eventually. It might take him a day or two, but he wouldn't die in that time.

Luke climbed back up the ladder and replaced the other sacks. This time when he left the shed, he didn't encounter anyone else, so he was able to untie the gray and lead the horse away from the shed. He didn't mount up and urge the gray into a run until he was several hundred yards from the judge's house and the edge of town.

Then he headed for the box canyon where he had left Judd Tyler without wasting any time.

Luke's innate sense of direction once again came in handy. He was able to retrace his trail without much trouble, and the time was still a little shy of midnight when he reached the canyon. Knowing that Tyler might be standing guard just inside the entrance, he called out, "It's me."

"Come ahead, Luke," Tyler replied.

Luke was cautious as he rode into the canyon. If some of Axtell's killer deputies had found the hideout — as unlikely as that seemed — they might be using Tyler as bait to trap him, too. Luke figured if that had happened, Tyler would try to find some way to warn him, as he had in the past, but anything was possible.

So being careful was a lot better than a bullet out of the dark.

In this case, however, the concern turned out not to be necessary. With Luke's Winchester cradled in his arms, Tyler met the bounty hunter where the passage widened out into the hidden canyon.

"What happened?" Tyler asked before Luke could even get off the horse. "Were you able to talk to Judge Keller?"

"I did," Luke said as he swung down from the saddle. "I talked to both the judge and his wife."

"They're mighty fine people."

"That's the impression I got, as well. I don't know if the judge believes your story, but I think Mrs. Keller does."

"I'm not surprised," Tyler said. "She would've mother-henned me as much as I'd let her." He sighed. "Maybe I should have.

Things might've turned out a whole heap different."

"Dwelling on the past won't do us any good. Let's just concentrate on the future, and the first step is the trial. The judge has agreed to hold it tomorrow morning, so we need to get back to White Fork tonight."

Tyler let out a low whistle of admiration and said, "Man, you don't mess around once you start getting things done, do you?"

"I don't believe in wasting time," Luke said. "Saddle up that pony. You're going to spend what's left of the night at the Keller house."

"Axtell's bound to have guards out," Tyler said. Luke could hear the worry in the young man's voice even though in the stygian gloom of the canyon he couldn't see the frown on Tyler's face.

"The sheriff's already posted guards around the judge's house. He's making it sound like you want to kill Keller so he'll have a good excuse for gunning us both down if he or his men get the chance."

"What? I wouldn't hurt a hair on that old man's head!"

"The judge knows that, and so does Mrs. Keller."

"But how are we gonna get past the guards?"

"I know a way," Luke said. "How do you feel about being underground?"

"As long as it's not six feet deep in a grave, I don't reckon I mind."

The moon had set by the time they reached the settlement. Luke was counting on the darkness to help them reach the judge's house without being spotted.

He reined in while they were still half a mile away and said, "We'd better leave the horses here. We don't want any of Axtell's men stumbling over them. Even this far out, there's a chance of that, but we'll have to risk it."

"I purely do hate to walk any time I don't have to," Tyler said with a sigh, expressing the true Westerner's attitude about being afoot. "But I reckon you're right."

They dismounted, stripped the saddles from the horses, and picketed the animals where there was some graze. Then they started toward the judge's house.

"I hope you know where you're goin'," Tyler muttered. "I can't see a blasted thing."

"Which means they'll be a lot less likely to see you," Luke said.

He led Tyler toward the shed, stopping frequently to listen. No one seemed to be prowling around in the darkness except the two of them.

They reached the shed without incident. Luke moved the sacks and lifted the trapdoor.

"There's a ladder here, like I told you," he said. He had explained to Tyler about the tunnel while they were riding to White Fork from the box canyon. "You'll have to work your way down by feel. Once you're in the tunnel, be careful not to trip over the deputy who's tied up down there. I don't think he can do anything, bound like he is, but it's probably best to avoid him anyway."

"You sure do get yourself in some mighty strange circumstances, Luke."

"Yes, that thought has crossed my mind as well. Let's go."

Tyler went down the ladder first. When he called back up softly to let Luke know he'd reached the tunnel, Luke descended, too. He heard a muffled noise and realized it came from the prisoner he had left here earlier.

Tyler chuckled and said, "Sounds like that fella's cussin' you out pretty good."

"I wouldn't doubt it, but that's all he can do. Although maybe I should tap him over the head with a gun butt, just to make sure he stays quiet if he were to work that gag loose."

The incoherent cursing stopped.

Luke found Tyler's arm in the darkness and urged him toward the basement underneath Keller's house. He slipped one of the Remingtons from its holster, bent over, and grabbed the deputy's shirt collar. The man knew what was coming and tried to writhe out of Luke's grip, but Luke struck swiftly and surely. The gun butt thudded home, and the prisoner went limp again.

Luke checked the bonds and the gag and found them still secure. A few more hours and it wouldn't matter, he thought. The eastern sky had held a faint tinge of gray when he and Tyler got here, so dawn wasn't too far away.

Keeping his left fingers brushing the tunnel wall on that side, Luke knew when he reached the basement. He felt broken cobwebs brush against his face, too. Knowing it was safe now, he fished a lucifer from his shirt pocket and snapped it to life with his thumbnail.

Tyler winced from the sudden light and said, "Warn an *hombre* next time, why don't you?"

The basement looked just like it had when Luke saw it a few hours earlier. He pointed to the stairs and said, "That leads up to the kitchen. Be careful when you go out. Judge

Keller's liable to be sitting there with a Henry rifle across his knees. We don't want to spook him."

"He'll hear us coming up the stairs, won't he?"

"He will if he's awake, but he might have dozed off."

"Yeah, he's not as young as he used to be, I reckon, and it's pretty late. I'll stomp pretty hard."

"You do that," Luke said.

They went up the stairs, Tyler making plenty of clattering racket as promised. When he swung open the door and he and Luke stepped out into the kitchen, the judge was standing beside the stove pouring coffee in three cups. Keller still wore his dressing gown and had the Henry tucked under his left arm.

"Figured it was you boys," he said. "Either that, or a herd of buffalo was coming up from my basement."

Tyler grinned and said, "Howdy, Judge. It's good to see you again."

Keller *harummphed* and replied, "I wish I could say the same, young man. Or that the circumstances were different, anyway."

Luke said, "Your Honor, I need to tell you that one of Axtell's deputies is tied up down in that tunnel. I ran into him on my way out earlier and left him there."

"Good Lord, Jensen! If this turns out badly, you're putting me in a position where I'll likely be thrown off the bench."

Tyler said, "If this turns out badly, Your Honor, I'll wind up either full of lead or twistin' in the breeze at the end of a rope. So I reckon I've got even more at stake than you do."

"Well, no doubt about that," Keller said, frowning.

"Anyway, Your Honor," Luke went on, "I figured I'd better tell you about that fellow, just in case something happens to me. I wouldn't want him to die of thirst down there."

"I don't want a corpse under my house, either. I'll see to it that he's set free, if it becomes necessary. In the meantime, I've been thinking about how we're going to proceed in the morning. Or, I should say, in a few hours." The judge gestured toward the coffee. "Let's sit down and figure this out."

CHAPTER 38

When they were all sitting around the kitchen table sipping the strong black brew, Luke asked, "Where's your wife, Your Honor?"

"Mildred had to turn in," Keller said. "She wanted to stay up, but she was just too tired. None of us are as young as we used to be."

"I was just sayin' —" Tyler began, but Luke silenced him with a kick to the shin.

"Saying what?"

Tyler shook his head and said, "Never mind. How are we gonna get to the court-house without Axtell or some of his men spotting us?"

"I can go to the courthouse any time I want to. They're not watching me. They won't pay any attention if I drive up to the rear door in my buggy. I thought you could ride behind the seat, under a blanket, Judd, and then we'll whisk you inside so you'll be

410

safe in my courtroom before anyone knows you're there."

"And there's nothing stopping me from simply walking up the street to the courthouse," Luke said. "Axtell and his men probably don't know what I look like, so if I'm not with you, there's a good chance they won't recognize me."

Tyler thought about it and nodded. He said, "Yeah, it sounds like it ought to work. The biggest risk will be in the few seconds it takes to get from the buggy to inside the courthouse."

Luke said, "I'll leave here first and be in position to cover you if necessary. I don't think it will be, though. I believe we stand a good chance of taking Axtell by surprise."

"He's gonna be surprised, all right. And so are Spence and his pa. When the trial's over, you're gonna need to issue an arrest warrant for Spence, Your Honor, but I don't think Axtell will carry it out."

"If that turns out to be the case — and that's a big *if,* I'll remind you, I can declare an emergency, remove Sheriff Axtell from office, and appoint an acting sheriff to uphold the law. Perhaps . . . you, Mr. Jensen?"

"Me?" Luke said. "I've never worn a badge."

"There's always a first time for every-thing."

"Well, no offense, Your Honor, but I hope it doesn't come to that."

Tyler said, "It'll come to that, or worse, mark my words. Manfred and Axtell aren't gonna let anything happen to Spence. Not without putting up a fight."

Keller cleared his throat and said, "All of this, of course, depends entirely on the evidence you claim to have, young man. I don't suppose you'd care to tell me what it is."

"Now, Judge," Tyler said with a grin, "that wouldn't be legal and proper-like, would it? Doesn't all the evidence have to be pre-sented in court?"

Keller scowled and said, "No one knows the law better than a reprobate."

"Sounds like one of your quotes, Luke."

"I'll leave matters of jurisprudence to you two," Luke said as he picked up his coffee cup. "It's been a long night, and morning will be here before you know it."

Luke got a few odd looks as he walked toward the courthouse at the north end of White Fork's Main Street, but he assumed that was because the townspeople he passed didn't know who he was. Folks who lived in these western settlements were always interested in strangers.

He didn't think any of Axtell's deputies he had encountered during the dangerous trek from Bent Creek had gotten a good enough look at him to have passed on his description, but he couldn't be certain of that. He remained alert, especially when he saw anybody wearing a badge. Luke passed a couple of them during his walk to the courthouse, but he didn't see Sheriff Gus Axtell himself.

The sheriff's office was in a smaller stone building next to the courthouse, Judge Keller had told him while they were waiting for the sun to come up. The same building housed the jail. So the closer Luke came to the courthouse, the greater the odds of him running into Axtell.

If any of the crooked lawmen came after him, he would find some cover and hole up, keeping their attention on him instead of what was going on in Judge Keller's courtroom. That might not be a bad thing, but it would be risky. Luke might wind up dead before he ever knew the outcome of the trial.

He reached the courthouse a few minutes later. The hour was still fairly early, but most of the businesses in town appeared to be open and quite a few people were on the street. That was good, because Keller would need to empanel a jury, and the sooner the better.

Luke circled the courthouse, which sat in the middle of a rather sparse lawn with some tired-looking cottonwood trees around it. The rear of the building was deserted.

A few minutes later, he spotted a buggy rolling toward the courthouse. It was easy to recognize the burly, black-suited figure of the judge with his white mustache.

Keller hauled back on the reins and brought the vehicle to a halt near the stone steps that led up to the courthouse's rear door. He nodded to Luke and asked, "Any sign of trouble?"

Luke shook his head and said, "I don't think Axtell's expecting us to be right under his nose like this."

The judge nodded. He spoke over his shoulder, saying, "All right, Mr. Tyler. You can come out now, and please be quick about it."

Tyler pushed aside an old wool blanket bundled up behind the seat and stepped to the ground next to the buggy. He looked scared, Luke thought, and he couldn't blame the young man for that.

For Tyler, everything depended on what happened in the next couple of hours. Keller had made it clear that this was a real trial. If Tyler's story and the evidence he claimed to possess didn't convince the jury and he was found guilty of murdering Rachel Montgomery, Keller would pass sentence on him as the law required.

Tyler would hang by the neck until dead.

Luke's head turned from side to side as he followed Keller and Tyler up the steps. He watched all around them, but White Fork was still quiet and peaceful this morning.

"I'm much obliged to Mrs. Keller for fixing that good breakfast for us," Tyler said as they went inside. "You know what they say about the condemned man gettin' a hearty last meal."

"You're not condemned yet," Keller said. "Innocent until proven guilty is still the law of the land, and it's sure not going to change in my courtroom."

The three of them started along a hallway, their footsteps echoing from its high ceiling. Ahead of them, a door opened. Luke's hand hovered near a gun butt, but the man who stepped out into the corridor didn't appear to be a threat. He was short, slight, wore spectacles, and possessed a head of brown hair that seemed to have a mind of its own. He was trying to pat it down as he noticed the three men coming toward him. He stopped what he was doing and stared instead.

"It's all right, Eustace," Judge Keller said.

"But . . . but that's Judd Tyler!"

"I know. We're going to have a trial this morning. I realize it's a bit irregular, but we have to seize the opportunity." Keller looked at Luke and Tyler and added, "My court clerk, gentlemen, Eustace Adams."

"Shoot, I remember Eustace," Tyler said. "We were in school at the same time, what little I actually went to school. You're a couple years older than me, aren't you, Eustace?"

The clerk's mouth was still opening and closing in surprise. He didn't answer Tyler's question.

Keller beckoned him closer and said, "Eustace, Mr. Tyler has placed himself in my custody and will stand trial immediately. I have a very important job for you."

Eustace made a visible effort to gather his wits about him and nodded.

"Of course, Your Honor," he said. "Whatever you need."

"I want you to go along the street and find fifteen or twenty men who are honest, trustworthy citizens of White Fork. Tell them I need them to come up here right away, but don't let on what it's about."

"You're putting together a jury."

"That's right. You'll need to fetch Carson Delahanty, too. Can you do that?"

Eustace's head bobbed up and down. He said, "Certainly. What about a bailiff? One of Sheriff Axtell's deputies usually —"

"No, don't say anything to the sheriff or any of his men. Mr. Jensen here will serve as bailiff."

"You're just determined to make me official in one capacity or another, aren't you?" Luke asked.

"There's only so far I'll bend the law. We'll follow regular court procedure."

"All right," Luke said, nodding. "I reckon I can be a bailiff, for a little while, anyway."

Eustace hurried out of the building while Keller ushered Luke and Tyler through a pair of double doors into the courtroom. It was a typical scene of frontier jurisprudence with the judge's bench at the front of the room, a couple of plain tables for the defense and prosecution, and chairs for the spectators behind a railing. The jury box was to the right of the bench. One wall had a picture of the president on it.

The only other decoration, oddly enough, was a stuffed moose head hanging on the opposite wall. That was appropriate, Luke thought, because in his opinion most politicians' heads were full of sawdust, too.

"Who's this fellow Delahanty you sent Eustace after?" Luke asked.

"The district attorney. Can't have a trial without a prosecutor, you know." Keller looked at Tyler. "Do you want me to see if I can rustle up one of the lawyers in town for you?"

"There are only three that I know of," Tyler said. "One of 'em works for Manfred Douglas, one of them is eighty years old and might doze off during a trial, and the other hasn't been sober as far back as I can remember. I reckon I'll represent myself."

"There's a saying about how a man who serves as his own lawyer has a fool for a client."

"I'll take my chances, Your Honor. It's a pretty simple case. The jury's either going to believe me . . . or else they'll hang me."

CHAPTER 39

Judge Keller told Luke and Tyler to wait in his chambers, out of sight until court was actually in session. Luke wasn't fond of the idea of not knowing what was going on, but he understood the judge's reasoning. Keller wanted to keep the defendant out of sight for as long as possible.

"Are you going to tell the prosecutor what's about to happen?" Luke asked.

"I have no choice." Keller grimaced slightly. "And once the trial is under way, Carson Delahanty will do everything he can to drag it out. The prosecution gets to present its case first, you know. I can't get around that."

"Let me guess. Delahanty is friends with Manfred Douglas."

"Every elected official in the county owes a debt to Douglas except me," Keller said. "I was here before him. All the other old-timers have been swept out."

Tyler said, "I'm glad you're as stubborn as you are, Judge."

Keller smiled wryly and said, "This may be my last big case. I've had about enough. This could be my chance to go out on a high note."

The judge went back out into the courtroom, leaving Luke and Tyler in his chambers to wait. Or to fidget, in Tyler's case. He couldn't keep still. Luke would have told him to take it easy, but he didn't figure it would do any good. Tyler had too much riding on this.

Time dragged by. Tyler paced back and forth, stopping occasionally to part the curtains over the room's single window and peer out.

Finally he said, "What's taking so long? You don't reckon the judge has double-crossed us, do you, Luke? How long does it take to round up a jury?"

"I'm sure Judge Keller is moving things along as quickly as possible," Luke said. He fished his turnip watch out of his pocket and flipped it open. "It really hasn't been as long as it probably seems to you."

"Well, it's been long enough, that's for damn —"

The door opened. Keller strode into the room. A frown creased his forehead.

"All right, bailiff," he said to Luke. "Escort the prisoner into the courtroom and seat him at the defense table."

"And how will I know which one that is?" Luke asked.

"There'll be a snake in a brown tweed suit at the other one."

"Ah," Luke said. "The Honorable Carson Delahanty, Esquire."

"That would be the snake in question."

Luke took off his hat and dropped it on a chair, then held out his hand toward Tyler.

"Come on, Judd. Time to face a jury of your peers."

Tyler was pale now under his tan. He swallowed hard.

"I'm sorta startin' to wish I'd just kept running," he said.

"No, this is for the best," Keller said. "You'll get a fair trial, son, and if you're found innocent, all that weight will lift off your shoulders."

"Like you said earlier, Judge, that's a mighty big *if.*"

Keller raised a finger and said, "One more thing, Mr. Jensen . . . Sheriff Axtell is out there. I don't know how he got wind that something's going on. Probably heard about Eustace rounding up men and thought it sounded like a trial was about to take place.

But he's there, so you should watch out for him."

"I saw him in your study last night, Your Honor," Luke said. "I'll know him when I see him."

Tyler said, "He's liable to try to shoot me."

Keller shook his head.

"Not in my courtroom. He wouldn't dare."

"I'd like to believe that you're right, Your Honor," Luke said, "but I'm not sure Sheriff Axtell respects the sanctity of the court as much as you do."

"Well, if you have to shoot him, all hell's liable to break loose, so try to avoid that if you can."

With a grim smile, Luke nodded, then motioned again for Tyler to come with him.

The day of reckoning was at hand.

Word had gotten around White Fork that something was going on. More than the fifteen or twenty men Eustace had summoned for possible jury duty had crowded into the courtroom. All the chairs were full, and men stood along the rear and side walls, too, Luke saw as he led Tyler into the room.

He spotted Sheriff Axtell right away. The crooked lawman was standing at one of the tables with a man who was thin almost to the point of gauntness. The man had a high forehead and a Van Dyke beard and wore an expensive frock coat. Luke knew he had to be Carson Delahanty, the prosecutor.

Axtell and Delahanty were talking animatedly, and both of them appeared to be angry. Their conversation stopped abruptly as they turned their heads to glare at Luke and Tyler. Luke saw the way Axtell's right arm tensed. The sheriff wanted to draw his gun and put a bullet through Tyler, but all the witnesses in the room prevented him from doing so.

Luke took Tyler to the defense table and sat him down.

"Better be thinking about what you're going to say once you get up there on the witness stand," Luke told him quietly. "You'll have to question yourself, I suppose."

"Maybe I should have had you be my lawyer," Tyler said.

Luke grunted and said, "All you people seem to have forgotten that I'm just a bounty hunter. A simple man who's only interested in blood money, remember?"

"I reckon there's a lot more to you than that, Luke. It just took me a while to realize it."

Luke shook his head and went back to stand next to the door into Judge Keller's chambers. He waited for the judge to step out, and when Keller emerged, now wearing the long black robe of his office, Luke called, "All rise."

Everyone stood while Keller went to the chair behind the bench. He picked up the gavel, rapped it sharply, and said, "This court is now in session. Sit down."

Luke remained standing next to the bench. Carson Delahanty stayed on his feet, too. The prosecutor said in the deep, sonorous voice of a career politician — and windbag — "Your Honor, this is highly irregular. I received no advance notice that there would be any court proceedings today."

"Our Constitution guarantees a man the right to a speedy trial, Mr. Delahanty," Keller said. "I apologize for any inconvenience, but given the sensational nature of the case at hand, I thought it best to proceed as swiftly as possible. The court clerk will read the charge."

Eustace was sitting at a small desk at the other end of the bench, not far from the witness stand. He said, "The Territory of Montana, in the matter of the death of Miss Rachel Montgomery, charges Judd Tyler with murder."

Even though everyone in the room knew

what was going on, hearing it in words like that caused a murmur to go through the crowd. Keller waited a moment but didn't have to resort to using his gavel to quiet the room. He said, "Does the prosecution wish to proceed with this charge, Mr. Delahanty?"

Hooking his thumbs in his vest, Delahanty said, "It most emphatically does, Your Honor, but I'd like to move for a delay —"

"Denied," the judge said, not letting Delahanty finish his motion. "We'll proceed. The first order of business is to empanel a jury." Keller looked at the men in the first couple of rows of chairs and rattled off a dozen names. Then he turned his attention to Delahanty again and asked, "Does the prosecution object to any of these potential jurors?"

Frowning, Delahanty nodded toward two of the men and repeated their names.

"Move to strike these two jurors for cause."

"And that would be?"

"They're known to have been friendly with the defendant."

"Very well." Keller spoke to the men in question. "You're excused. You can leave or stay to watch the trial."

One of the men said, "We'll stay if that's

all right with you, Your Honor. Not likely there'll be a better show in White Fork today."

That brought a ripple of laughter from the crowd. This time Keller reached for his gavel, but everyone quieted down before he picked it up.

He looked at Tyler and asked, "Does the defendant have any objection to any of the remaining jurors?"

"Nope, they're fine with me, Your Honor," Tyler said.

"Very well, then." Keller called out two more names, then looked at Delahanty and Tyler, each of whom nodded in turn. "Members of the jury, please take your seats and be sworn in. Eustace . . ."

"Yes, Your Honor," the court clerk said as he stood up. He waited until the jury had taken their seats in the chairs behind another railing that formed the "jury box," then administered the oath to them.

This was moving right along at a good clip, Luke thought.

Then the doors at the back of the courtroom opened and a man and a woman came in. They were middle-aged, but grief had made them look older. The man was slightly bent in his sober black suit. The woman wore black as well, and a hat with a veil that

426

covered her face.

Luke figured he was looking at Reverend and Mrs. Montgomery, the parents of the murdered girl. The way a couple of men in the front row of spectator seats stood up and offered their chairs to the newcomers seemed to confirm that hunch.

So did the stricken expression on Judd Tyler's face as he looked at them. He swallowed hard and turned back toward the front of the courtroom.

Judge Keller waited for the hubbub to die down, then said, "Mr. Delahanty, since you're representing the prosecution, you may now make your opening statement, if you have one."

"Oh, yes, Your Honor, I have one," Delahanty said. "I have one, indeed." He strode out into the open area between the tables and the judge's bench and proceeded to harangue Tyler for the next quarter of an hour, spewing out phrases like "heinous crime" and "wanton slaughter," calling Tyler "a crazed, brutal animal," and generally painting as dark a picture as he could. Luke saw the pallor that crept over Tyler's face as Delahanty described in graphic terms how Rachel was killed. Mrs. Montgomery bent forward in her chair, and her husband put his arm around her trembling shoulders.

Luke was damned glad when the prosecutor concluded his thunderous denunciation and took his seat. Judge Keller, who appeared a little shaken himself, looked over at Tyler and said, "Does the defendant wish to make an opening statement?"

Delahanty shot back to his feet before Tyler could say anything.

"Is the defendant represented by counsel, Your Honor?"

Tyler scraped his chair back, rose to his feet, and said, "I can speak for myself."

"Go ahead," Keller said, nodding.

"Can I talk to the jury?"

Keller indicated with a wave of a hand that he could.

Tyler walked over to the jury box, looked at the men sitting there, and said, "I reckon all you fellas know me, or know who I am, anyway. I admit I'm probably not the best citizen White Fork's ever seen. Far from it, in fact. But right here, right now, none of that matters. The only thing that's important is I didn't kill Rachel Montgomery. She was one of the finest ladies I've ever known, and I would have died myself before I'd ever harm a hair on her head."

At the prosecution table, Delahanty made a disgusted noise in his throat. Tyler looked around to glare at him, and the judge said,

"You've made your opening statement, counsel. Interrupt like that again and I'm liable to hold you in contempt of court."

"My apologies, Your Honor. I assure you, it's not the court that I'm in contempt of."

"Mr. Delahanty —"

The prosecutor held up his hands, palms out in surrender.

Tyler pointed at Delahanty and addressed the jurors again, saying, "You see, he doesn't believe me. But what he believes doesn't matter. The only thing that does . . . is what the twelve of you fellas believe. And I'm going to convince you that I didn't kill Rachel Montgomery." He started back toward the defense table, seeming not to see the skeptical expressions on the faces of several jurors. But then he stopped, looked back at them, and said, "You're going to believe I'm innocent because I know who the real killer is . . . and by the time this trial is over, you will, too."

Gus Axtell was standing near the doors. Luke saw the look of alarm that passed over the sheriff's face at Tyler's words. Axtell turned and left hurriedly.

Gone to make sure his master Manfred Douglas was on his way to town, Luke thought.

Tyler sat down, and Keller said to Delahanty, "The prosecution may now present its case."

CHAPTER 40

Judge Keller had warned them Delahanty probably would try to stretch out the trial, and that was exactly what the prosecutor did. He started by calling one of the deputies to the stand. The man had been the first peace officer on the scene the night of Rachel's murder, and he described in grim detail what he had found.

The local doctor came next, and even though he looked like he wished he was anywhere else, he answered Delahanty's questions about the condition of Rachel's body when he examined her later that night.

Delahanty called more witnesses, townspeople who had been at the church social that night and had seen Tyler there, talking to Rachel. Delahanty's questions slanted the answers they gave to make the whole thing sound more sinister, as if Tyler had been pestering Rachel and she didn't want to be around him.

Sitting at the defense table, Tyler just shook his head slowly. Luke thought the young man was doing an admirable job of keeping his emotions under control. He knew Tyler probably wanted to leap to his feet and shout out that things hadn't been the way they were making it sound at all.

After a while, Judge Keller said, "You seem to be covering the same ground with all these witnesses, Mr. Delahanty. Are you prepared to follow any new trails any time soon?"

"The prosecution should be allowed to present its case as it sees fit, Your Honor."

"Agreed, but the court's time is worth something, too."

Before Delahanty could proceed, the double doors at the back of the courtroom opened and several men strode in. The one in front was tall and rawboned, with a weathered face, hawk-like nose, thin mustache, and gray hair under his black Stetson. The man's arrogant, imperious attitude instantly told Luke that he was looking at Manfred Douglas.

Right behind Douglas was a younger version of him with dark hair and a face with more handsome but weaker features. That would be Spence, Luke thought. Father and son were both dressed in expensive clothing, a simple dark, Western-cut suit for Manfred, sharply creased denim trousers and a colorful shirt with pearl buttons for Spence.

The two men behind them wore range clothes and had the look of hardcases. Riders for the Circle M who had been hired more for their gun skills than their abilities as ranch hands.

As had happened when the Montgomerys came in, a couple of spectators immediately gave up their seats to Manfred and Spence Douglas.

Delahanty looked pleased as he said, "The prosecution calls Tom Borden, Your Honor."

One of Douglas's men came forward. He wasn't carrying a gun — no one in the courtroom was armed, at least openly, except Luke — but he looked like a threat anyway. Eustace swore him in, and Delahanty said, "Tell us about your role in the affairs of the night in question, Mr. Borden."

The witness didn't have to ask what night that was. Clearly, Douglas, his son, and the men who worked for him all knew exactly what was going on here before they'd ever walked into the courtroom.

Borden testified that he and some of the other Circle M riders had been in White Fork that night for the social, and after it was over, as they were leaving, they'd heard a commotion in the woods near the church.

"We figured we'd better take a look, and when we did, we ran smack into Judd Tyler, running away from the body of the Montgomery girl. Wasn't any doubt in our minds that he'd killed her, or else he wouldn't have been trying to get away. We did our best to corral him, but he gave us the slip."

"You're sure it was the defendant?"

"I got a good look at him," Borden said. He pointed at Tyler. "There he sits. He's the killer, not a doubt in my mind."

"Thank you." Delahanty smirked at Tyler and added, "Your witness."

So far, Tyler had declined every opportunity to cross-examine the witnesses. This time, however, he got to his feet. He walked toward the witness stand and asked, "Where did you run into me that night?"

"I just said, in the woods."

"In the woods themselves?"

"Well . . . right at the edge of 'em."

"And what's the first thing you did when you saw me?"

"I don't remember, exactly. Seems like I yelled for you to stop."

"What you said was that I'd killed the Montgomery girl."

"Maybe. What was I supposed to say?"

Tyler scratched just in front of his ear and asked, "How'd you know she was dead? You couldn't see her body from where you were, could you?"

"Well . . . well, I guess I must've been able to, since I knew you'd killed her."

"You think so? You want to wait until it gets dark tonight, and then we'll all go out there and stand where you say we were and find out just how far somebody can see into the shadows under those trees?"

Delahanty stood up and said, "Objection, Your Honor. Such an experiment is irrelevant."

Tyler said, "Seems to me like it ties right in with what Borden just testified to, Your Honor."

"Objection overruled, Mr. Delahanty," Keller said. "Sit down."

"Well, how about it?" Tyler said. "You want to meet out there at the edge of the woods tonight so we can figure this out?"

"You'll be at the end of a hangrope by then!" Borden said. "Anyway, all these words don't change the facts. You killed that girl. I must've been able to tell that, or I wouldn't have said it. How else would I have known what was goin' on?"

Tyler turned his head and looked for a second at Spence Douglas before he said,

"That's a mighty good question. Unless you want to answer it for us, I don't have anything else."

Luke saw that several of the jurors were frowning now. Delahanty had overplayed his hand by having Borden testify without making sure every detail of what he was going to say was nailed down. Tyler had managed to raise some doubt in the minds of at least a few of the jurors.

Borden stepped down, and Keller asked, "Does the prosecution have any more witnesses?"

"The prosecution calls Reverend Wilfred Montgomery, Your Honor."

Tyler stood up and said, "Blast it, you don't have to do that! The preacher and his wife had already gone home. They weren't anywhere around when . . . when . . ."

"Your Honor?" Delahanty said.

Keller sighed and said, "Sit down, Mr. Tyler. The prosecution has called Reverend Montgomery, and I see no legal reason to disallow it."

The reverend was Delahanty's emotional hole card. Montgomery's highly visible grief might be enough to erase any doubts Tyler had created in the minds of the jurors.

But as Keller had said, there was no way to prevent the testimony, gut-wrenching though it might be.

If anything, the preacher's words were worse even than Luke expected. Clearly, his daughter's death had torn his heart out. Mrs. Montgomery began to sob as her husband described how they had gone to the doctor's house that night to view Rachel's body. Her crying intensified as the reverend talked about the agonizing hole her death had left in their lives.

Delahanty was less bombastic in his questioning this time. He didn't need showmanship now.

All he needed was a couple of grief-stricken parents, and he had them.

By the time Reverend Montgomery left the stand, nearly every man in the courtroom was looking at Judd Tyler like they were ready to go get a rope right then and there. Tyler had shaken his head mutely when asked if he had any questions for the preacher. That would have been futile, and Tyler knew it as well as Luke did.

"The prosecution rests, Your Honor," Delahanty said.

"Very well. You may present your case now, Mr. Tyler. Do you have any witnesses?"

Tyler got to his feet and said, "Only me, Your Honor. Am I allowed to call myself to the stand?"

Keller waved toward Eustace and said, "Go ahead and be sworn in."

When that formality was taken care of, Tyler sat down. The judge said to him, "Am I to understand that you want to tell your side of the story, Mr. Tyler?"

"That's right, Your Honor."

"And you're aware that the prosecution will have the right to cross-examine you?"

"Sure." Tyler smiled. "I reckon I can answer any questions Mr. Delahanty wants to ask me."

"We'll see about that," Delahanty said.

"That's enough," Keller said. "Confine your remarks to cross-examination, counselor." He nodded to Tyler. "Go ahead."

Luke had heard the story before, more than once, and it hadn't changed. It still had the ring of truth. But it was still simply Tyler's word against that of everyone else who had testified. Without any eyewitnesses or physical evidence, Tyler's conviction or acquittal would come down to whether the jury wanted to believe a young, admitted outlaw.

Luke kept waiting for Tyler to reveal whatever the evidence was he claimed to have, but Tyler just told his story straight through without adding anything to it.

When he was finished, Judge Keller said, "Would you like to cross-examine, Mr. Delahanty?"

Standing up and hooking his thumbs in his vest again, Delahanty said confidently, "I hardly need to ask any questions to discredit such a flimsy tissue of lies, Your Honor."

"I didn't ask for a closing statement, counselor."

"No questions." Delahanty sat down with a self-satisfied smile on his face.

Keller looked at Tyler and said, "I suppose you can step down, if there's nothing else."

Tyler stood up and started toward the defense table, then paused and said, "Actually, I think I would like to call a witness, Your Honor."

"It's your prerogative to do so."

"I'd like to call Spence Douglas."

It was Manfred who came to his feet, exclaiming, "This is outrageous. I won't have my son subjected to —"

"Spence is a grown man, and the defense has a right to call him as a witness," Keller said. "Get on up here, Spence."

Luke saw the frightened look in Spence's eyes. If he'd had any doubts about it before, he no longer did. Spence Douglas was guilty as hell, and Luke knew it.

Spence stood up and went hesitantly to the witness stand. When Eustace asked him if he swore to tell the truth, the whole truth, and nothing but the truth, he had to clear his throat a couple of times before he could say, "I do."

When Spence was sitting down, Tyler approached him and said, "You had words with Rachel Montgomery at the social that night, didn't you, Spence?"

"I spoke to her, yes. I wouldn't call it having words."

"That wasn't the first time you'd argued with her, either."

"I told you, we didn't argue."

Tyler ignored that and said, "You'd been after Rachel for quite a while, hadn't you?"

Spence glared at him and said, "I don't have to put up with your ugly implications, Tyler. I admired Miss Montgomery. She was a fine young woman."

"That why you called her a tease and even worse things? Remember, there are folks here who were at the social and probably heard what you had to say to her."

Spence leaned forward and clenched his hands into fists.

"Whatever was between Rachel Montgomery and me doesn't have anything to do

440

with you killing her. Everybody in White Fork knows what a no-account you are! Just like your worthless, booze hound of an old man!"

Keller rapped his gavel to quiet the ensuing muttering and murmuring in the room and said, "That's enough. The witness will confine himself to answering questions." He nodded to Tyler. "Proceed."

Tyler rubbed his chin and said, "You like those fancy shirts like that one you're wearing, don't you, Spence?"

Spence leaned back in the witness chair and frowned, clearly confused by the question.

"What? What do my shirts have to do with anything?"

"Well, I've seen for years how you like to dress nice." Tyler raised his right index finger and tapped it a couple of times against his lips. "You've got one, I recall, that's a bright blue, like the sky, and it has these turquoise and silver conchos on it . . . You know the one I'm talking about?"

Delahanty stood up and said, "Your Honor, this is totally irrelevant to the case."

"Not really, Your Honor," Tyler said.

Keller thought about it, then said, "Go ahead, Mr. Tyler, but I want to know how it connects, so don't waste the court's time."

"No, sir, I sure won't, if the witness will answer the question —"

"All right!" Spence burst out. "For God's sake, yes, I have a shirt like that. You've seen me wear it. Probably everybody in here has seen me wear it, even the judge!"

"Seems to me like you were wearing it the night of the social, weren't you?"

"What if I was?"

"Have you worn it since then?"

"No, it's missing one of the conchos, I lost it somewhere —"

Spence stopped short and turned pale. Luke fought off the impulse to smile as he finally understood what Tyler was after. He knew he wasn't the only one who had figured it out, because he saw Sheriff Axtell and several deputies crowding into the back of the courtroom, obviously ready for trouble. Manfred Douglas and his men were tense as well.

"You lost a concho somewhere," Tyler said. "Well, I think I may have found it." He slid a hand into his pocket and brought out a round, turquoise and silver decoration. "Is this it, Spence?"

"I . . . I . . ."

"Because this is the one Rachel Montgomery was clutching in her hand when I found her body, the night you killed her.

This is the one she tore off your shirt while you were choking her to death."

"I . . . I . . . That bitch! I never thought . . . I never would have hurt her if she'd just stopped fighting!"

Spence broke then, launching himself at Tyler from the witness chair, hands reaching out for Tyler's throat.

"I'll kill you, too!" Spence bellowed.

Behind the railing, Manfred Douglas shot to his feet. As Tyler and Spence fought, falling to the floor in front of the bench, Douglas shouted, "That bastard's trying to kill my son! Stop him! Shoot him!"

Axtell and the deputies surged forward, drawing their guns, eager to do murder in their real employer's behalf. Shouts and curses filled the courtroom as the spectators leaped and scrambled to get out of the line of fire. Luke stepped forward and reached for his Remingtons, and at the same time, Judge Keller brought an old percussion revolver from somewhere under the bench. Even Eustace yanked a pistol from a drawer in his desk.

The courtroom exploded in gunfire.

CHAPTER 41

Axtell was the closest to Tyler, so as Luke drew his guns he moved swiftly to intercept the sheriff. Axtell hesitated. The way the two young men were rolling around on the floor as they fought, a shot aimed at Tyler might well hit Spence instead.

So Axtell shifted his aim toward Luke and opened fire. Flame spouted from the lawman's gun. A slug whined past Luke's ear.

Luke triggered the Remingtons. Both .44 slugs hammered into Axtell's chest, bracketing the badge. Luke didn't like shooting a lawman, even a crooked one who didn't hesitate to stoop to murder, but since Judge Keller was trading shots with Axtell's deputies and so was Eustace, the court clerk, he figured no one was going to hold it against him.

Axtell went over backward, dropping his gun. Tom Borden dived forward, scooped it up, and snapped a shot at the judge, who rocked back from the bullet's impact. The next instant, Luke shot Borden in the head.

Keller might be wounded, but he wasn't out of the fight. His ancient cap and ball revolver boomed thunderously. One of Axtell's deputies spun off his feet as the judge's shot tore through him.

Eustace was bleeding from a bullet-torn left arm, but the gun in his right hand still spoke. He shot another deputy, who collapsed backward and scattered some of the spectators' chairs. Luke drilled another corrupt badge-toter who doubled over and toppled face-first over the railing behind the defense and prosecution tables.

Carson Delahanty was cowering under the prosecution table, both arms shielding his head as he tried to curl up in as small a ball as possible.

The blasts died away, although echoes of the gun-thunder continued to fill the courtroom for several long seconds after the shooting stopped. Some of the spectators were pressed against the walls on both sides of the room. Others had managed to flee out the open double doors.

Left standing in the front of the courtroom were Luke, Judge Keller, Eustace . . . and Manfred Douglas.

The rancher stood with clenched fists,

pale under his permanent tan and trembling with fury. Slowly, he lifted his hand and pointed at the judge.

"You! You're a murderer, Keller! I'll see that you hang for what you've done here today!"

All the color had washed out of Keller's face, too. He sank down into his chair, but he kept the percussion revolver leveled at Douglas.

"The only murderer here is your boy!" Keller thundered back. "Everybody in this room heard him admit to killing the Montgomery girl!" He finally put down the gun and picked up the gavel instead. As he slammed it down on the bench, he said, "The charge against Judd Tyler is dismissed!"

Meanwhile, Tyler still had his hands full with Spence Douglas. They wrestled and slugged at each other and rolled back and forth. Finally, Spence wound up on top. He locked his hands around Tyler's throat and started to squeeze.

"Is this . . . the way . . . you choked Rachel . . . to death?" Tyler forced out as he tried to pull Spence's hands loose.

"Shut up!" Spence shouted. "She had it coming, just like you, you piece of gutter trash! If that stupid sheriff and his deputies had just killed you like my father told them to, you never would've —"

Luke had heard enough. He stepped toward Spence, intending to slam the young man over the head with a gun and knock him out, but before he could strike, Manfred Douglas jerked a derringer from under his coat and fired. The bullet plucked at Luke's shirt along his ribs but didn't break the skin.

Douglas had another shot left in the derringer, though. Luke fired before Douglas could squeeze off the second round. The bullet caught the rancher in the chest and knocked him back a step. Douglas bumped into the chair where he'd been sitting. He sank onto it again, his eyes widening in shock and pain. His mouth opened and closed a couple of times before his arms fell loosely at his sides and his head sagged forward on his chest. He didn't move again.

The shots and the bullets whipping back and forth above his head had distracted Spence enough for Tyler to break free. Tyler's fist sledged into Spence's jaw and knocked him to the side. Tyler was gasping for air, but he didn't let that stop him from going after Spence. He planted a knee in the other man's belly and started hitting him in the face, again and again.

Tyler didn't stop until Eustace dragged

447

him off and said, "You don't want to kill him, Judd. If you do, we won't get to watch the son of a bitch hang for what he's done."

Luke had to smile. The mild-looking little court clerk was pretty fierce when he got his dander up.

Recalling that Judge Keller had been wounded, Luke swung around, pouched his irons, and hurried to see how bad the judge was hurt. As Luke pulled up the black robe, Keller said, "I'm all right, damn it."

"There's a considerable amount of blood, Your Honor."

"It looks worse than it is, I tell you. Did I say that court is adjourned?"

"No, you just dismissed the murder charge against Tyler."

"Well, then, court is adjourned!"

With that, the judge passed out and slumped forward over the bench.

It had taken a courtroom full of gunsmoke to accomplish it, but justice had been done.

The judge was a better jurist than he was a sawbones. The wound in his side was more serious than he claimed. The local doctor said that he would be laid up for a while, but with plenty of care — which he was sure to get from his wife — Keller would recover just fine, in the doc's opinion.

After the doctor examined him in the courtroom, Keller was coherent enough to appoint Luke acting sheriff, over Luke's strenuous objections. But with Gus Axtell and several of his deputies dead, along with Manfred Douglas, and the rest of the deputies having taken off for the tall and uncut as soon as they found out their payday was over, White Fork would be without any law if Luke refused.

"All right," he said, "but I won't wear a badge. I've had too many lawmen give me trouble to start packing a star now. And it's only until you can get a U.S. Marshal in here to restore law and order."

Luke's first official duty as acting sheriff was to lock up Spence Douglas. Eustace had been holding him at gunpoint, and the expression on the pistol-packing court clerk's face made it clear he would welcome an excuse to blow a few holes in the prisoner. A much abashed Carson Delahanty promised that Spence would be prosecuted for murder and would undoubtedly hang since there were several dozen witnesses to his confession.

The second thing Luke did as acting sheriff, after talking again with the judge, was to lock up Judd Tyler.

"What the hell!" Tyler said as Luke pushed

him in the cell across from Spence and slammed the door. "You can't do this, Luke!"

"There's a little matter of rustling and stagecoach robbery to deal with," Luke said. "And a cache of loot from those jobs."

"You think I'm gonna tell you where to find it now? You're loco!"

"If you've got any sense, you'll tell me. I just had a little talk with the judge, and we worked out a deal. You tell me where that money is, and I'll use it to make good for what you stole, with the people you stole from. You'll still have to do some jail time, more than likely, but maybe only a year or so. By then, those folks from the wagon train will be here and will have established farms and ranches in the area. I suspect Deborah Howard and her father would be glad to have some help on their homestead."

"Me? A sodbuster?"

"On the other hand, there'll be a new sheriff in office by then — an honest sheriff — and I'm sure he might be interested in hiring an honest young deputy who has some . . . experience, shall we say? . . . with lawbreakers."

"A deputy?" Tyler practically yelped. "You want me to be a *deputy*?"

"It's entirely up to you. But I think Miss

Howard would be more inclined to accept a proposal of marriage from a young man who had a decent job that's not illegal."

Tyler raked his fingers through his hair and then scrubbed his hands over his face. Finally, he said, "All right. I'll tell you where to find that loot, and I'll go along with whatever deal you and the judge worked out. But I want one thing in return."

"What's that?"

Tyler pointed across the cell block at Spence Douglas and said, "Don't leave me locked up in here with that . . . that . . . I can't even come up with a word bad enough for him!"

"I suppose we can arrange bail, as long as you give me your word you won't try to run again."

"And what if I do?"

"Then I'll track you down again," Luke said, "and you know how much hell breaks loose when I have to do that!"

The employees of Thorndike Press hope you have enjoyed this Large Print book. All our Thorndike, Wheeler, and Kennebec Large Print titles are designed for easy reading, and all our books are made to last. Other Thorndike Press Large Print books are available at your library, through selected bookstores, or directly from us.

For information about titles, please call:
  (800) 223-1244

or visit our Web site at:
  http://gale.cengage.com/thorndike

To share your comments, please write:
Publisher
Thorndike Press
10 Water St., Suite 310
Waterville, ME 04901